AOIFE *of* LEINSTER

THE PRICE OF A THRONE

Seán J. FitzGerald

The Hiberno-Norman Chronicles

© Sean J. Fitzgerald 2024

All rights reserved. No part of this publication may be reproduced, stored in a retrieval system, or transmitted in any form or by any means, electronic mechanical, photocopying, recording or otherwise, without the prior permission of the author.

This book is sold subject to the condition that it shall not, by way of trade or otherwise, be lent, re-sold, hired out or otherwise circulated without the author's prior consent in any form of binding or cover other than that in which it is published and without a similar condition including this condition being imposed on the subsequent purchaser.

This novel is entirely a work of fiction. The names, characters and incidents portrayed in it, while at times based on historical figures, are the work of the author's imagination.

First published in Ireland by Coldwater Publishing House 2024

ISBN(eBook): 978-1-7395332-1-2
ISBN(Paperback): 978-1-7395332-0-5
ISBN(Jacketed Hardcover): 978-1-7395332-2-9
ISBN(Audiobook): 978-1-7395332-3-6

www.seanjfitzgerald.com

Title Production By The BookWhisperer

Contents

The Descendants of Nesta ferch Rhys, Princess of Wales	vii
The Families of Aoife MacMurrough and Strongbow	ix
Map 1166-1167	xi
Map 1168-1169	xiii
Irish Language & Pronunciation guide	xv
Place Names	xvii

PART I
Escape and Despair   1

PART II
Allies and Anger   23

PART III
Impulse and Hate   117

PART IV
Return and Understanding 187

Author's Note	277
Acknowledgments	283
About the Author	285

For Déirdre with all my love

The Descendants of Nesta ferch Rhys, Princess of Wales

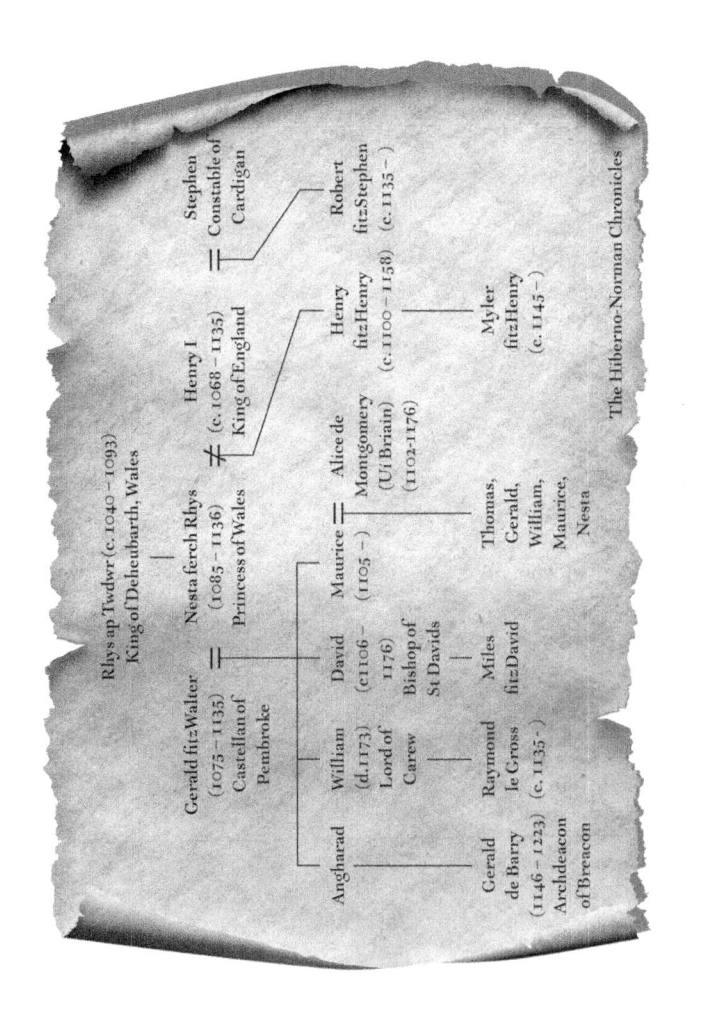

```
                    Rhys ap Twdwr (c. 1040 – 1093)
                       King of Deheubarth, Wales
                                 |
        ┌────────────────────────┼────────────────────────┐
        │                        │                        │
   Nesta ferch Rhys  ══  Henry I (c. 1068 – 1135)    Stephen
   (1085 – 1136)      ≠   King of England          Constable of
   Princess of Wales                                 Cardigan
                                 │
                    ┌────────────┴────────────┐
           Henry fitzHenry              Robert fitzStephen
           (c. 1100 – 1158)                 (c. 1135 – )
                    │
              Myler fitzHenry
                 (c. 1145 – )

   Gerald fitzWalter ══ Nesta ferch Rhys
   (1075 – 1135)
   Castellan of
   Pembroke
        │
   ┌────┼────────┬────────────┐
   │    │        │            │
Angharad William  David      Maurice ══ Alice de Montgomery
        (d.1173) (c.1106 –   (1105 – )    (Uí Briain)
        Lord of  1176)                    (1102-1176)
        Carew    Bishop of                     │
                 St Davids              Thomas, Gerald,
                    │                   William, Maurice,
                    │                   Nesta
              Miles fitzDavid
   │
   Raymond le Gross
   (c. 1135 – )
   │
   Gerald de Barry
   (1146 – 1223)
   Archdeacon
   of Breacon
```

The Hiberno-Norman Chronicles

The Families of Aoife MacMurrough and Strongbow

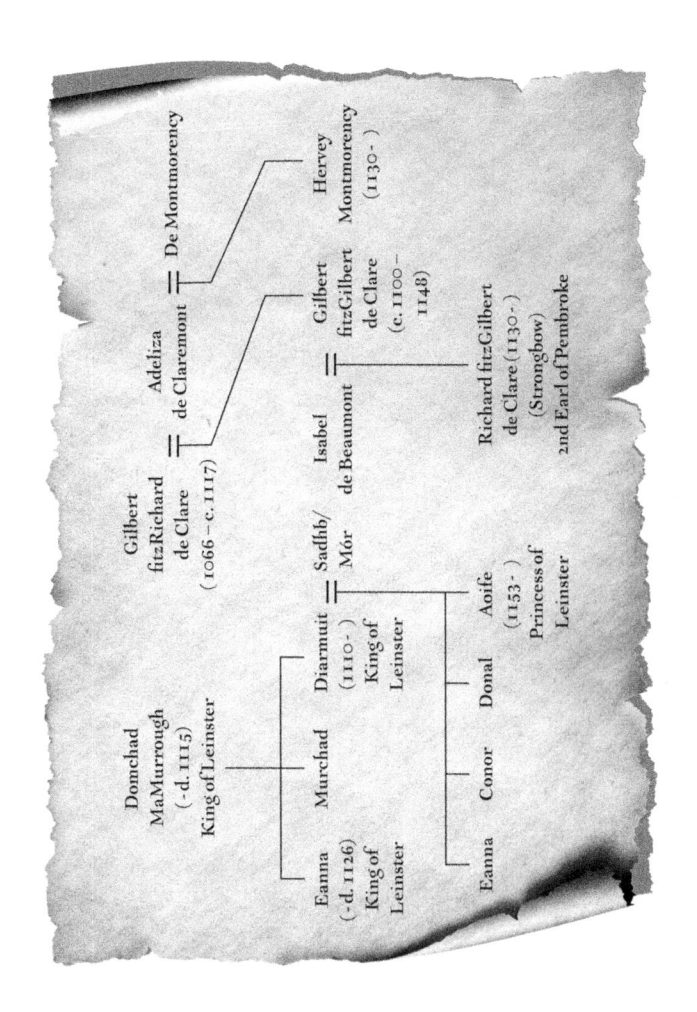

```
Gilbert fitzRichard de Clare (1066 – c. 1117) ═ Adeliza de Claremont ═ De Montmorency
                                                          │
                    ┌─────────────────────────────────────┴──────────────────┐
        Gilbert fitzGilbert de Clare (c. 1100–1148) ═ Isabel de Beaumont    Hervey Montmorency (1130- )
                                │
                Richard fitzGilbert de Clare (1130- )
                        (Strongbow)
                     2nd Earl of Pembroke

Domchad MaMurrough (-d. 1115) King of Leinster
        │
   ┌────┼─────────┬──────────┐
 Eanna  Murchad  Diarmuit   Sadhb/Mór
(-d. 1126)       (1110- )
King of          King of Leinster
Leinster
                     │
         ┌───────┬───┴───┬────────┐
       Eanna   Conor   Donal    Aoife (1153- )
                               Princess of Leinster
```

THE HIBERNO-NORMAN CHRONICLES

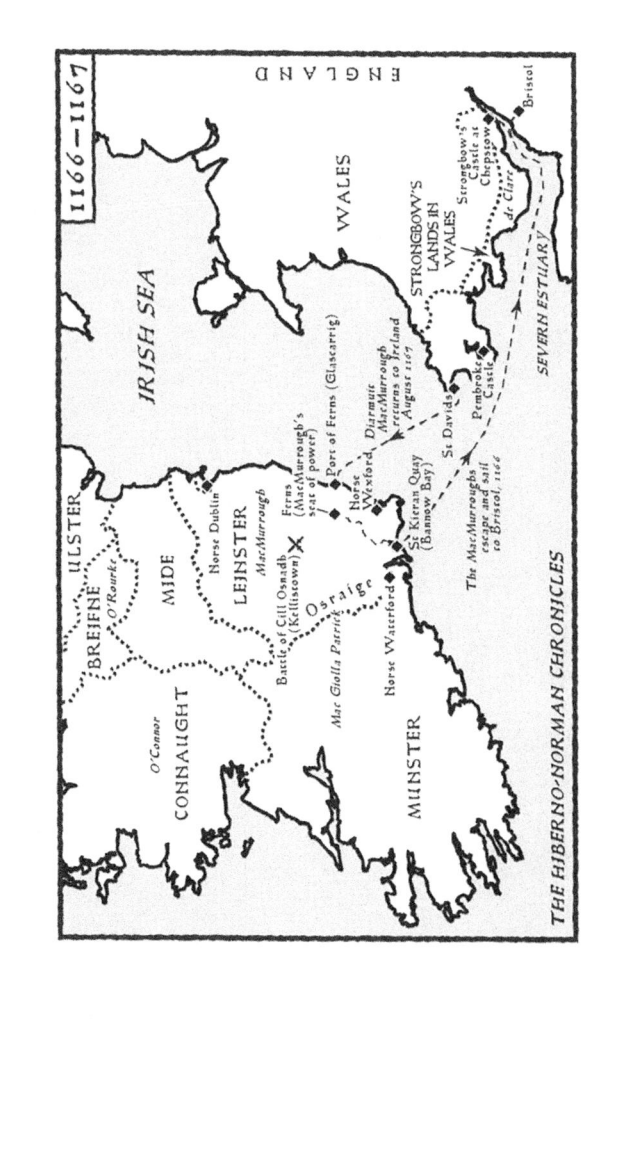

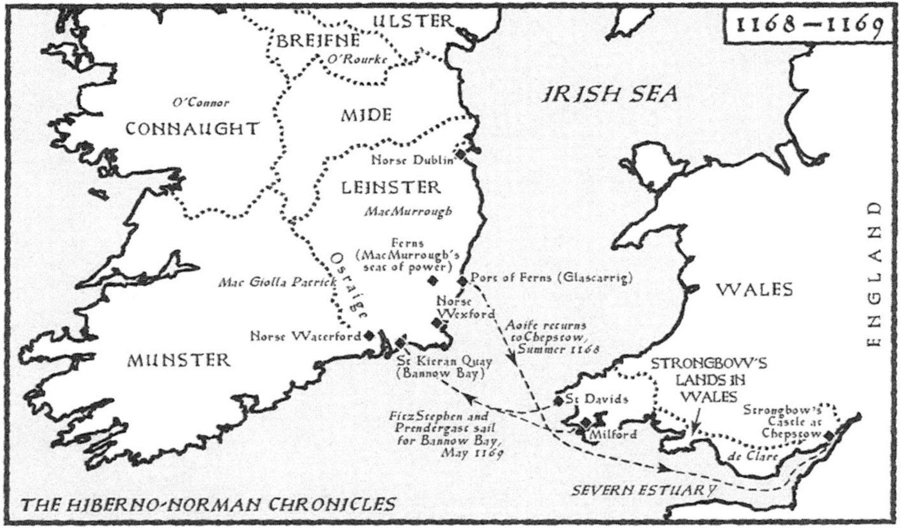

THE HIBERNO-NORMAN CHRONICLES

Irish Language & Pronunciation guide

Fáinleog – *fawnleog* – swallow
Garsún – *garsoon* – young lad
Mo chailín – *mu khaleen* – my girl
Mo grá – *mu graw* – my love
Mór – *more* – big
Mo ghrá sa – *mu graw sa* – my own love
Póg mo thóin – *powg mu hoan* – kiss my arse
Seanchaí – *shanakhee* – historian or storyteller
Slán – *slawn* – goodbye
Thóin – *hoan* – arsehole
Tóg go bog é – *toeg guh bug ae*e – take it easy

Place Names

Ferns – Ferns, County Wexford
Glascarrig – Port of Ferns, 20km due east of Ferns
St Kieran Quay – on north shore of Bannow Bay
Wexford – Walled town controlled by the Norse
Waterford – Walled town controlled by the Norse
Chepstow – Welsh town on the Wye river in Strongbow's lands
Bristol – English port on Severn river controlled by Henry II
Cill Osnadh – Kellistown, County Carlow

Part I

Escape and Despair

Chapter One
THE BURNING OF FERNS

Wexford, 1166

I had never killed before that night. Before the dawn came, that would all change.

It was closer now. I could hear the clashing of swords in the courtyard below, panicked voices in the great hall beyond the corridor leading to our chambers. Though I had barred the heavy oak door, I knew it was of little use against the approaching horror. Where was my father now? Had he fallen in the attack?

I knew what they would do to me. I had seen the girls and young women, slaves, abused at will by the warriors and young men. Mercilessly worked like pack horses, they moved like ghosts, like the dead, through the camps. As with all livestock, they served a purpose and would be discarded and replaced in time, revolting wretches dying pitiful deaths.

I wept silently, trying to calm Eanna and Conor. I knew what I had to do, and though my body shook convulsively, my mind was calm and clear. I remember thinking it strange, this calmness, but I was resolute—it would be by my own hand, with the light short sword in my skirts. Donal, my older brother, who commanded the Household Guard, had shown me how to make it fast, should the time come.

My tears were for my two beautiful brothers gripping tightly to my waist. Their fate would be worse than mine if they were taken. As male heirs to the king of Leinster, they would die anyway, but their killing would have to be witnessed by many. It would be obscene, degrading and slow, serving as a warning and the final vengeful humiliation of the house of MacMurrough for crossing O'Rourke.

In my long and storied life, that moment stands alone, unique in itself. My story is one of betrayal, hatred, rage, revenge and sorrow, but it is also one of love, passion, joy and happiness. Taken in various measures in the sweep of time, I have embraced my station. We do not choose our provenance, but our duty is written in our blood. This can be a curse or a blessing, so I am told. Yet even now, at the end of my life, I'm not sure where I sit on that scale. And in truth, it is of no consequence. I have done my duty, led our armies in battle, governed our lands. I have striven to do so fairly, as an example to my children of the power of justice to bind our lands and people. But governing involves decisions and choices: balancing outcomes, weighing probabilities, consulting and persuading in the midst of ambiguity. This has been my life since that moment.

Back then, in the thick blackness of that musty room, there was a purity in the certainty of what I was about to do. I was very young at the time, and that probably helped—the certainty of youth, the call of duty. It is chilling to think of it now, that at that tender age, I was ready to kill my beautiful brothers. But under those circumstances, it would have been the right thing to do, putting an end to it.

A grunt and the metallic ring of a weapon hitting the flagstones. Just outside the door now. A dark red pool seeped under my feet. I leant my weight against the door, my feet slipping in the blood. I held my brothers to me, their heads buried in my skirts. Two swift upward jabs under their rib cages to the heart was all it would take. I remember I could taste my tears.

Then the heavy, lurching thumps which shook through my body as they tried to force the door. The screaming as the battering heightened. The cracking as the boards strained and hinges loosened; I leant back with all my weight.

It had to be now. Holding them in a final, tight embrace, each face pressed into my young bosom, I gripped my short sword two-handed, the point at Eanna's back. I screamed my fury to the gods and filled my lungs, ready to deliver the first thrust cleanly.

The heavy door behind me shattered in a cloud of wood splinter and iron rivets. Knocked to the floor, the sword spun from my hand and my brothers fell from my grip and tumbled across the room. Recovering from the shock, I saw my blade lying close to my outstretched hand, returnig in my time of need, as always—Fáinleog, my short sword.

Seizing the grip, I spun and struck wildly, driving the blade upward into the belly of the dark shadow of the warrior moving towards me. There was a jar as I felt the light blade stop abruptly on a thick mail coat. The weight of the man drove me back. I twisted the sharp point viciously, trying to work through small chain links to the flesh beneath, as I had been taught.

Light flooded the room. I stared up into the bloodied face of my father, Diarmuit MacMurrough. His sunken dark eyes shone with a cold battle-madness. The whites of his eyes blazed bright against his thick black beard and smoke-charred face. There was, for a moment, no hint of recognition from him. I thought he would cut me down.

Staring blankly, he seemed to emerge from the humanity-draining bloodlust where men go in their minds during battle.

'Gods.' He slapped the sword from my hand, seeing me afresh.

'Where are your brothers, Aoife,' he snapped as Donal, my older brother, stumbled into the room over the broken remains of the shattered door. His helmet bore the scar of a hard blow, probably from an axe. His battered willow shield was barely held together by the tight band of iron on its edge. Bright red blood glistened, smearing his sword, the edges nicked and dulled from the fight.

'They're here,' I said. Conor and Eanna scrambled from the debris and ran to my side, whimpering. 'I'm keeping them with me.'

'And your mother?'

'She's waiting with the horses, hidden at the back of the stales.'

'What?' he snarled.

'The horses,' I said. 'We have a chance, Father!' I pleaded, knowing he was loath to run from Ferns, the seat of power in Leinster of his father and forefathers for generations. He would not be the one to lose it, chased away like a diseased dog. He stared at me with cold venom.

'Father, please! I beg you. We must leave immediately. Ferns is lost. They are attacking from the west, but the eastern gate is still free. We must go now!' I knew my father's dangerous rage, but there was no time.

'She's right, Father,' Donal said now. 'They are through the palisade and swamping the lower town. It's a slaughter now. They'll reach the palace soon enough. We don't have the swords to hold them.' He looked exhausted from the day's long fighting as wave upon wave of O'Rourke's army stormed the wooden palisade of the town. I think he was relieved that I had been blunt with our father.

Turning on him, my father growled. 'We'll never make Wexford, and what when we get there? They'll have us cornered.' Slamming his shield into Donal's chest, he shouted, 'You! You should have held them at the wall and driven them back.' Lifting his sword, he levelled it at Donal's chest. There was a madness on him—a battle-madness that takes some men beyond fear and most beyond reason. It was not bravery; bravery is feeling the fear and riding on. To lead in battle, you must be brave, but also clear-headed. He was neither now.

His eyes remained fixed on Donal, who didn't move. I could see his clenched teeth through the grimace of his beard. This was dangerous. My father could be a violent, unforgiving man, unpredictable in a fit of rage—a rage heightened now by the fury of battle. I quickly stepped in front of Donal. Facing my father, I reached out and held his sword hand. He stared fixedly at Donal with a raging, silent intensity. I could feel the pent-up fury in his iron grip.

'Father, please, I sent the pack horses with everything we need to a ship yesterday. The ship's master has it waiting on the quay at St Kieran in Bannow Bay.'

He looked at me, hesitating.

'Father, you're right!' I tried. 'Wexford is too dangerous. They won't be watching St Kieran. The ship can take us all. But we must go now. Please, Father!' I knew it had to be now, but only he could decide. Donal would not take his orders from me.

'You must listen, Father,' Donal said evenly.

Still my father didn't move, his gaze scorching Donal's face.

Nothing.

The fighting edging close.

I exploded. 'You will have us all killed! And for what? All is lost here!' I screamed. 'I am taking the boys and Mother to the boat with what men will accompany us. You can stay and die if you wish. Wallow in your stupidity. You have lost us everything, but we will not die for you now!'

Stunned from his stupor, my father turned on me, but the allowance a father will often give a daughter but deny a son stopped him. He groaned deeply and eased the sword from Donal's chest, dropping it to the ground by his side. The loud metallic clash on the stone floor bounced off the chamber walls. Sitting heavily on a bench, he buried his head in his hands.

'No, no! I have never run.' He shook his head. 'If I go now, I lose everything—my crown, my lands, Leinster. Everything!' I could see the battle-madness seeping from him as his despair grew.

'Father?' Donal said. 'Father? Please, you must decide!'

Exasperated, I picked up my father's sword and slammed it on the table in front of him and gripped his face in my hands, staring into his eyes. 'Father, you are Diarmuit MacMurrough, king of Leinster. You will return to take our family's rightful place here. Today your duty is to survive.'

He dropped his head. A strained silence held us frozen, waiting in death's certain shadow as time slowed. In what seemed an eternity but was only an instant, he slowly raised his head and, with a distant look, nodded faintly. That was all I needed.

'Donal, bring the household troops to the east gate. We leave immediately,' I said as I helped my father rise to his feet.

❦

MY FATHER LEAPT onto his horse and made to break for the gate before it was taken. It was our only hope.

'Stop! We don't have enough horses; you must take Eanna and Conor,' I insisted. 'I'll bring Mother and the others.'

He hesitated. 'Gods,' he said. Roughly placing both boys before his saddle, he made to leave. Then, turning, he ordered the man on his right to have the guards put the town to the torch as they fled. 'Leave nothing standing. Everything must burn,' he spat. 'The bastards will win a pile of ashes.' He lashed his stallion, which, already maddened by the din of battle, surged forwards through the narrow street, scattering the fleeing townspeople caught under its thundering, iron-shod hooves.

My mother, Mór, clung tightly to my waist as we galloped through the close lanes and alleyways trying to catch him. The thatch on the low houses was burning on every side, sending showers of fire and choking smoke into the reddening dark sky. The attackers had reached this side of the town as I had feared. I only hoped they hadn't taken the gate.

My heart sank as we emerged from the smoke-filled alley into a small, open square in front of the large gates embedded in the wooden palisade walls. More than the height of two men, the trunks of oak trees were buried deep into the ground to form a strong defensive barrier. The wall was erected and had expanded around the town as it had grown over the centuries. It was half castellated by cutting the trunks at regular places. Here the guards watched over the approaches to the town from the timber platform which skirted the inner side.

I pulled my horse to a fast stand, feeling the heat from the chasing flames as the wind swept the fire in sheets across the tinder-dry thatch of the houses, lighting the night. Through the thickening smoke I saw mail-clad warriors struggling to close the gates. They heaved their bodies against the stubborn weight, which responded slowly, closing our escape. They were on the walls too, firing arrows into the townsfolk fleeing the fire and slaughter. I knew that meant they commanded the other gates; this was our last chance.

If we got through the gates, we would be within bowshot of the walls as we made our way down the slope to the bridge over the river, the Bann. It ran along the eastern wall through the open meadow, which stretched to the forests that encircled the town. Its sturdy wooden bridge carried the road the hour's ride to Glascarrig, the port on the east coast that served Ferns. O'Rourke's men would be on that road by now, so we would turn south and ride hard for Bannow Bay. The king's roads radiated in all directions from Ferns, cut through the impenetrable forests from the ancient seat of royal and spiritual power of Ireland. I only hoped they had not reached the road south.

My father didn't hesitate. Whipping his crazed horse onwards toward the gate, he rode hard, hooves pounding on the dry earth. Abandoning the gate, the warriors turned to face his charge, gathering in the gap to prevent any escape. There was no time to ready their weapons as the maddened animal surged forwards, a snorting, sweating mass of muscle and flesh bearing down on them, unstoppable. His momentum scattered them like straw in the wind.

Through the dull light and thickening smoke, I saw Conor grasping the horse's mane before he tumbled backwards and slipped from the withers to the ground. Through the gate my father wheeled his horse. Seeing O'Rourke's men recover themselves, he seemed to hesitate. Our eyes met momentarily.

Another pause.

Then he turned his horse and sped into the darkness towards St Kieran and the waiting boat.

A few men on the palisade wall loosed a flurry of arrows pointlessly in his wake. A huge, heavily bearded man standing in the gate barked at them to stop wasting their arrows—my father was well gone. He carried a large double-bladed battleaxe of the Norse kind. The weight alone was enough to split the strongest helmet, but he carried it lightly in one hand, the weapon dangling loosely by his side. It had seen much use that day. Removing his helmet, he stood over Conor, who sat at his feet, dazed from the fall. Slowly coming to his senses, Conor rubbed the smoke from his eyes with the backs of his hands, as all small children do. Then he lifted his gaze to take in the bulk of the enormous man who towered above him. He watched, transfixed, as the man sneered and hefted the battleaxe above his head.

Time slowed. I remember the paralysing shock; my father had left his son there. Panic, revulsion, my stomach heaving bile, filling my mouth, a dry acidic bile. The flames raged about us, reflected by the sharpened metal of the battleaxe, which was poised to deliver a death blow to Conor. The gripping tightness in my chest allowed no breath. A moment more and Conor would die in the gates of Ferns.

I let loose a howl from the core of my being—a sole plea to the mother Goddess to aid the child—and I dug my heels hard into my mare. She sprung forwards, almost unseating my mother, but she gripped tight enough, her head buried in my back. It was a desperate move, but I was beyond sense now. I pulled Fáinleog from her scabbard and hoped the long practice days in sword skill with Donal would pay and guide my hand. I needed it now.

My shout seemed to distract the axeman, giving me a few precious moments to cover the ground across the courtyard to the gate. The men on the wall remained occupied with the fading silhouette of my father. The axeman paused for an instant and looked at me, a woman…two women…with a short sword on a palfrey mare. He grinned.

The arrow hit his left shoulder. The chainmail slowed the speed and the padded jerkin he wore underneath took the force from it. It had barely reached his flesh. It was more the shock of it that gave me what I needed to reach him before he could release the swing of his axe on Conor. Guiding my mare with my thighs and calves was as instinctive as breathing. I had learned to ride bareback, in the Irish style, from early childhood. I gripped Fáinleog's hilt with both hands, holding the blade high. Two strides out I swung the mare with a squeeze of my thighs and a press of my right leg to pass behind the axeman for fear of trammelling Conor. The look of surprise on the axeman's face was his last. I was well practiced and knew to keep the blade level and connect with the neck as close to the hilt as possible—the forte, the strongest part of the blade. My speed did the rest. There was a splash of blood, and I felt its warmth on my hand; his head rolled. I heard his axe clatter to the ground behind me. He was the first man I had killed. The first of many, I am not proud to say.

Before I had time to gather myself, I heard Donal call, 'Keep riding, Aoife,' as he galloped through the gate after me, bow in one hand. Without breaking stride, I saw him lean from his saddle to snatch Conor from the ground. Securing him across his horse's neck, he turned and loosed an arrow at the men on the palisade. Then we sped from the gate into the safety of the darkness beyond the orange glow, which was spreading far from the burning town. Pounding over the bridge, we wheeled the horses south up the slope towards the welcoming blackness of the forest.

The fire threw a broad sweeping light across the meadows around the town and gathered pace. Reaching the cover of the forest, we paused to gather whatever remaining household guards had escaped. It would be safer to ride in strength, as O'Rourke's men could already be on the road ahead of us. As the last of the men galloped in, Donal checked their numbers and, sending scouts ahead, set a troop to guard our rear as we prepared to move south.

He drew level with me, throwing his bow across his shoulder. 'Nice sword-work, Aoife! I see you were paying attention some of the time.' He grinned but I could see the strain on his face, lit by the shifting orange glow where we stood at the edge of the forest.

'The arrow, it was you?' I asked, keeping my mare in hand. Her blood was up. She was spooked by the flickering shadows thrown from the fire.

'Yes…although it was meant for his neck, the bastard. You did the rest.' He paused, pushing his long hair from his sweating brow. He turned to look at the fire. 'I saw what happened. Gods, he's some bastard!' There was a twist of despair in his face, or perhaps it was a quiet rage that had his hand shaking as he spoke.

'How could he?' I asked.

Ignoring my question, Donal shook his head. We sat, mesmerised by the inferno. The tinder-dry thatch of the parched buildings seemed to bristle, then burst, sending columns of sparks skyward to merge into a narrowing, twisting heavenly spiral, reaching far into the darkness to the very gods themselves. I would not easily forget the grief of witnessing the destruction of Ferns that night. The seat of our power, the place of our youth, the centre of our kingdom —little would survive this.

'Look, Aoife, now's not the time,' he said, turning to me, his horse pawing impatiently at the mud. 'We got everyone out. This fire will sow confusion and give us a bit of time… but not for long. So let's get to your boat and get the hell out of here.'

Turning our backs on our home, we kicked our heels and rode hard after my father, south for St Kieran in Bannow Bay.

Chapter Two
THE FLIGHT FROM ST KIERAN

Bannow Bay, Wexford
August 1166

A steady south-westerly wind swept across the bay as we rode cautiously down the gentle slope of a narrow tree-lined lane which led to the coast road and the deep-water quay of St Kieran. The horses dropped their heads, exhausted from the long ride through the night. The steam rising from their sweating bodies embraced us, merging into a ghostly pallor in the grey light of the early dawn. The quay where I had arranged to meet the boat that would take us to Bristol was an hour's ride from the village that bridged the Corock River. The narrow, boarded walkway by the riverbank there could not water the larger seagoing vessels that plied the coast and trading routes to Britain.

To my relief, the scouts had returned with the welcome news that the boat was waiting for us. Through the trees I could see the torches on the wooden quay from where the brownish, bulky silhouette of the twin-masted boat emerged, skeletal-like, from the mist.

O'Rourke's men were not here. They would be watching the docks at Waterford and Wexford for certain. Amlaib, the old Norse shipmaster who owned the deep-bellied trading barque that would carry us to Bristol, had suggested the small fishing village on the river Corock, knowing it would likely miss the attention of our pursuers. He made frequent use of the quay, which had the water depth to accommodate the draft of his boat, when he wished to evade the attention of ever-watchful eyes at the ports. He was an experienced Norse navigator who knew the south Irish coast as smugglers must.

'The tide is ebbing, but it'll turn soon. You must hurry!' Amlaib shouted as we dismounted and made our way along the creaking boards over the swirling sea beneath. He would use the strong tidal current of the wide bay to help his crew row the boat swiftly from the lee of the land into the wind. When the tide turned, it would be hard to get out of the bay with that westerly wind against us, as it could drive the boat onto the shore if it rose high enough. With O'Rourke's men certain to make their presence felt soon enough, we had to catch this tide. However, if we could get through the channel between the far headland and Bannow Island to its west, it would be harder for any boat to follow, Amlaib explained, as it would be fighting both tide and wind. The depth in the tidal channel would quickly lessen, forcing any pursuing craft to skirt to the west of the island.

As Amlaib continued ushering everyone aboard, O'Rourke's two scouts were spotted cresting the low hill above the quay. The horsemen were lightly armed, as scouts were for swift travel. Staying on the hilltop, they waved and shouted frantically, clearly summoning to their comrades that we were found.

'Set the horses loose and get everyone on board now,' Donal shouted to his men in the rising panic on the quay. 'They won't be far behind. Leave everything, get on board!' Our men chased the loose horses onto the road up the hill, hoping to delay any attack. They then formed a shield wall at the lip of the quay while the last of us clambered onto the boat.

I hurried my mother and Conor down the gangplank and pushed through the mass of men towards the stern of the boat. I caught sight of my father at the bow shouting at the crew to cut loose as men scrambled aboard.

There was panic now as a large troop of riders crested the hill and rode hard towards the quay, their spears held skywards as they pushed through the loose horses. Momentarily delayed, we got everyone aboard and Donal ordered the retreat of the last guardsmen from the quay. They scrambled aboard as my father screamed at the crew to cut the guy ropes holding us to the quay.

'Lord King! If you please. My crew will take their orders from me while aboard my ship. Stand down!' Amlaib shouted angrily through the noise. Standing at the prow with his sword in hand, my father seethed, not accustomed to the tone of the grizzled seaman. For once, he held his tongue; in seafaring matters, a captain's word trumps that of a king.

'Get the last of them aboard,' Amlaib's voice boomed, practised at besting the roar of the sea and wind. 'Pull the gangplank! Hold the lines. Loose the bow. Steady!'

The bow of the boat swung into the bay. 'Oars! Ready; loose the stern. Heave!' The boat shot forward into the kindly current, causing the less seaworthy amongst us to steady ourselves. I saw the pursuing horsemen reach the shore by the quayside; abandoning their mounts they crowded onto the quay. Some threw spears, but the boat was quickly beyond them. Several men with bows aimed them skywards and strained the bowstrings, readying to let loose a volley of arrows.

'Shields!' Donal shouted, and the men scrambled. 'Get down here,' he ordered, and the rest of us jumped down amongst the benches where the sailors manning the oars sat. He had the men cover the belly of the boat with their shields in a protective wall above us. Through a gap, I could see Amlaib standing impassively on the stern deck, holding the massive oak tiller. He concentrated on the bay ahead, following the narrow, hidden channel to the headland and safety. Only the gods knew how—only the gods and Amlaib.

'Amlaib, get down!' I screamed as the arrows slammed into the shields above us.

'Really, m'lady. And how would you suppose we get this barque from here into that sea if I rest my arse down there with you?' He leant into the tiller, guiding the boat through unseen sandbanks. If the boat grounded, low tide would leave us at O'Rourke's mercy. 'Heave, lads. Heave!' And soon the powerful strokes and ebbing waters carried the boat safely out of bowshot from the shore.

The boat moved swiftly in the current now, propelled forwards by the sweating oarsmen, murmuring a low chant that guided their rhythm. As more pursuing riders arrived, they moved along the shore, keeping pace. Donal's men shouted insults in response to their taunts, but their arrows splashed harmlessly in the swirling green waters. I recognised some of these riders, kinsmen of the families that sought our destruction.

I remember my mother, shivering and weeping silently as I held her tightly, comforting her with the knowledge that all her children were safe. I wrapped her in a heavy cloak against the chill of the wind that lifted the waves under the bow. The barque rose and then plunged shudderingly, sending a salty spray carried by the strong wind lashing into our faces. The gulls gathered in our wake, screaming their indignant protest, expectant of an easy meal from the fishing boats of the bay. Nature dances on, the Goddess, I thought, oblivious of our plight, or worse, regarding it as of no consequence.

'Bring them to me, Aoife,' my mother said.

I pushed Conor into her arms and moved forward through the belly of the boat, calling for Donal to fetch Eanna from the bow where father stood facing the shore. The boat glided through the narrow channel between the island and the headland. Smoke rising from the houses in the village of Bannow was swept eastward in the favourable wind.

'He's not there!' Donal returned, ashen faced.

'What do you mean? Where is he? Father brought him.' I said.

Donal shook his head just as a piercing wail from my mother caused us to look to the headland where she pointed.

In front of a group of mounted riders, one man stood. Helmet removed, he wanted us to know it was him, O'Rourke. He was unmistakable, a squat barrel of a man with bowed legs from a life in the saddle. The wind whipped his long, flame-red hair to expose the twisted sneer through his matted beard. Kneeling in front of him was a small boy, weeping, on whose shoulder O'Rourke rested his bloodied longsword.

'Eanna!' I screamed and turned to find my father.

'Father, Father! He was with you...'

He stared impassively at the scene on the headland, aware that the deafening silence of the boat was focused on him.

'Father?'

Turning to me, he shook his head. 'He slipped from my saddle. I couldn't...'

'You left him! You left him! You saved yourself and left

him!' And for the second time that day I was ready to kill family—this time willingly.

'Bastard!' I lunged at him, snatching at Fáinleog to free her from her scabbard. But Donal moved quicker. 'No, Aoife! No! Stop. You can't,' he said, holding me tightly, pinning my arms. I thrashed wildly, my fury needing to vent, but Donal's firm clasp would not be broken. As my strength ebbed into a sobbing despair, he gently eased me free and, brushing the hair from my face, kissed my forehead softly, his own tears welling from his pale blue eyes, MacMurrough eyes.

'We will come back for him, Aoife. I promise you.'

'Eanna,' I cried, louder and louder. A howl that carried to the small boy, shivering on his knees on the shore as we rounded the headland and Amlaib turned the tiller to point the prow eastward.

But O'Rourke did not lift his sword. He did not do so as the seamen shipped the oars and hoisted the sails. Hanging limp, the sails shimmered and then bellied with a snap as the wind filled the enormous square linen cloths. I could feel the powerful surge as the boat lifted over the waves, ploughing due east for Bristol at the mouth of the Severn River on the Welsh-English border. There we could expect some sympathy and hopefully a welcome from the English king's appointed reeve of the town, Robert Harding, who governed the important port on his behalf.

Harding and my father had built a strong, mutually beneficial relationship over the years as trade between his town and Leinster had flourished. Trading barques plied the short sea routes to Bristol, and the wharves in the port had continually expanded to accommodate their ever-increasing numbers and size. The reeve's coffers benefitted substantially from the tariffs levied on the shipped goods, and the English king's treasury gained accordingly. Both men would be keen to ensure that this important source of finance would not be put at risk by the turmoil overtaking Leinster.

I watched until my eyes strained as our boat sailed steadily in the following wind. I knew that Eanna lived. O'Rourke would have killed him there for the pleasure of it, but he was a clever man; he knew Eanna was more valuable as a hostage. He was a son of the once great king, Diarmuit MacMurrough, a bitter enemy on whom O'Rourke had sworn vengeance for the humiliation he had brought to him these fifteen years past. Although fugitives now, the MacMurroughs were not without support. O'Rourke knew that, like him, my father would not care who he had to kill, evict or blind to regain his throne. Somehow, somewhere, he would return. So, for now, until MacMurrough power was forever broken, Eanna would live as a bargaining tool. And in that calculation by O'Rourke, there was hope for me to save my brother.

While my father wanted his kingdom, I wanted Eanna. I knew then that my path to saving him was through my father's lust for power and revenge. He would seek the support of the English king, Henry II, to regain his throne. Henry had long sought the pretext to add Ireland to his dominions; the profusion of feuding, petty kingdoms there were ripe for conquering and unification.

However, there would be a heavy price to pay for this help, but whatever that price, I would stop at nothing to make sure my father secured that army to return to regain his kingdom. I would use that army to bring Eanna home.

As the receding shore faded into the sea mist, my despair turned to anger—a bitter anger at the man standing at the bow of the boat. Was there no price he was unwilling to pay for his own gratification? I knew he was a ruthless man, as all kings with many rivals must be. But did that price now include the lives of his own children? This was not the father

I knew. The father I had loved and who I know had loved me, as he had cherished all his children. While he had never been overly affectionate, I had always sensed his devotion to us, and sometimes as I grew and began to notice things in people, I saw the burden he carried in his desire to keep us free from harm in this turbulent world. Being a man of his time and more importantly a king, he was not one to express his deep-felt thoughts. While others could regard him a cruel man, bordering on a tyranny that had alienated his enemies and kinsmen alike, I had seen him as a child wishes to see her father: as a caring man of deep sensibility in a depraved world, dedicating himself selflessly to the protection, well-being and future of his family.

My anger on that day reflected a more profound grief—grief at the loss of my belief in the basic goodness of my father. If he could abandon Eanna to the clutches and depraved appetites of a man like O'Rourke, he was not the father I had believed him to be. It was as if a veil was lifted and I saw the world anew. I felt horribly alone, unanchored from my past self. A biting, bitter coldness crept within me, which took no comfort as I grasped the heavy woollen cloak against the cold wind. The salt from the sea spray mingled with my silent tears as I watched the disappearing land. I was leaving more than my beloved brother on that shore that day; in the floatsam I saw my shattered home, the father I thought I knew and my very childhood itself.

Part II

Allies and Anger

Chapter Three
POLITICS

Chepstow Castle, Wales
Spring 1167

'Must I give my time to meeting her now? Don't we have enough to do, Sir Raymond?' Strongbow didn't look up from a list of supplies he was studying. As he rose from his seat behind a long oak table, the scrape of the chair on the flagstone floor was lost in the vast hall. Retrieving another parchment from the mass of orderly documents along the length of the table, he resumed his seat while seeming to cross-reference the contents. Without lifting his head, he instructed an attendant to close a window against the chill from the early morning spring breeze drifting across the River Wye. The seven high, round-headed windows were all arranged on the north-facing wall, opposite from where Strongbow sat. The south-facing wall gathered scant light, and the candles on the long table burned incessantly, throwing a shifting light on his work. The Great Tower—built by his ancestor, Gilbert Fitz-Gilbert—stretched over a hundred and twenty paces, had high sandstone walls and was capped with a low gabled timber roof. The pure white plaster and decorative tiles made the most of the weak northern light that seeped into the hall.

'M'lord,' Raymond tried again, leaning into a touch of flattery. 'It is a great honour for MacMurrough that you have accepted his daughter's hand in marriage.' He paused, carefully weighing his next words. 'Which means you will, in all probability, wed the princess within months. With all that that entails...' He purposefully stopped now, letting the silence finish his sentence, hoping it was enough to get Strongbow's attention.

Not seeming satisfied with what he was reading, Strongbow reached for his quill and, scratching some alterations, remained engrossed in the papers. He was rare amongst the Norman nobility in his mastery of reading and writing. A militaristic race, the Normans valued the skills of the sword far more than those of the quill, and while Strongbow was no delinquent in matters of arms, his father had taught him that the stroke of a quill could, at times, carry far more power than the stroke of a sword. At his father's insistence, he had been tutored by monks from a very young age. In time, albeit reluctantly at first, he had learned the wisdom of his father's words.

'Sir Raymond. The clerks' manifest for bodkin arrowheads for the second transport ship does not accord with what we ordered from the smithy.' He held up the two lists.

Raymond wished he had learned his letters. He had not wanted this position as Strongbow's secretary for the campaign. His place was in the saddle, not buried in books. But Strongbow had insisted. 'It's never too late, Raymond. If you can't learn, then sharpen your memory. That's what I did before I could read. A sword only cuts so deep,' he had said, 'but a quill wins wars and holds kingdoms.'

Raymond would berate the clerks again—they should know Strongbow by now.

Strongbow placed the lists on the table and looked through the windows over the river, as if first noticing the morning. 'A pleasant day, Raymond,' he observed.

Raymond tensed. Strongbow was not one for pleasantries in the morning. 'Indeed, m'lord.' He waited.

Strongbow turned to him. 'A morning made even more enchanting by the silence which accompanies it,' he said. He rose and walked to the window, pulling the shutter open. The scene was dramatic. A sheer drop, the height of forty men, to the slow-moving broad river. Heavy wooden quays stretched along the riverbank around the eastward bend in the Wye. The town, Chepstow, had developed around the castle and priory which sat just outside the walls.

It was a prosperous town. Benefitting from the deep river, which could accommodate the largest of ships, it also had the advantage of the presence of the large garrison the castle afforded. The quays normally bustled with the noisy chaos of the thriving port trade, while the river crowded with trading barques and merchant ships carrying wine, grain, wool, hides and all manner of goods. The boats were sometimes tied three deep along the quays.

Just after dawn, it was still quiet this morning. 'That silence, Raymond,' Strongbow continued, 'is costing me time and money. The shipwrights are contracted to work from dawn to dusk.' He gestured at the sun, already clear of the low hill across the river in the east. 'Last chance; if it happens again, cancel the contract.'

'I'll see to it immediately, m'lord. It won't happen again.' He was sure of that. It wasn't the contract the master shipwright had to worry about; it was removing Raymond's dagger from his arse if he had to suffer this from Strongbow again.

However, now he had to contend with Aoife MacMurrough. For Raymond, the Earl of Pembroke was his liege lord, the man who had his oath and loyalty. Known to his followers as Strongbow, the nom de guerre the earl had inherited from his father, whose renown in his skill with the Welsh longbow had not passed to his son. He was not one for frivolity or coarse words. Any suggestion touching upon what Strongbow considered highly private matters would provoke instant reproach. But Raymond needed his attention.

'M'lord,' he tried again, adopting a tone of bonhomie, 'not wishing to sound like a crass purveyor of goods, but I'm sure a man of your appetites would wish to cast his experienced eye on the spoils...to see what intimate joys the girl has in store for your attention, so to speak. I don't think you'll be disappointed.' He forced a conspiratorial laugh, paused and dearly hoped he hadn't gone too far.

It had the desired effect. The quill stopped scratching; a loud silence followed. Raymond felt decidedly uncomfortable. He would have sworn the attendants had thrown the windows open to the cold northerly wind. Strongbow placed the quill on the table. Slowly lifting his head, he set his sharp gaze on him and held it. Raymond thought he'd prefer a small cut from a shortsword than this, but eventually Strongbow responded.

'That *girl*, as you refer to her, Sir Raymond, is a princess. The Princess of Leinster.' He paused. 'You will do well to remind yourself of her status.' A longer pause.

There was a quiet fury in him.

'Pay heed, and the proper respect, for, as you say, she will occupy a position of considerable importance in my household should my plans come to pass.'

Raymond felt the chill. But needs must. He knew that should they reach Ireland, Strongbow would secure his position as the King of Leinster's heir by wedding his daughter, Aoife. More importantly, he had just been forcefully, and rather uncomfortably, reminded of this fact when he had encountered Aoife and her retinue crossing the blustery courtyard of the castle on his way to the Great Tower.

※

RAYMOND HAD ENJOYED A FILLING LUNCH, which he took these days in the warmth of the kitchens, with their ever-glowing fires. Strongbow demanded discipline from the men, but his kitchens at Chepstow Castle turned out the best victuals and ale in copious quantities. You could demand a lot from men who had full bellies and the promise of more. And it was this excessive time in the kitchens which had earned Raymond the nickname 'Le Gros', the Fat.

Bracing himself against the wind, he wrapped his heavy cloak tightly to preserve the warmth from the fires. He was surprised to see MacMurrough's daughter, Aoife, in his path, and he smiled benignly at the girl as she approached. He had had no cause to have any dealings with her as he had negotiated the wedding with her father. As yet, she was unaware, and they would leave it that way for a while; she had no need to know. From what he knew of her, she was of fine figure and considerable beauty. She would serve her purpose well enough, which was to provide Strongbow with the heirs he needed to carry the de Clare family name and bloodline forward.

'Sir Raymond,' she addressed him formally. 'Good day to you, sir.'

Surprised but ever gracious, Raymond responded, 'Good day, m'lady,' and he and his clerk stepped aside to let the ladies pass before going about their business.

Just as the men were about to continue on their way, her voice came from behind, rooting him to the spot: 'Le Gros.'

Very few men addressed him in that manner and tone—those who wanted to remain living, anyway—and certainly no women. Turning, he was surprised to see the girl moving closer. As she did so, she pulled back the hood of her cloak. Her long, flaming red hair was quickly taken by the gusting wind, obscuring her face. A big man, he was more than a head taller. Uncomfortably close, she stopped, and using her hands to tame and part her whipping hair, she revealed her striking pale blue eyes and clear skin. Unusually, her beauty was amplified by its proximity. She stared at him expectantly, unnervingly.

'Apologies, m'lady, if I did something to offend. I…I…' He gathered himself, regretting that second tankard of ale, which had muffled his thoughts slightly. He lacked the sharpness of mind to handle this kind of ambush.

'No apologies necessary. I understand you are acting as the Earl of Pembroke's secretary at present.' She beamed now.

'You are correct, m'lady,' he said with an authority he didn't quite feel just then.

'Excellent. Could you inform His Lordship that I would be pleased to visit him presently—this afternoon—to discuss matters of mutual interest.' She continued in a most pleasant manner.

A bit of spirit indeed, Raymond thought, somewhat recovering himself and smiling. He was responsible for Strongbow's diary of meetings, and as was expected of him, it was planned meticulously and rarely changed. 'Forgive me, m'lady, but His Lordship is busy attending to serious matters at present.' Confidence restored now, he charged on: 'However, I'm sure you have important lady's matters to attend which will well occupy you. I will raise the matter with His

Lordship in the coming weeks, and we'll see what we can do. Now, if you'll excuse me...' He made to resume his walk to the Great Tower.

Standing back, Aoife faced the wind and let it take her hair. A quiet disappointment gathered from her full lips to her sculpted jawline and long neck. A hint of snow-white flesh cresting her bosom was exposed by the lifting wind. An allure, almost bewitching—it was not a sight that a man with blood in his veins could easily ignore.

Eventually she spoke, more slowly now and with a tinge of sadness: 'You seem to misunderstand me, Sir Raymond. I am not making a request of you.' She paused, then looked at him.

Raymond was feeling very uncomfortable. His clerk stared dumbfounded at the girl and dropped a sheaf of parchments. She glanced pitifully at the handsome young man as he scrambled to collect the documents in the blustering wind. Then she seemed to sigh, stilled her hair, and returned her gaze to Raymond. 'I am making the assumption, at this stage, that you are competent.' She spoke deliberately. 'Please don't regard this in any way as a test, but I do so truly hope that I can rely on you as a trusted member of our nobility in Ireland.'

It took Raymond a while to absorb and recover from the shock of the implied threat. How much did this girl know? However, he was quick on the uptake, and if you had to get a tongue-lashing from someone, he couldn't think of a more beautiful face to deliver the blow.

'Of course, m'lady. I fully understand. I will of course see to it immediately. Please let me apologise. I was somewhat preoccupied.' He stumbled on.

'Oh, no need whatsoever.' She smiled. 'Shall we say three o'clock, then?' The girl's face lit up like an angel's.

'As you wish, Princess Aoife.'

'Please, please. No need for formalities. We shall be seeing so much of each other. Slán.'

And one man's blessing is another man's curse, he thought, as the girl replaced her hood and curtseyed. Smiling at them both, she flashed her cloak, summoned her retinue, and went on her way.

Raymond now regretted that first tankard of ale. Moments ago, his world had looked good. The plans were going well; he had a full belly and a packed afternoon of audiences arranged for Strongbow. They would stick rigidly to the schedule, no exceptions. And now this.

Staring after her, the two men stood transfixed. 'If this is what their women are like, maybe we should rethink the whole damn thing.' Raymond grinned with a friendly nudge to his companion, regaining some of his natural good humour.

'Well, she certainly is a beauty,' said Myler, his young cousin who was acting as his clerk. He stood open-mouthed, watching her withdraw with an intensity Raymond suspected went beyond surprise.

He paused and turned to Myler. 'Now, you listen to me, m'boy. I know what's going through your stupid head right now.' He wagged a finger in his face. 'You keep that little sword of yours in its scabbard, if you gather my meaning, or an even smaller, shrivelled version of it—if that's possible—will be found hanging above Strongbow's mantel. You know well whose bed she'll be warming.' He prodded Myler's chest for effect, gently scolding this likeable but impulsive young man.

'Prudent advice, Cousin Raymond.' Myler smiled. 'I always take my example from you.' And he even managed to keep a straight face before they both laughed loudly, knowing full well Raymond's reputation and form with the ladies.

However, Raymond's good humour was short-lived as he approached the Great Tower. How to explain to Strongbow that he had arranged an unscheduled audience with MacMurrough's daughter?

No turning back now. Onwards into the breach.

※

HAVING SUITABLY CHASTISED Raymond for his crass language concerning the princess, Strongbow resumed his study. Scribbling notes, he quickly consumed the mass of logistical information for the campaign spread before him on the large oak table.

'What's next on the list?' he asked. 'Have we finalised the horse transport arrangements?'

'M'lord, if I could just suggest a short interview. There is a small gap in your plans this afternoon…' Raymond persisted; time was against him now.

'Gap! Gap in my plans, Raymond?' Strongbow, exasperated now, dropped the formalities with his old friend. 'There is not, and never has been, a gap in my plans, to the best of my knowledge.' He sat back and rested the quill carefully aside. He wasn't a big man. He had a weather-worn, chiselled face and a sharp, penetrating gaze that carried an easy intelligence like a spotlight. It settled on Raymond.

'As you said yourself, m'lord, she is of royal birth, and it might be appropriate to afford her the respect, of which you have just spoken; after all, as I said, you will be… you know… I'd strongly advise… just a few moments…' Raymond was panicking now. He could hear the rustling of skirts and footsteps mounting the wooden staircase which led to the hall.

'Raymond, you look a bit flustered. What's going on?'

The bell rang three o'clock.

'I think you should meet her, m'lord.' Raymond spoke quickly.

There was a knock on the door. Raymond jumped.

'Well,' Strongbow finished, looking to the door. 'It seems the matter is out of my hands.'

❦

THESE NORMANS COULD BUILD castles to defy arrows and armies, but wind and drafts seemed to elude them—our chambers in Ferns were far more comfortable. This large dusky hall was cold, its scattered candles flickered in the dampness despite the large fire cracking and spitting in the broad open hearth

The flames seemed to pause and then surge as a door opened in a far wall and a party of four men entered, engrossed in conversation. Seeing me, they fell silent. The handsome young man who had accompanied Le Gros in the courtyard smiled broadly; I did not know the others.

The smaller one was a well-built, sturdy man of military bearing with a quiet but fierce expression. His padded gambeson—the thick overcoat worn under the mail shirt for protection against heavy blows—added to his barrel-like appearance. A functional leather belt carried the weight of his undecorated longsword over saddle-worn leather breeches and knee-high boots. Dressed for effect rather than display, he would seldom be seen otherwise. His name, I was to discover, was Robert FitzStephen.

The dullness of his attire amplified the opulence of his companion's. Dressed in a long blood-red damask robe, hemmed with ivory embroidery signifying seniority in the church, he carried a sheaf of rolled manuscripts under his left arm. The ornate chain of office that hung about his shoulders carried an overly large wooden crucifix, carved and embossed with gold at the edges. He seemed the antithesis of the military man—the priests of their church dressing for display, not effect. Their God, it seemed, would impoverish a people to cow them into submission with their gold-and-jewel-laced dresses, cathedrals and palaces. Even the very gates of their paradise, they said, were carved from pearl, as if to say, 'Give us what meagre means you possess in this life, and we promise you riches in the next.' At least there was a brutal honesty with which the dullness of the sword stole wealth, rather than the deceit of this fine-robed promise, playing on the gullibility of the vulnerable—penury for salvation.

Standing apart from the others was a tall grey-bearded man with prominent eyes and a refined manner. His style of dress differed from what I had seen of the Norman nobility in Chepstow; I was to learn it was acquired in France from where this man, Sir Hervey de Montmorency, had recently arrived. The man's apparently agreeable manner and open disposition were to quickly dissipate as a salutary reminder of how unsound first impressions can be, particularly those of the practiced courtier.

Le Gros glanced nervously from me to the man seated behind the large oak table, whom I knew, only by sight, to be Strongbow, the Earl of Pembroke. He was a man more than twice my age: not as old as my father, but there was little difference. Tall, he leant over the papers arranged on his desk from his high-backed chair. His reddish hair and freckles were more of my race than I had expected.

Ever mannerly, Le Gros, despite having been coerced into this audience, made a great show of genuine courtesy as I strode the long length of the hall to where they were gathered. They were clearly surprised by my arrival.

'Delighted you could make the time, m'lady,' Strongbow said, rising to take my hand. His manner was impeccable.

'And please do let me apologise for having neglected to pay my respects to date. Our planning for the assistance we will provide your father has completely consumed me.'

'M'lord,' I said, offering him a curtsey. 'I fully understand, and your help is greatly appreciated.'

'And to what do we owe the pleasure?' the grey-bearded man cut in, giving a show of courtesy that was not, I thought, matched in his tone, which had a rasp of impatience about it. I was feeling very unsure of myself, and his nearly abrupt manner unnerved me. I hadn't expected hostility, but then again, I had entered their domain with very little warning.

But our father had chosen not to keep us informed of his negotiations with these Normans. We survived on the scraps of hints and whispered conversations amongst the servants. From these Donal learned that our father had, at the very least, promised my hand to Strongbow when he brought his army to Ireland. While being of marriageable age, I was dismayed at this, not least because in the Irish custom the consent of the bride was required—Brehon law did not tolerate marriage by coercion. In time I was to learn that the secrecy that shrouded the marriage was owing to the Norman law that required the permission of the English king for any such marriage, a permission that would not be forthcoming from Henry II, who remained hostile to Strongbow. So my betrothal was to be a tightly guarded secret, even from me.

Furthermore, I had seen Strongbow for the first time late one evening as I strolled on the battlements. There was a strong wind blowing, and the hooded crows careened through the sky. They had made the recesses in the roof of the Great Tower their own but seemed to abandon the refuge of their nests there in high winds, to screech their cackle at me as I strode the walls.

Gusts carried rain, dampening my whipping hair.

Through the wind, the noise of iron-shod hooves clattered over the cobbles, echoing around the courtyard of the lower bailey. The main gates to the castle were like nothing I had ever seen in Ireland. Two enormous towers, built close together and pocked with arrow loops and murder holes, straddled the iron-clad gates and protected the entrance. For added security, two immense iron portcullises could be easily dropped into place by a system of counterweights. Donal, captivated by the system of levers and pullies, had explained to me how they worked.

Retreating into the shadow of the late evening light, I had watched as Strongbow rode with his attendants through the middle bailey gate to the Great Tower in the upper reaches of the castle. Dismounting with the agility of a much younger man, for I knew him to be over forty, he handed his reins to a young groom and thanked him. I heard him enquire after the boy's mother on some matter of her health. Then he bounded up the wide timber stairs that approached a balustraded platform opening in front of a large ornate doorway. While the castle was built with military intentions, the intricate saltire carvings in the stone lintel and arches surrounding the diamond-shaped patterns embedded in orange mortar spoke of the pride and wealth that had flourished in times past in Strongbow's family, the de Clares. In the frame of the doorway, the light thrown from the fire within threw his shadow across the courtyard, and for a moment I thought he paused and looked my way. I withdrew deeper into the shadow of the wall. Delaying momentarily, he turned and entered the hall, his shadow vanishing with the light.

This was not the stuff of my dreams. I, like all young girls, had woven the tapestry of my future in sunlit meadows, rich colours of cloth and laughter bathed in the passion and love of a handsome suitor who prospered on his devotion to me and our life together. This dream had withered on the flotsam-stained shoreline of Ireland along with other childish notions. I mourned the loss of my hopes, at the spirit-sapping price I would have to pay to bring Eanna to safety. But it was a lesser burden to bear than the gripping underbelly of pain I felt in Eanna's pale blue eyes, fearful and lonely. His childish bewilderment at the cruelty, his anguished cries, his silent weeping. I saw it all as though through a fog, which would allow no touch or words of comfort…just to witness the pain, the uncomprehending pain of the child.

So it would be done. I would marry Strongbow. Donal, although sensitive to my disappointments, felt that the offer would give us some sway with the Normans if we played our hand carefully. We could use it to discover their plans and ultimately influence the course of events. It would require great care and a deal more brazenness on my part for it to succeed, but it could work. I wasn't at all as confident as he was about it, but it was important that they take heed of us now. 'That's more the case for you than for me, Aoife,' he said. 'If you are to marry Strongbow, you should show him your steel now.' He laughed. 'And more so with his leading men. They need to respect you, at the very least.'

So we had planned this encounter with Strongbow. I would be alone, and in that it would carry all the more weight, he tried to assure me.

However, alone in the expanse of the hall of the Great Tower for the first time, I could feel the uncontrolled tremor of a rising sob in my chest. The barely suppressed hostility of the grey-bearded man disturbed me. My throat tightened and would allow no words to form. My tears welled and I lowered my head to hide them from the gaze of the men, so many men, in the hall. I had expected to see Strongbow alone, and now the bustle of the hall petered out to a silence matched by the intensity of their scrutiny of me, the uninvited guest—

an expectant silence.

The hush intensified and seemed to stretch indefinitely as Strongbow, close now, my hand resting in his, watched me intently as I stared at his feet. Feeling the shake extending to my hand, he seemed to grasp my predicament and, stepping closer and whispering for my benefit alone, said, 'M'lady, forgive me. You are most brave. Leave this to me.' Then, departing from our private moment, he raised his voice for all to hear:

'Please forgive me, m'lady. I forget myself. It is most remiss of me.' Gesturing to the grey-bearded man. 'Allow me to introduce my uncle, Sir Hervey de Montmorency.' He went on: 'Please forgive Sir Hervey his impatience.' There was a downward twist to his mouth as he threw a barely noticeable glance at him. 'He is keen to further your father's cause expeditiously.'

'Our scholar and font of all knowledge is the Most Reverend Archdeacon of Brecon, Gerald de Barry,' he continued. 'And I believe you are acquainted with Sir Raymond Le Gros and his young cousin Sir Myler FitzHenry.' The young man stepped forward, took my hand and bowed, his lips brushing my skin. The moist warmth of his breath clung to my cold hand, chilled more from a cold sweat than from the damp of the room. His long, thick dark hair was matched with fierce deep eyes, which journeyed from my hand to meet and hold my gaze.

'And my brave and reliable commander, Robert FitzStephen.' The military man took my hand, bowing with great gallantry.

'Gentlemen, delighted.' I curtseyed, recovering myself, saying a silent prayer that the words would come as Strongbow offered me a chair and ordered some refreshments. I politely declined and, things having settled somewhat, turned to him.

'And how might our plans be progressing, m'lord?' I addressed him directly. He paused at this. A faint look of amusement flickered across his face, barely perceptible. Deciding his course, he nodded his head once as if in acquiescence and approached the table, indicating that I should accompany him. Relieved, I presumed he was about to show me something of the preparations that were underway. However, before we could reach the table, Montmorency intervened loudly.

'If you'll allow me, m'lord,' he put in. Then, turning to me, he continued in a dismissive manner. 'These matters are somewhat complex, m'lady. So we won't burden you with the troublesome details.' He smiled derisively to the others and motioned, somewhat flamboyantly, for me to accompany him towards the door, his manner and accent heavily influenced by his life in France.

'Well, you might just indulge me, Sir Hervey,' I said, not moving and holding Strongbow's gaze. I could sense Le Gros becoming decidedly uncomfortable, and to this day, I would swear he moved to put more distance between himself and Montmorency. For his part, Montmorency now made no effort to conceal his frustration with me.

'I really think, m'lord, we don't have time for such trivia with this troublesome girl,' he spat.

Strongbow winced at this, seeming to shudder with revulsion. He turned and slowly approached Montmorency. With an intense gaze, he spoke so quietly that I strained to hear. 'You will never speak of the princess again in such terms.' The great beams and of the hall's high roof boomed his whisper; the flickering candles and crackling fire seemed stilled with the force of his words. Montmorency recoiled from the undisguised venom.

'Apologies, m'lord,' he mumbled.

'I'm sure he meant no offense,' Le Gros added.

There was a controlled ferocity in Strongbow's eyes, but he seemed to check himself.

In time, I was to learn that Strongbow had taken Montmorency into his court at the request of the English king. Montmorency had won the king's trust while doing his bidding in Aquitaine in France, where the king held extensive lands. As such, he was the king's man and required the respect that came with that position.

'Forgive my vehemence, Sir Hervey. I mistakenly believed you were being disrespectful to the princess,' he smiled as he returned to the table, a smile that did not reach his eyes.

'Not at all, m'Lord. A complete misunderstanding,' Montmorency waved the incident away.

'Now, Sir Hervey'—Strongbow was suddenly as affable as he had been threatening a moment ago—'please explain your plan and thinking to the princess.'

Straining under the effort to appear civil, Montmorency went on: 'M'lady. Broadly speaking, our sources tell us that the land seems to be in some turmoil at present. And while this is not unusual, we think we could take some advantage from it if we act quickly. Hence, we plan to send an initial exploratory force to land—'

'Exploratory?' I interrupted him. 'What do you mean by exploratory?' I did not want to stretch Strongbow's goodwill in his tolerance of my intervention, but Donal and I had discussed what was required for any expedition to succeed. We knew our land, our coast, our people and our enemies. And increasingly, we doubted our father's judgement. Consumed by a vicious rage and craving for vengeance at the wrongs, treachery and ill fortune that had befallen him, he had withdrawn deeper into himself and seldom sought our company or counsel.

We needed to ensure that the Normans got this right or Eanna would die. Our army needed to be overwhelming in both size and the pace at which it would sweep through southern Leinster in the first days of any campaign. Loyalty was fickle and followed the strong in Ireland. The kindred families would flock to join us if they thought we would win. Otherwise, they would unite against us with the armies of our enemies: O'Conner, the self-declared high king of Ireland; O'Rourke, the king of Bréifne; and Mac Giolla Patrick, the king of Osraige to the west of Leinster, who had seized half our kingdom when we fled these nine months past.

Montmorency clearly resented my impertinence, but keen not to offend Strongbow again, he continued: 'Well, if you must, m'lady. We believe a force of twenty knights, with the accompanying men at arms and archers. Approximately one hundred and fifty in total, I estimate, should be sufficient.'

'And that's *your* plan, is it, Sir Hervey?' I asked pointedly. I did not want to alienate Strongbow if he was an architect of this expedition, which I was certain would fail. I would need to tread carefully.

'It is, m'lady. And I am confident of its success,' he added.

'M'lord,' I addressed Strongbow directly. 'This number is far too small. It will fail. The families will know it will fail and will unite with our enemies and drive us into the sea once more. Except this time, they will have an even larger force against us, and I doubt we will reach the sea to escape again. It is rank stupidity!'

Montmorency was seething, bristling with a suppressed violence which I suspected he would not be slow to unleash against me in different circumstances. He dared not speak for a moment, struggling to contain his rage.

However, I could see Le Gros and FitzStephen nodding

and murmuring some agreement or approval of my outburst. This, I thought, was not the first time Montmorency's plan had been questioned. Donal had far more confidence in the soundness of judgement in military matters of these gentlemen than he had in our father. He feared they would be overconfident and make the mistake of sending an overly small, unprepared force to a disadvantaged landing on our shore. I was very relieved they were here now. FitzStephen spoke up in favour of landing with a far bigger force to seize the initiative. His battle-scarred face suggested he was well experienced in these matters, and Strongbow clearly respected his views.

Furious, Montmorency moved to place himself between Strongbow and myself, as if to physically obstruct the flow of events over which, he sensed, he was losing control.

'Indeed I admire your enthusiasm, m'lady,' he said. 'However, this plan, of which you are so dismissive, has been drawn up not only by me but by your father as well. You'd agree that he might be more knowledgeable in these matters than you?' He snorted dismissively, heightening the confrontation by goading me into challenging my father's judgement. It would, as Montmorency knew, take a brave person to question Diarmuit MacMurrough's prowess in war, considering the many battles he had fought and won. His reputation was fierce and feared, but as most who live by the sword seldom die in bed, he had now failed and fled his kingdom. His star had fallen somewhat, and his judgement certainly had.

Donal had told me not to plead under any circumstances. Their determination to come to Ireland was not a spoil-seeking raid, from which they would return enriched with plunder. We had come to understand in those early months in Chepstow that, for reasons that would soon become clear, these Normans intended to come to Ireland to settle permanently amongst us. Strongbow's willingness to marry me confirmed this intent. Norman dynasties would be planted to take root in Ireland. In the fertile soil of my own royal womb, through this marriage, the seed of their bloodlines would be legitimised.

Their need for legitimacy was where our power in this relationship with the Normans lay. What I had yet to say about the marriage would undoubtedly shock them. Nonetheless, it was necessary that I establish some sense of respect now if we were to have some influence over events.

Consequently, they must believe I was resolute. Comportment amplified power, just as pity weakened it, Donal had said. 'So hold your head up and speak confidently.'

At that time, standing in the large hall alone, I remember trying hard not to show my panic and wishing Donal was there. I could feel droplets of sweat shivering down my back. Searching for the words we had rehearsed, I recalled nothing…but I knew what I wanted to say.

'My father lost his kingdom. He almost had us all killed. He did stupid things, and now our brother is a prisoner. This plan is more stupidity,' I almost shouted at him. 'They will kill Eanna.' I regretted this at once. I was supposed to avoid mentioning Eanna. The Normans had no interest in saving him. Quite the opposite for some of them, Donal thought. The fewer male heirs to the MacMurrough dynasty around the better.

Strongbow's gaze never faltered during these exchanges. I could feel the intensity of his scrutiny. I have come to see that my thoughts are as impenetrable to others as their own are to me, yet back then I felt he reached behind my eyes with ease.

Now there was a smugness about Montmorency after my childish outburst. 'M'lord, I think the princess may be over-tired. These matters are best left in our hands.' He appeared as if vindicated.

After a long pause, Strongbow looked to Le Gros, who seemed glad to take the opportunity to question Montmorency's plan: 'What harm in listening to what the princess has to say, m'lord.' This seemed to infuriate Montmorency, but Strongbow silenced him with a casual gesture, then turned to me.

'And what so would you suggest, m'lady?' he asked quietly as he invited me to the table where the manuscripts and maps of the campaign plan were arrayed. He wasn't much younger than my father, but there was a warm and thoughtful way about him.

'Thank you, m'lord.' I could feel my hands shaking, so I held them clasped to my skirts. Donal had told me to be clear and assured when it came to the campaign. Uncertainty bred fear. 'Could I ask where you propose to land?' I asked.

'Sir Hervey, please show the princess what you have proposed,' Strongbow instructed Montmorency.

'Well, obviously the closest point to Ferns on the east coast would be most advantageous,' he responded loudly, with a bit more confidence than his nervous appearance suggested at this stage. He pointed to the coast roughly halfway between the coastal towns of Wexford and Dublin.

'M'lady?' Strongbow said, turning to me and inviting my opinion.

Any knowledge of the geography of the east coast of Ireland would expose the risk of this landing. The towns of Dublin, Wexford and Waterford were fortified Norse settlements, with formidable armies and seagoing fleets. Their wealth derived from their long-established trading links across Europe in furs, wines, timber and slaves. They were self-ruled by powerful Norse lords who acknowledged the Irish kings as required but with a fickle loyalty. Of these,

Dublin was by far the largest and most powerful. They would not take kindly to the arrival of the Normans in their hinterland on the east coast, threatening their interests. They would be certain to react.

'In doing so, m'lord, you place our forces within easy reach of the Norse army of Dublin. If they march, we will not even make it to our boats. And if we do, their fleet will sink us,' I said, regaining some composure.

He returned to the table and examined the large parchment map, stretched and anchored between several large ornately decorated silver candlesticks. While he was absorbed with the others joining him at the table, Montmorency stepped forward, passing uncomfortably close. With the others momentarily distracted, he caught my eye, lowered his gaze to my bosom, half sneered and moved to the table. My jaw quivered as I felt the sharp chill of his threat.

'M'lord, the princess's father, the king, assures me that this area of the coast is most suited for our landing,' he said, pointing at the small port of Glascarrig that served Ferns. He went on, 'I wholeheartedly agree and respect his knowledge and experience.'

But Strongbow never lifted his head from the map. There was clear sense in what I was saying. Now was my chance.

'With your permission, m'lord.' I moved to the table, purposefully requiring Sir Hervey to step aside. 'We will be expected in the east, whereas there are better places here for us to land,' I said, pointing to the south coast.

'I see,' Strongbow said eventually. 'And where exactly do you believe might be most advantageous for us to land?'

'There are several places, m'lord. But here,' I said, pointing to a large bay. 'This is Bannow Bay. It has a small tidal island, not shown on this map, actually. From here, it is easy to pass to the mainland on foot at low tide. I know it well. It could also be easily defended. And we would be within striking distance of both Wexford and Waterford, but far enough from Dublin.'

Le Gros, FitzStephen and FitzHenry were clearly in favour and gathered with around the map with Strongow. He pulled several other parchments, which he seemed to examine; he confirmed that none of the others were familiar with this coast and that the Norse army and fleet of Dublin were the most formidable in Ireland. He seemed to place far more weight on the views of FitzStephen and Le Gros in this discussion, which didn't please Montmorency at all. He seemed humiliated, and I was the cause. He looked contemptuously at me and then at the others, who were largely ignoring him now. He seemed to make a decision.

'M'lord, the king and I are in full agreement. We should not cause him any displeasure by questioning the plan. He has, after all, given you the princess's hand in return,' he said to the shock of everyone within earshot. All eyes turned from the table in the silence. They would have believed I was unaware. Le Gros stared at him, an angry twist to his jaw. FitzHenry's eyes darted from me to Strongbow. Strongbow, in turn, glared at Montmorency in disbelief.

Now it had come to the matter which I knew could cause the most upset. Strongbow was clearly embarrassed. Such a delicate matter between us should first be discussed privately. Unhindered by the presence of others, a man and a woman could slowly navigate the delicate currents of their fate, that mix of fortune, duty, the heart and the bedchamber. Whatever it came to, its basis was best laid away from the scrutiny of others. This was highly inappropriate. Strongbow was angry, but I had to deal with it now.

'I beg your pardon, Sir Hervey.' I turned on Montmorency.

'Indeed,' he replied, almost sounding sorry for me. There

was a smugness about him now. A swish of his cloak as he moved to Strongbow's side. 'You may not have been aware, but I have agreed with your father that you are to marry Strongbow upon his arrival in Ireland.' There was a vindictive core in this man, and he clearly wanted to shock and provoke me. He was not aware that I already knew.

Strongbow looked uncomfortable. My first impressions of him were good, but as had been expected, these men had little understanding of Irish customs and law in these matters. Neither the Celts nor the church had managed to fully quench the important role women played in our ways. The deep sinews of ancient Brehon law survived and stretched into the present day, across all aspects of our lives. In that tradition, Danu, the earth mother, was all-important, and this echo sounded today in our customs. Women were not only valued for childbearing; we were also regarded as equal and seen as a balancing force in the great scheme of life. With great power in daily life, we also had rights to own property, rule kingdoms, wage war and decide our own futures.

And today that meant that no marriage could take place without my consent.

'My father may have suggested this, but I have agreed to no such arrangement,' I said bluntly. I had to tread carefully, as I needed to retain Strongbow's sympathy while not diminishing the force of my words.

Undeterred Montmorency continued, 'I'm sure it's a surprise, m'lady, but you will become accustomed to it in time. Your father has already agreed to it,' He was almost smiling now.

Not fully recovered from Montmorency's indiscretion and the turn in the conversation, Strongbow nonetheless, and probably unconsciously, distanced himself from him. He would take no part in adding to my discomfort at learning of my betrothal in such a manner. However, this concern was quickly overwhelmed by his shock upon learning of the illegitimacy of that promise, as I now made clear.

Avoiding Strongbow's gaze, I purposefully spoke directly to Montmorency; it was better to deliver these unpalatable truths to him. 'My hand in marriage is not my father's to give. You clearly need to acquaint yourself with our ways, Sir Hervey. That choice is mine, and mine alone.'

A shuffle of disbelief rippled through the hall. I held my gaze on Montmorency, trying to gauge Strongbow's reaction reflected in Montmorency's confusion. His rattled eyes darted around me, his jaw agape. I remember his broken yellow teeth. Muted, he mouthed nothings. The hush of his companions amplified their bewilderment.

In the Norman tradition, women were tools of diplomacy, married to further a family's interests through alliances. Male relatives decided their futures. A woman's wishes played no part whatsoever, and these men standing in the Great Tower with me today were obviously wholly unaccustomed to anything different. No one spoke, fearful; words had consequences now.

Collecting himself, Strongbow, otherwise expressionless, regarded me now with a searching gaze that never wavered. He eventually spoke into the silence.

'Archdeacon, what is your knowledge of these matters?'

'Yes, m'lord. I was meaning to bring some trivial matters to your attention.'

'Trivial?' Strongbow said.

Ignoring this, the archdeacon continued. 'M'lord. There are some archaic pagan customs still surviving in Ireland which the church has not entirely suppressed, as yet. However, they have no legitimacy in the eyes of God and may be safely ignored.'

Strongbow said nothing. The archdeacon's hand drifted

to the crucifix hanging from his neck. His fingers found the splayed figure of his god and stroked. He swallowed, his throat suddenly dry. He looked uncomfortable under the searing gaze of Strongbow as he proceeded to tell how the church in Ireland struggled to eradicate the deep sinews of Brehon law and the ancient pulse: that slow pagan heartbeat buried in the soil and blood of its land and 'uncivilised' people; how the foundations of these beliefs differed fundamentally from Christianity in their emphasis of the Goddess as opposed to the God: female over male. Primitive superstitions of how she controlled the rain, sunshine and the harvest; the health and fertility of man, woman and beast; indeed, the soil itself. Nothing was inseparable in this belief system, and the Goddess, the female, the woman, was at its core.

'Absurd heresies,' he said. 'They claim that this ancient code of lawful behaviour, Brehon law, emerged from the mist of times preceding the Celts and probably the Druids themselves. In this they are correct,' he continued, warming to his task. 'It is nothing more than a collection of confused primitive beliefs from heathen times before the arrival of God's teachings on earth. God be praised,' he intoned, opening his arms to give thanks to the heavens. 'For these pagans, not having the God-given gift of letters, it was an unreliable oral tradition, passed down fitfully through the centuries by word of mouth until it was eventually put to paper by the lawgivers sect, the Brehons—descendants of the Druids who had carried the lineage of the law through the ages in the great tomb, the Senchus Mór—a diabolical incantation of the devil's work I myself have been witness to.' He shuddered at the memory.

He went on to explain how the 'tentacles' of these laws had grown over thousands of years, expanding through the experience of daily life into 'a myriad of absurd laws to establish rights, obligations and punishments through a system of fines. Wholly ludicrous, it upended the Christian truth of the law deriving solely from the king by divine right. It was a common, poorly managed system of law, developed from the people by the people for the people. Every man and woman, from king or queen to servant or slave, was subject to the law. 'Perfectly ridiculous,' he concluded, appealing to his audience, laughing at the absurdity of it all.

Strongbow sat down. His hand coursing the skin on his clean-shaven chin, he said, 'If I understand you correctly, Archdeacon, and correct me if I'm wrong here, with this system of law—Brehon law—a king does not make the law. In a sense, the law is independent of the king, and he, like all his subjects, must obey the law. Correct?'

'Exactly!' exclaimed the archdeacon. 'I can't tell you how absurd it is.'

'No, I think you can,' Strongbow said. 'Please go on.' He sat back and listened, captivated as he learnt of our law.

I was impressed by the archdeacon's depth of knowledge, which was far greater than mine. While he could recount large tracts of the Senchus Mór at will, I could remember little of what my tutors had earnestly tried to teach. And despite the archdeacon's animated disdain, that knowledge was certainly fascinating to Strongbow, who sat forward, inching his frame over the table as if imbibing as sustenance what he was hearing.

As the afternoon drew into early evening, he listened intently. He learned that the objective of the law was fairness, justice and peace. Rejecting savage reprisals or revenge, the death penalty was all but prohibited. It sought harmony above retribution in the people it governed with detailed laws covering every aspect of daily life. Humane at its core, it contained overriding provisions to protect the innate rights of the less fortunate.

'M'lord, most astonishing of all, you will accuse me of jesting when I tell you that the penalty for unlawfully killing a man is a fine!' He paused. 'A fine! Yes, it is true. There is a detailed set of fines extending from slander, injury and theft to murder itself. Most incredible of all, there is a sizeable fine for what they term as the serious offence of insulting a woman!' At this, as if remembering my presence, he bowed in apology, claiming he was merely recounting the laws themselves for the benefit of those present.

We had all taken seats by the time the archdeacon explained how judgement was in the hands of the Brehons, the lawgivers. They studied and practised at the feet of their seniors for decades before presiding. Their wealth and lands were held independently and subject to no lord or king. They were regarded with a mystic reverence in the land and, as far as he was concerned, were a living embodiment of Satan despoiling God's earth.

'Archdeacon. How could this system of law, unique from anything I know in many lands, have existed, wholly different from ours?' Strongbow enquired.

'The island, m'lord, has not been blessed with the civilising influence of those who came to our shores over the centuries—particularly the Romans, who brought the gift of Christ to our land. God be praised.'

Strongbow raised an eyebrow and smiled. 'You're referring to the hordes of raiders who have repeatedly swept across the continent onto these shores over the centuries, I presume?' he asked, not expecting an answer. 'The very ones who visited quite a bit of devastation on this land before the civilising benefits became obvious, and I include us Normans in that, gentlemen.' He laughed. 'But before us, there were the Angles, Saxons, Norse and of course the Romans. Amazingly, none of them ever made it to Ireland.'

'The Norse did, my lord,' the archdeacon interjected. 'But

still, compared to Britain, the island has remained relatively unscarred—unblessed, I mean—its laws for thousands of years virtually unchanged.'

'Remarkable, truly remarkable!' Strongbow said, rising, animated now. 'A system whereby a king cannot arbitrarily make laws and impose them on his subjects, strip them of their wealth, deny them of their inheritance…it seems to me we have found a paradise, gentlemen!' He laughed, throwing a knowing look to his men, who joined him. I would later understand the meaning in his words.

'However, m'lord, we need pay no heed to these pagan ways,' said Montmorency, not fully grasping the implications of what they had all just heard. But I could sense a depth of understanding dawning upon Strongbow, a man of more refined sensibilities.

Thus, I spoke clearly into the silence. 'In doing so, Sir Hervey, your race will never have any legitimacy in Ireland.' I knew Strongbow and the others fully understood the importance of that fact. They would forever be seen as a transitory presence with no legitimate right woven into the permanent fabric of our ways. They could claim no lineage on which to build a permanent dynasty and would forever be regarded as bagmen and freebooters. And this was not the Norman way.

The Normans had an established reputation for successful conquest. From their humble origins in Norway to Normandy in France, from where they had seized one of the most valuable crowns in Europe in the lands of our neighbours, the Britons. Through southern Italy to the eastern Mediterranean, their power would extend and take root. Their goal was permanency, and this was achieved by settling and adopting local ways and legitimising their presence.

Strongbow, having fully grasped the importance of what I had said, seemed resigned but certain as he approached me, taking my hand again. 'M'lady, again I must apologise. I seem to be doing a lot of that today,' he said with a gentle smile. 'I was remiss in not acquainting myself with your fine traditions and culture.' Looking directly at me, his penetrating gaze lingered as if conversing with my thoughts.

Then, resolute, he purposefully released my hand as if releasing me of any obligation, acknowledging my free will. He turned to his men and announced quietly, 'There will be no marriage without the freely given consent of the princess.'

The shock seemed to rock the others in unison. Startled looks were exchanged, despairing heads shook, a rising murmur of dissent eventually broke into voiced objections: 'The very success of the venture is predicated on the marriage!' 'It is a necessity!' 'It has to happen!' 'This is madness!' On and on they went, their cackles lost in the high-beamed roof of the Great Tower.

Having heard enough, Strongbow eventually silenced them with a sharp glance.

The men, now helpless spectators of an exchange between a man and a woman. An exchange that would determine their futures and those of their families for generations to come. An exchange entangled in matters of state, kingdoms and wealth, which by their very nature were somewhat malleable. But most chillingly, this exchange was subject to matters of the heart, of human attraction; matters of little certainty, tempered by no reason, ever incomprehensible.

Their fears were etched on their faces. The woman, whose next words would determine their fates, was barely free from the blushes of childhood. A young woman who probably harboured the childish notions of romance, uncorrupted as yet by the mosaic of experience that life would inevitably bring.

Little did they realise that, far beyond them, it was the very fate of Ireland that would be decided.

'M'lord, thank you for your understanding.' I paused. I could hear the frantic whispering and shuffling feet on the worn flagstones, then a deafening silence. My pounding heart seemed to muffle everything. I was trying to find the words.

'I understand duty, m'lord.' I hesitated and looked directly at him now. 'But I must also have respect. Respect for my wishes, my ways and my advice. I will not be passive, I will not be idle and I must be involved.' I looked away momentarily from the intensity of his gaze. 'If you can respect these wishes, I will consent to be your wife upon your arrival in Ireland.'

A collective sigh, a release of tension, a taking of breath—a sense of airiness released into the hall. The archdeacon steadied himself before taking a seat.

'M'lady. You have my word of honour,' Strongbow said, placing a kiss on my hand. 'I would be honoured, truly honoured, if you would be my wife.' He paused and looked to his stunned men. 'And we will land in Bannow Bay.'

'In that case, m'lord, I will be your wife.' I curtseyed, turned and walked the long length of the hall, feeling the searing gaze of the men on my back, nearly driving the chill from my body.

And as the heavy door closed behind me, I heard Le Gros break the leaden silence with his characteristic good wit: 'It's at moments like these that I yearn for the tranquillity of battle.'

Chapter Four
LOVE AND DUTY

Chepstow Castle, Wales
Spring 1167

The sharp white light of the rising sun skimmed through the patches of mist lingering in the hollows surrounding Chepstow Castle. It was cold for late spring, and the frost hadn't yet left the land, delaying its wake from the winter slumber. But the sharpness was gone from the chill, with teasing hints of warmth quickly snatched away to remind us that the Goddess wasn't quite ready to let her children of the summer tumble from the earth.

The castle was wakening. From the ramparts I could see the men beyond the sowing fields hunting the cover at the edge of the forest with the hounds, making the most of the dawn chill, which held a prey's scent to the ground. The concentrated silence of their frenetic, haphazard search was shattered when a howl rose and the pack formed as one, then quickly flowed away, the men scrambling before disappearing into the forest.

The farrier's voice boomed in the courtyard below as he harangued the boys who were bringing the last of the horses in from the paddocks just outside the walls. The breath of horse and man mixed in the heat of the forge as he worked, bare chested, the sweat of the younger nervous animals thick on his back as he murmured his calming charm to them, tending their hooves. He gently chided a younger animal to use its three legs to carry its weight rather than his back as he pared its fourth hoof secured between his knees.

'I'm not your fourth leg, Ness,' he said, shifting his weight. Ness was a common name for much-loved mares, named after the great Welsh princess Nesta, I suspected. The care for the horses had surprised me, but I was to learn of their importance to these people.

The Normans had created an empire from the saddle. When battles were still fought on foot, they had perfected warfare on horseback. The horses—destriers—were bred to carry the weight of a knight in full armour; they were trained to be brave and to kick and bite in the fight. The knights themselves trained incessantly, fighting from the saddle—at the gallop and in close quarters—riding formations, charges and feigned retreats. This was how William the Conqueror had vanquished this land one hundred years ago at a decisive battle at Hastings, so Myler told me. With a force of six thousand men, he had landed from Normandy and defeated a far superior force of forty thousand Anglo-Saxons to take the English crown. Like the Irish, the Anglo-Saxons used the horse mainly for transport. They had dismounted and arranged themselves in the formation used in battles of the day—and still used in Ireland today—the shield wall: men on foot in lines and rows, their shields locked together. The battles would be fought at close quarters, in the breath, smell, sweat and blood of one's enemy, in long pushing, pulsing crushes.

But the Normans hadn't obliged that day. They attacked the shield wall on horseback. Using the skills and tactics I witnessed them practicing every day, they had prevailed and taken the crown. Donal and I watched them train, knowing Irish armies would be no match in an open field. Although Donal had charge of our cavalry in Ireland, he knew he had much to learn from these men and was training daily with FitzStephen and Le Gros.

On this morning, in the sand-covered practice area to the side of the forge, Myler was showing Donal the techniques used with a favoured weapon of the Normans, the longsword. A weighty two-handed sword, half the length of a tall man, it was double edged and had a heavy pommel below the grip. Mostly decorative, the pommel could also be used to bludgeon an opponent with a heavy blow. I watched as he demonstrated an array of guard positions, inviting Donal to strike and each time absorbing the attack on the thick part of the blade near the grip. He then countered with a variety of cuts using a rotating motion of the sword to deliver blows of sufficient power that would easily cut through anything but the best plate armour. Taller than Donal, Myler moved with a practiced grace that made light of the heavy blade as it flashed and whirled around him.

He caught a glimpse of me watching from the ramparts, and I noticed his movements becoming more exaggerated and overly flamboyant—he was showing off now. Without acknowledging my presence, he removed his leather tunic and untied the bind on his long shoulder-length hair. With his shirt unlaced and his hair dancing, he flowed through the swordplay; it had the intended effect. He was certainly a handsome young man, and I suspected his beauty was only surpassed by his confidence. Donal was putting up a good fight, but he wasn't used to the weight of the sword.

We had learned to fight up close with a stabbing spear or

short sword. The battleaxe, which had been brought to Ireland by the Norsemen, was the preference of some. It was used where more brute force was required, but it was too heavy for me. We had also taken on the practice of naming our swords from the Norse. It was a long tradition among them to imbue the power of their gods into the steel of their blades with names that put fear into the hearts of their enemies, such as Skullsplitter, Warflame or Manslayer. And when my father had given me my own short sword, he had told me to name it carefully: 'Name it from your dreams, for a sword can mark your destiny, girl. Take your time and don't worry, the name will come to you, and you will know.'

The sword was magnificent. As long as my arm, it was deceptively strong for its lightness. Swirling flight-like patterns flowed along and through the blade, repeating and ever changing in a binding unity, the result of a long forging process in which the layers of iron were pressed and twisted before being hammered and polished into form. My father had spent a considerable sum with the best Norse sword forger in Dublin to produce it, and he had not been disappointed

Nearly a full season passed without the name coming to me, until one sweltering day, as I lay alone, drifting on my thoughts, in the long swirling yellow-green grass of the meadow, with the blade pressed to my chest. I was young and dreamt of the things that fill a young girl's head as she wakens to life's possibilities. I wanted to be beautiful, happy, admired, graceful, swift, loyal, joyous . . . and as my mind wandered, the swallows flashed above me, skimming the waves of rolling grass, screaming and careering with effortless ease, diving recklessly one moment, speeding skyward the next.

'Fáinleog!' That was it: Swallow. I would name my sword

after the bird that sang of everything I wished for. I jumped up and ran to find my father.

'I like it,' he said. 'They are deadly to their prey; they never see them coming.' And I suppose there was that truth too.

I had learned the sword skills from Donal. He taught me to use the round wooden shield to deflect a blow before getting close to the body of an opponent, using sharp stabbing lunges while moving swiftly to unbalance my foe. And that day in Chepstow, after Donal had taken another rap to the side of the head from the flat of Myler's sword, I shouted down, 'Get closer, Donal. Don't let him room to swing at you!' The practice arena was full of sparring couplets and groups under the instruction of the arming sergeants. It was difficult for Donal to make himself heard above the noisy clacking of wooden training swords and metallic rings as the iron swords met.

'It's not so easy,' he shouted as they paused their bout and looked up at me. Myler bowed, as if just seeing me there on the ramparts. 'He's quite good,' Donal said, 'in case you haven't noticed.' He held up his half sword, which was a good deal shorter than Myler's longsword. 'And this isn't long enough.'

'Well, if you take a step forward it'll be plenty long,' I responded, and Myler grinned at Donal's discomfort. Some of the men going through their paces sniggered. They enjoyed seeing the great Irish warrior belittled by his sister.

'Well, if it's that simple, why don't you just get down here and show us all how it's done properly, why don't you?' He was a bit testy now and fully expected me to back down. He was by far a better swordsman than I, and he knew Myler would easily best me.

'I will so,' I responded and strutted down to the cheers of the men, who, happy for the break, gathered to watch the

AOIFE OF LEINSTER

entertainment. I had no idea of what to do as I marched into the arena, but I wasn't going to be humiliated by not trying after the goading from Donal. However, Myler was overconfident, and I'd see how I could use that.

'Thank you,' I said, to the man who handed me his wooden practice sword. I purposefully handled it awkwardly and asked if they had one with a softer grip, as it was quite coarse on my skin. 'I could get a splinter,' I complained loudly to the grins and laughter of the men gathered to watch.

Donal started to look a bit worried; he knew I was well capable of handling a sword. 'Now you behave yourself, Aoife,' he said under his breath as he took my cloak. 'He's a good lad; there's no badness in him, and he's on our side . . . remember that!'

'Well, you started it!' I snapped at him and strode into the centre to face Myler, dragging the sword after me for effect.

'There's really no need, m'lady,' Myler said quietly. His chest was exposed in the mid-morning heat. I could see the sweat glistening on his forehead and neck. His knee-length leather boots and tight breeches sat under the flowing white linen shirt. His dark eyes reflected a soft kindness which seemed to seep through into his gentle smile.

'Yes, there is!' I insisted. Turning to the crowd now gathered, I said, 'When do we start, Sergeant? Is there a horn or something?'

Grinning and shaking his head, the sergeant gestured as if to suggest he would have nothing to do with it but we could assume the bout had begun.

'Great, so we've started,' I said, and Myler shrugged his shoulders and stared at me. 'Would you mind just showing me a few of those stances you take at the start?' I went on, lifting the light wooden sword.

'Certainly, m'lady. I'd be delighted.' He seemed to relax

now, far more comfortable to be in teaching mode with me. 'There are three common stances, which suit most purposes.' Turning side-on, he lifted the long blade to rest over his right shoulder. 'In this stance, I might appear somewhat relaxed, when in fact I can quickly deliver a variety of cuts . . . so if you might just stand back.' When I obliged, he quickly delivered a dazzling array of sword strokes to the general murmur of approval of the onlookers.

'The second is more aggressive, used more to intimidate.' He stepped back, holding the blade directly above his head, the pommel facing me. 'For that reason, it's known as the offensive.'

I could sense a weary boredom creeping into the crowd as a few wandered away, disappointed in the show. Although I could see Donal starting to look a bit agitated, pacing around. I thought he might be trying to get Myler's attention.

'Fascinating,' I encouraged Myler, sensing something was coming. 'And the third?'

'Well, that's a more nuanced stance, used to throw your opponent off guard by seeming to drop your own. It's called the 'inviting stance.' He spread his arms by his sides in an inviting manner, standing with feet planted squarely but apart. And there it was.

Already close, I quickly stepped my left foot forward and swung my good leg, using my weight to deliver a forceful kick to his exposed manhood. And it was one of my better ones. It had always amazed me how nature had chosen to leave such an important and delicate part of the male body hanging around in such a vulnerable place, particularly with little girls like me in the vicinity. Myler was probably thinking something along those lines as he collapsed to his knees and clutched the offended area. If anything, I thought, it proved that the Goddess was definitely in charge and had a sense of humour.

Anyway, the thump of the kick landing home seemed to reverberate around the courtyard. There was a shocked momentary silence followed by a collective groan from all the men. Donal had his head in his hands. But always being one to finish a job, I delivered a swift rap with my practice sword to the back of Myler's head. The crowd seemed to recover themselves and broke into uproarious laughter as Myler, still kneeling, clutched the back of his head. But then, seeing me still within kicking distance, he decided it better to protect his manhood and hastily dropped his hands again. The crowd was in convulsions, and I have to say it was funny to see and I couldn't help but join in. And that was probably my mistake.

With a determined look, he sprung to his feet and rushed me. I managed to get a swinging glancing blow to the side of his head, but his weight and speed easily bowled me to the ground. Tumbling around he managed to use his weight to pin me down before holding my wrists above my head to stop my wild sword sweeps. I kicked at him furiously as the onlookers roared. He grappled, using his weight and hips to eventually still me, leaving me with my legs wrapped around his waist in a most unladylike manner. Well, unladylike for the centre of the practice arena with half the garrison looking on.

Stilled now, under his weight, his breathing heavy, matching mine, his lips brushed my nose as we settled. I could have kissed his eyes—and almost did. Instinctively, I wetted my dry lips with my tongue. His eyes left mine and moved to my lips, and his tongue moistened his own. Almost touching, I felt the draft of his warm breath.

'I think you have beaten me, Sir Myler,' I spoke softly, enjoying the moment. When he didn't react but held my gaze, I went on. 'Sir Myler, I submit.'

'M'lady?' He seemed to somewhat recover but still made no effort to remove himself.

'Is this the way you Normans always finish a fight?' I asked, goading him a little.

'M'lady?'

'It seems the swelling has set in rather quickly where I kicked you,' I said, our eyes still locked. That seemed to snap him out of it, and he quickly jumped up to the applause of the crowd, who were cheering loudly. He helped me up and, after adjusting our clothing, we bowed and curtseyed to the onlookers.

As we made our way from the centre of the arena—Myler with a certain hesitancy in his step—I quietly whispered, 'It was most impressive, actually.' He looked puzzled and turned to face me.

'Impressive. What?'

'Well, it was hardly your swordplay.' I smiled. Grasping my meaning, he threw his head back, laughing, and lifted me by the waist onto a grain cart by the entrance. He turned to the crowds, who were thoroughly enjoying this. 'To the honourable men and women and gallant warriors of Chepstow and Leinster, I give you your new champion, Aoife of Leinster.' And the crowd roared and some of the men hoisted me playfully and marched me around the arena to thunderous applause and laughter.

As THE SPRING drew to a close, the frantic pace of the castle settled into the slower routines of summer labour, the rising heat tempering exertions by mid-morning. Strongbow had taken to inviting me to dine or walk with him when he was in the castle, which was not often. He dined in the Great Tower, where the servants set a table close to the large open hearth, taking advantage of the expansive view of the River Wye. The broad tidal river swept past the vast north-facing windows of the castle, turning sharply east and then south on its slow, relentless journey into the vast estuary of Severn at Bristol, less than an hour's ride away. He jokingly told me that his nickname, Strongbow, derived from this—*striguil*, which in Welsh meant 'river bend'—rather than the story that his father had been rather adept with the Welsh war bow. Quite the contrary, like him his father couldn't hit the ground with an arrow. The glassy water reflected the listless sails of the boats moving sluggishly under oar below the castle.

Ferns would also be settling into its season's rhythm; the sowing, tending, and harvesting would not wait, the new masters imposing themselves and the townsfolk submitting to creeping acceptance. Eanna imprisoned, in fetters? Every day that passed lessened the threat of the return of the MacMurroughs. Every such day diminished Eanna's value as a hostage and magnified his threat as the remaining male MacMurrough heir on the island, the blade inching closer with each dawn.

On evenings when the summer sun swept along the river, Strongbow would invite me to join him on a small castellated private terrace close to the kitchens and storerooms. The river ran directly below this part of the castle, under a sheer wall where, when the tide was right, the provisioning barques of the traders would tie up. A large ratcheted heavy oak winch reached out from the kitchens over the river and was used to haul barrels of wine, dry goods and household wares. The heavier barrels dangled and, wind-buffeted, occasionally bounced dangerously against the wall; but the staff worked quickly and, with Strongbow watching, seemed to manage well enough.

I preferred walking or watching the views and activity

from the terrace to dining in the hall with him. Initially the conversations were quite strained, so the river and boats provided a distraction and eased the tension. Pleasantries were a labour to him; he was not naturally at ease with a woman less than half his age. He was unmarried, which was not unusual for lords in constrained circumstances. I was sure he had mistresses and probably children as old as me. It was quite normal, indeed expected, for Norman lords to take mistresses. Not much different from Ireland, really, where men could take two wives, although under our Brehon law, the first could divorce the man and take a sizeable portion of his wealth with her, if she so wished. That tended to keep everyone reasonable, and it seemed to suit some women, who had tired of their husband's attentions.

And women also had their own appetites, although we have always been far more discriminating than men. Recognising this, our ways allowed women to take lovers with or without the approval of their families, and this indulgence was protected in our laws. Indeed, I was no angel myself in these matters and fully expected Strongbow to behave as men do.

Gradually our conversations became more relaxed. He was quite witty, in a dry sort of way, and he asked a lot of questions and listened attentively as I described the land, laws and people of Ireland. He paid particular attention to my father's enemies and the events leading to our escape to Bristol. I described the night of the attack on Ferns and how we barely got through the gate and how my father had abandoned Eanna who, unseen by us in the dim light, had slipped from his horse just outside the gate and fled.

'I'm not sure I would have acted much differently,' he replied, shocking me as we stood on the terrace one evening. Seeing my reaction and realising what he had said, he went on: 'I'm sorry, Aoife. I didn't mean it that way.' He paused and seemed to search my face for his next words.

'Aoife. Your father holds the weight of the inheritance of your bloodline on his shoulders. God knows, I understand that burden.' Seeing how shaken I was by what he had said, he took my hand and continued, almost pleadingly. 'Aoife, please listen. Any lord or king holds his place in the shadow of his ancestors. These unbroken lines stretch deep into the past, and it is a heavy duty for us to ensure that it carries cleanly into the future.' He was very earnest now. 'That is seldom achieved with clean hands or a clean conscience.' He paused again, and I could see he felt that burden's weight in his own life. 'That is a luxury that is not in the destiny of people with bloodlines like yours and mine.'

'But he left him in the gate and fled!' I almost wept now; the thought made me shudder.

'I know . . . but listen to me. Please. I wasn't there, but if he had turned back, he would have blocked your escape and the enemy bowmen would have concentrated their arrows on you. I don't think any of you would have made it through that gate.'

I was stunned into silence.

He continued. 'Whatever his motives, he did the right thing. Most of you escaped. The bloodline survives. And I doubt that this sits easily on your father's conscience. It is possibly why he behaves as badly as he does.'

Turning to face the river, glittering with flashes of low evening sun across the dark waters, he placed his hands on the smooth granite topstone and stared at the meadow, which reached down to the far bank.

'Having said that, and forgive me if I offend you, but I'm not sure your father has the character that is required to make a great king.' He paused, waiting to see my reaction. Seeing none, he continued, 'Difficult decisions can be explained and understood. I believe you must encourage men to follow you with the better virtues, rather than coercing them.' He paused again, judging his next words before he spoke.

'However, I do understand your father and his position. In fact, I have agreed to support him, as it is not so very much different from my own.' He waited, as if expecting me to say something.

When I said nothing, he went on to tell me of his own family and how events had brought him to his strained relationship with the English king, Henry II. Henry had come to the throne in 1154 after a long civil war in which Strongbow sided with the losing side—King Stephen. Stephen had, not long previously, come to the rescue of Strongbow's family, and as a consequence, Strongbow, unlike his own father, had wholeheartedly thrown his support behind him in the war against King Henry.

'But you behaved honourably,' I objected. 'You stood by your loyalties . . . unlike my father, who will betray anyone and anything to preserve his crown.'

Turning to look at me, he spoke, his voice now strained: 'And so he should—as my own father did! He died during the war, but before that he changed allegiances many times depending on which side held the upper hand and was most likely to win at that particular moment in time. He was fickle in his loyalties.' He was angry now, but his frustration was with himself and what he considered his own naivety at the time. 'I was young and idealistic, and when he died, I became the earl and committed fully to Stephen. He lost,' he spat, 'and now I have been stripped of great swaths of land and King Henry won't even recognise me as the earl.' His hands gripped the wall. He looked miserable now, staring at his feet.

'I was stupid.' He shrugged, shaking his head. 'My father

told me that loyalty ebbs and flows, that there are no absolutes in it, that we must sense the wind and bend with it. But me, I thought I knew better, and look at where that has got me, my family, my followers, my inheritance . . . everything.'

He went on. 'Don't you see? A lot of people are suffering, and my bloodline could end because of my silly notions of honour.' His voice was lower now. These were his innermost thoughts—thoughts I doubted he shared with many—and I could see his grief. I moved beside him by the wall and placed my hand on his. He turned to hold my gaze, and I saw he was close to tears.

'But you,' I said, purposefully setting him apart from my father, 'you think of others first. Not only of yourself. Your men choose to follow you. Their families are cared for and happy.' I thought for a moment that he might not know how his people spoke so warmly and respectfully of him. 'This place, your home, is a happy, prosperous place. These people will not hear a word against you! Don't you know this?' I nearly pleaded with him, exasperated.

'Yes,' he said, nodding his head. 'Yes, I know . . . and that makes it all the harder to bear.' He shuddered. 'They place great trust in me, all their faith in me, Aoife.' He sighed and then, seeming to collect himself, straightened and continued: 'So I must do everything to repay that trust and secure their future. I owe that to them. Even if that means I must bend a little every now and then.' He was smiling now as he once again turned to look at me.

I sensed he had spoken more than he intended. After a moment, he went to pour each of us a glass of rich burgundy wine, which I had grown to enjoy sharing with him when we met in the evenings. The wine was decanted from the oak barrels that were stored in the cellar down the flagstone steps leading from the kitchens. The crystal decanter was set on an embroidered-linen-covered trestle table near the back wall of the terrace. The cloth flapped gently in the warm evening breeze.

'Enough of me, Aoife. What about you? What is it you wish for in all this?'

By now, after our many evening strolls and conversations, I had become very comfortable in his company. He was a good man, and I had grown to like and trust him. His wasn't a blind, naked self-serving ambition. Although not immune to the lure of higher status and wealth—who is?—he was not solely driven by them. They were more a consequence of his burning need to preserve the heritage of his ancestry and to pass it on to future generations. This, and the responsibility he felt for the care and wellbeing of the wider families and followers of the de Clares, was what drove him. I thought this most admirable, but frankly, at the beginning, I had hardly understood the most of it. I felt embarrassed at my own trivial, girlish musings and was initially reluctant to expose my innermost thoughts. But as the weeks passed, he put me at my ease and teased them from me.

'I want Eanna back,' I said, deciding he could hear my truth. 'I want him back, and I want to keep Conor safe from it all.' I told him I wanted us all to live happily in our home in Ferns in Leinster and not to be bothered by the waves of strife that constantly swept back and forth across our land. I wanted us to be left alone, and we would not bother anyone in our neighbouring kingdoms. Why were they constantly fighting, year on year? Over and over the cycle repeated, bordering farmlands raided for cattle, slaves, and plunder, reprisals made. Armies would gather, alliances were formed and broken just as fast, battles were fought, and all the while killing, rape, hostage taking, slavery, maiming and grief continued.

Listening, his hand resting soothingly on my bare forearm as we sat, side by side, in the cushion-lined chairs, he eventually spoke: 'Aoife. I understand. I know what you long for, and it is also my wish. I also want for all our families to live like this. But peace in a land is only safe with strong borders that neighbours know to respect. And that respect is won by the sword.' He had listened and learned much about Ireland in the past months. He understood that none of the many kings who claimed sovereignty in some part of the island had grown sufficiently strong enough to impose his will on the others. The result was constant squabbling and conflict as one or another sought to take advantage of some momentary turn of events to further their interests. The lack of a dominant power and the collective, mutual weakness was a recipe for turmoil, and as far as he could judge, the chaos was set to continue indefinitely, with all the suffering that brought.

'They are fools. They break their strength on the rocks of their neighbours, not lifting their heads to see the powerful force which will engulf them and sweep them all away.' He laughed, shaking his head at their stupidity.

'You?' I asked, a bit taken aback.

'No.' He waved his hand dismissively. 'Not me.' He paused now. 'If anything, I can help, Aoife. But I am not the one they need to fear most.'

'Who, then? What are you talking about?'

Refilling our glasses, he offered me some almonds and black olives, which a merchant in Bristol had imported from France. He laughed at my reaction to the salty bitterness of the olives and assured me I'd grow to like it. Then he continued.

'Aoife, it's the English king, Henry II, you need to fear. And in that we have common cause.'

As I sat there, sipping the strong wine and looking out over the Wye, he told me of how the fate of Ireland had long been decided. Just over ten years past in 1155, the young

King Henry II had decided to take his army to conquer Ireland. He regarded Ireland as part of his dominions and had been granted permission to invade and take the island by the then pope, Adrian IV. Adrian, as an Englishman, was quite sympathetic to Henry's ambitions and approved the scheme in a papal bull known as the Laudabiliter.

'Have you heard of the crusades, Aoife?' he asked. 'They had always looked to Jerusalem until recent times, when the popes began turning their eyes closer to home when it suited them and their benefactors. Firstly, it was to rid the northern lands of paganism, and then it was the west, with this Laudabiliter, to cleanse and enlarge the boundaries of the church in Ireland. It suited Adrian to please Henry.'

The forces the king could gather would easily overwhelm and subjugate the island. He had only been dissuaded from the expedition at the last moment by his mother, the powerful empress Matilda, whom Strongbow had battled in the civil war before the young Henry came of age and to the throne. Before then, she had secured the throne for the young Henry by battling Stephen, whom Strongbow had supported. She regarded the subjugation of Ireland as a lesser issue to the reestablishment of royal authority over some rebellious knights in their domains in France. Ireland could wait.

However, this was only a temporary reprieve for Ireland. Henry fully intended to return as soon as he had pacified his rebellious lords in his French lands, hence his approval for my father to gather support from Norman lords willing to come to his aid. In addition, the invitation of my father to Henry to intervene added significant legitimacy to Henry's ambition to assimilate Ireland under the authority of his crown. However, this permission for the Norman lords to assist my father was not extended to Strongbow, owing to the distrust between them. The king did not want a mistrusted lord establishing a powerful foothold on his western flank. Hence, he had refused Strongbow's request for permission to go to Ireland, much to Strongbow's growing frustration. He had not been called by Henry to campaign in France as most of the leading barons of the realm had. I was sure my father was not fully aware of the extent of Strongbow's disfavour with the king. Regardless, my father had few options with the bulk of the Norman lords in France and those who remained unwilling to go act without Strongbow.

'So the king won't let me prosper here, but he also won't give me leave to sail to Ireland. This is impossible for me. I will make one last try to appease him, but this can't continue.' He spoke quietly now, for he was aware that if his words reached the king's ears, he would not be pleased. Any hope of reconciliation and approval would vanish. Worse could follow if Strongbow's enemies leaked whispers of treason into the king's willing ears.

'Aoife, if Henry comes to Ireland with his army, he will lay waste to everything. His army, drunk with crusading fervour, would be merciless. He is ruthless and driven to expand his royal lands at any cost. He has taken mine, and he will take yours and all of Ireland. It will be bloody. Compromise is not his way when he holds the whip hand and the papal bull.'

I had seen and been astounded at the weaponry, skill and battle effectiveness of Strongbow's garrison at Chepstow. An army of many thousand well-trained, properly equipped, disciplined and battle-hardened Normans, led by King Henry, would crush any opposing force in Ireland. There was no hope for us if what Strongbow told me was true. But was it not also inevitable?

'But won't he come anyway? If not now, surely, it's only a matter of time.'

'Yes, Aoife. It is. He will come.' He stood and paced across the small terrace, relieving the tension. He was also checking that no one was in earshot on the battlements above us or in the corridor that led to the kitchens from the terrace. He closed the heavy oak door.

'Aoife, if we do nothing, both you and I, our two families, will lose everything. That's the path we are on now.' He paused, and I could sense his dismay. 'The way things stand, I doubt I will be reconciled with the king, but there *is* a way.' Looking at me, I knew he was weighing carefully what he was about to say, and I soon understood why.

'If we can establish a strong foothold in Leinster, together we can secure the futures of both our families and followers. That bond will be strengthened by our marriage.' He waited for my reaction and, almost relieved, smiled when I nodded, showing my continued consent. 'With a strong base and the people with us, we will be in a position to negotiate with Henry. He will not want to fight our armies unnecessarily and will agree to letting us keep most, in return for some painful concessions on our part. But it will be worth it. We will have to give up a lot, acknowledge him as king, but we will survive and prosper. Then, let us see what the future holds.

'So I will come to Ireland, with or without his permission. But not just yet. I will try once more to gain his consent for me to sail,' he said.

His caution in laying bare his plans to me was justified. What he had just told me was dangerously close to treason and could have him imprisoned and hanged. Kings don't take kindly to overt defiance from a disliked lord. This was dangerous talk. Still, I was encouraged by his intentions—I trusted him—though I feared for Eanna.

'We must trust each other, Aoife,' he finished.

MYLER WAS BESIDE ME AGAIN. He had taken to joining me, when his duties allowed, as I watched the dawn break from the wall walk on the castellated ramparts of the lower bailey. The wind whipped Strongbow's swallow-tailed banners on the Great Tower much to the annoyance of the large, hooded crows nesting high on its shallow turrets. The three deep-red chevrons on the sharp gold of Strongbow's family coat of arms snapped sharply against the wispish grey clouds scurrying eastward across the dull sky. I wondered if Eanna could see these clouds and feel this wind before they swept over the sea from Ireland.

I had heard his approach and felt the familiar weight of his heavy woollen cloak as he draped it across my shoulders. I banished my gloom before turning, lifting my chin to smile at him. He was an attentive man, and while I did enjoy his company, I also intentionally encouraged him, as we needed to know these men who would come to Ireland. 'Who are they, and why are they coming?' Donal had said. "They will be a formidable force once in Ireland, and we must learn how to harness and control them. Keep him interested and keep him talking, whatever it takes. That's your task, Aoife,' he'd said. 'I'll learn their battle skills.'

'You'll catch your death up here, Aoife,' Myler said.

'Surely the ever-chivalrous Sir Myler FitzHenry would not allow that,' I teased, wrapping myself in the warmth against the chilly gusts of the morning wind which rushed unimpeded across the river. The castle walls would gather the heat from the light reflected from the river as the sun rose and deliver a gentle warm breeze soon enough. For now, the sailors stirring on the boats below the castle huddled in the boat-waists, sheltering from the wind and the attention of the boat masters.

'That's why the work shy are known as waisters,' Myler quipped.

He gazed over the town. Shielding his eyes from the glare with one hand, he looked to be following the progress of an overladen cart towards the docks. 'What do you see when you dream of your home?' he asked almost casually. 'Is it to be a queen? Or would your brother want to be a king?'

Such a searching question from him, slipping almost unnoticed into the wind.

'There are so many boats. Where do they all come from?' I asked, pretending I had not heard.

He looked at me, hesitating, searching my face for my thoughts. He continued, 'Oh, France, Spain, Ireland of course . . . and they are even bringing dried fish in from Iceland now, I believe.' Ever more frequently they were seeing cargoes from northern Europe and the Mediterranean lands, the reason being, Myler explained, that any goods imported into England through Chepstow were exempt from the king's import tax. This was a concession that the English king had given to Strongbow's family, the de Clares, who had been tasked with guarding the border with Wales, or the Welsh Marches, as they were known. Hence, family dynasties who held the borders were known as the Marcher lords. The merchants took advantage of the lower taxes Strongbow imposed, and he received quite a sum each year in return. So the port of Chepstow thrived but still Strongbow fretted, worried that the king would someday act on his visceral distrust and seize the remaining lands he held in Wales and Aquitaine.

I was relieved at the turn in the conversation.

'That's why he is seldom in the castle,' Myler went on. 'He's constantly trying to appease Henry, trying to win his trust again.' Without thinking, he gently closed the cloak around my neck to protect me from a sudden sharp gust.

'But I'm not sure he'll get anywhere. The king bears grudges like his mistresses bear children—he has a lot of them.' He laughed and then became serious again. 'It's impossible for us all, Aoife.'

Further along the walls we watched as the stable lads led the bulky warhorses from the farrier's forge to the courtyard. They advanced through the vaulted castle gates out to the near paddocks in the castle dell, the natural ravine which ran to the south of the castle. There would be no hunting today, and they took care to keep the stallions apart as they made their way, stamping noisily through the cobbled entrance beneath the fortified gates.

In Strongbow's absence, the household had spent much of the past few weeks in the hunting preserves of the castle. The closer chases and parks were abundant with deer and foxes, whereas the more distant Forest of Wentworth provided much sport with the more dangerous wild boars. The large party would ride out before dawn with the hounds tethered, coupled and tightly controlled by the huntsmen before we reached the hunting grounds. Myler seemed to have appointed himself as my guardian, and as the weeks went on, he spent more time at my side than at the front of the chase with uncles and friends.

On the first day I was to accompany them, he presented me with a small palfrey, hunting horse sporting an elaborate embroidered breast cloth. The carved saddlebows were covered in what seemed to be another precious purple cloth. Having been taught to ride without a saddle in the Irish style, I was far more comfortable and confident with my hips and legs in close contact with the horse, particularly when I needed a lot of control in the hunting field. Much to the amusement of the party, I asked for the saddle to be removed and, refusing Myler's offer of a leg up to mount the horse, took a fistful of the mane in my left hand. I urged the animal forward and used the momentum to vault and swing myself comfortably onto its back, as was my way. There was a round of laughter from the men, although there was undoubtedly an added tinge of respect from these people who valued good horsemanship.

'Well, you learn something new every day.' Myler shrugged and instructed the groom to store the saddle. 'But don't say I didn't warn you. It's tricky out there, particularly with the boar. They can be very clever and too brave sometimes.' So off we went, and several hunts later, during which I spent more time on the horse's back than he did, he let the matter drop.

These Normans were obsessed with hunting, and it wasn't purely for entertainment. They used it as an integral part of their training and rehearsal for war. Riding their heavy destrier warhorses, they perfected their horsemanship and use of various arms from the saddle. In addition, the beasts of the chase were put to good use, providing a rich stock of food for the castle kitchens.

The wild boar in the Forest of Wentworth were smaller than those we hunted around Ferns. But what they lacked in weight they made up for in speed, making them nearly impossible to kill on horseback. They would easily outrun the horses in short spurts to find the cover of the dense undergrowth, where they secreted their dens. The huntsmen would chase them to ground, where the men would arm themselves with long-shafted spears and venture tentatively forward, goading and teasing each other. It was a dangerous game which all too frequently ended in the blood of the hunter finding the soil.

Not used to the burst of speed with which they would charge unseen from the thickets, I stood well back, spear in hand and Fáinleog drawn. She was a comfort by my side but wholly useless. She would not save me from a maddened, charging boar. The hunter's only hope was to impale it under its own speed and weight and use the length of the shaft to hold the sharp tusks and thrashing hooves at bay until it bled to death or was killed by the other huntsmen. They moved quickly through the forests on foot in the pursuit, and I would struggle to stay with them, following the baying of the hounds for direction.

On one such day, I heard a meek squealing over the gentle rustling of the trees in the gentle breeze. It silenced abruptly as I stepped into the small clearing in the speckled sunlight. Stilled, I softened my breathing and listened, waiting. The baying hounds grew distant, the leaves shivered, and there it was again, not two paces to my left in the dark undergrowth. Hardly turning, I parted the bush with my spear, slightly more, my eyes straining in the shadow. A startled chorus now of pink piglets, a mass of flesh not long of this world, nestled in the boar's den. She was clever, leading the hounds astray, away from her family. They were out of earshot now.

Sensing the light, their squealing heightened until I allowed the bramble to close above them. Their noise lessened as the comforting darkness gathered around them. It lessened just enough for me to hear the rising crashing of the boar mother descending upon me. The undergrowth beyond the clearing parted above her charge, straight as an arrow. At least I knew from where she was coming. I'd seen the men do it. Drop to the knee, plant the shaft, wait. There was hardly the time to do that. Her broad chest met the broad spear tip as the shaft met the ground. It held fast, the momentum carrying her forward, knocking me back, my shoulder hitting the ground. The thick oak shaft held her weight above me, the spear embedded deep in her chest. Her blood gushed down the shaft, its flow quickening over my slipping hands as she thrashed her tusks. Sharp teeth snapped in strong jaws; the stench was overwhelming. Her weight slowly, mesmerizingly carried her down the spear, her jaws inching closer. To reach for Fáinleog would mean lessening my grip on the shaft, which I strained with all my strength to hold. We would both die then.

A sudden shock broke the shaft and the blow to my head blackened everything. Stunned, I sensed the flash of steel, the stench of burst bowels and the sing of a sword silencing the boar's squeal as her head left her body. I felt the strong arms lift and place me gently in the soft grass. The cool water flowed over my lips, tickled down my cheek and gathered in my ears. Soothing fingertips cleaned my face, caressing my neck. The haze sharpened into the handsome features of Myler, sitting above me, the dancing canopy of the trees around him. He smiled.

'Sorry about that,' he said. 'I seem to have given you a bit of a bang when I knocked the boar off you.' He wet his hand and ran it along my neck. 'There, that should do it. You're half respectable now.'

His hand lingered. Without thinking, I lifted it to my lips and kissed his fingers. And again. 'Thank you,' I whispered. I held his hand to my lips. The desire had burned long in his eyes. He probably saw mine. But like me, his family and duty held him firm, so far anyway. Everything was at risk by this. The return to Ireland. Our family's fortunes for generations. Kingdoms were in the balance. Eanna's very life. I kissed his fingers again, he saw my invitation. Softly, he curled my lips open and, leaning forward, brushed my nose with his breath and kissed me.

The light danced in the trees above, throwing patterns around us. In time, we lay watching the songbirds racing across the sunlight, oblivious to our presence. Motionless, our breathing quietened, our nakedness absorbing the midday heat.

Chapter Five
THE THREAT WITHIN

Chepstow Castle, Wales
Spring 1167

From Myler first offering me his heavy fleeced cloak on particularly cold mornings we had taken to sharing it, quietly revelling in the luxurious body-heat warmth, but always out of sight. Unspoken, disguised by our talk, our bodies grew ever closer. I found myself delighted to wake when the morning dawned bitter cold and with a strong wind: all the more reason to bury myself in his arms, which were now no longer shy in the embrace.

Even though Myler was not much older than me, he was more than a head taller. His shoulder-length dark hair, left untied, stirred in the wind as we continued our stroll around the wall walk. His normally happy, good-natured disposition clouded when he spoke of Strongbow's troubles with the king. 'You see, we are also a Marcher family, the Geraldines,' he told me. 'We are part of Strongbow's following, and with him out of favour with the king, we are all disadvantaged,' he complained. 'I have a life to live. I want to prove myself worthy in the eyes of my uncles, earn their respect and my own fortune.'

'So why don't you just take up my father's invitation and come to Ireland to help us?' I couldn't understand why they didn't grasp the opportunity for land and wealth.

'We want to, all my uncles, but we can't without whipping up the king's displeasure. He knows we are Strongbow's men. He won't stand for it!' I could see his frustration plainly. 'You see, I have little family wealth or estates coming my way. I don't want to end like all those knights errant, roaming the kingdom trying to prove myself and hoping for fortune to look favourably on me.'

I knew this was a miserable and uncertain existence and the fate of many sons of the Norman nobility. Lacking inheritance but carrying noble names, many such knights ended destitute, maimed in the jousting tournaments or perishing as hired swords in near or far lands. Those who survived lived a pitiful existence. Fugitives from fortune, often attaching themselves to a willing lord's court, they scratched an existence from his charity. 'Look at Sir Hervey, that detestable snake. His tongue is poison. If he wasn't, by chance, Strongbow's uncle, he'd be long gone from here by now.

'The king will never favour me, even though—believe it or not—I am his cousin.' Myler explained how he shared a grandfather with the king, King Henry I. 'But that doesn't mean much. If you think our king resembles a feral dog in his appetites, our grandfather was worse. So, there are a lot of us around and not enough land and spoils to share.' The result being, he explained, that many ambitious young lords of military bearing, like himself, had to find their own fortunes. To do that they needed their lords, like Strongbow, to prosper and give them the opportunity to acquire land and wealth.

These young men were restless to put their skills to use to win the renown that came with martial prowess. Myler's broader family, the Geraldines, were replete with such men of varying ages. Raymond Le Gros, Robert FitzStephen and Maurice FitzGerald—Myler's cousin and uncles—were keen to build on their wealth and needed the release of Strongbow from the king's yoke. Gerald de Barry, the archdeacon of Brecon, another Geraldine cousin of Myler's, had ambitions to take the archbishop's seat in Canterbury, the highest church office in the land. To achieve this, he needed the wider family to prosper to garner support when the time came. He, like many more of the Geraldines' wider family who populated Strongbow's army, were eager to sail for Ireland, where they saw their fortunes rising. They were not an ancient dynasty that had the opportunity to establish a deep-seated wealth. They took their name from one of the husbands of the formidable Princess Nesta of Wales, whom they revered as the maternal founder of the family. 'Like you, Aoife, we too have our goddess of sorts,' he whispered.

The wind rose as the sky darkened from the west while the hooded crows wheeled recklessly in the strong gusts. Seeing me shivering, Myler took the cloak and, throwing it around his shoulders, wrapped me in a warm embrace, closing the cloak around us both with my back to his chest as he often did. Facing over the castellated wall, I relaxed in the warmth of his body beneath the heavy cloak. I could feel his chest rising and ebbing and the gentle sweep of his breath in my hair as he spoke.

'She died before I was born, but Maurice says you remind him of her, his mother. It's uncanny,' he said. 'I think it's why he's a bit afraid of you. They all are.' He laughed and tightened his embrace against the sharpening wind. He spoke more softly now. 'She too was very beautiful . . . and provoked great passions in many men.' He was silent now. I could sense my breathing deepening with his own. We had grown close over the past months, spending much time together. I now sought out his company and knew my feelings had deepened.

Suddenly a swallow, unhappy we were so close to her nest, flashed a warning swoop, almost touching my face before speeding away skyward. We both laughed and, woken from our reverie, he continued his story of Nesta, his grandmother.

A daughter of a Welsh king, she had married twice and taken many lovers. Her many children included one with King Henry I, Myler's grandfather. Her children, Myler's uncles, had become established in positions of importance in the Welsh reaches of the Normans, including in the church. They were driven by an ambition to further their prospects in any ventures that would offer the opportunity to build their dynasty—the dynasty of the Geraldines.

As we descended the narrow stone steps from the wall walk, I couldn't help thinking how these men always managed to diminish the women in their stories. It seemed to me that his entire family was descended from one common source, the matriarch Nesta, whom they all held in great reverence. Why, then, do they call themselves Geraldines, not Nestines? That would indeed be truer, yet it would give too much credit to a woman. I wondered if they would write me out of their history when the time came. Nonetheless, I wouldn't trouble Myler with these thoughts.

We moved wordlessly to the small turret built to provide shelter for the guards where the wall turned. It also provided shelter from prying eyes; we embraced immediately, our lips, breath and bodies merging with a desperate urgency that sharpened my desire. We would quickly emerge from these snatched moments to resume our innocent stroll for watchful eyes. And it was as well we did on this morning, for as we emerged, one of Sir Hervey's men, Dwain, could be seen skulking in the shadows of the courtyard. He slipped away from view behind a stone pillar.

'That bastard is watching us, Aoife,' Myler said under his breath, acting naturally. 'On his master's orders, no doubt,' he said with a bitter twist.

Sir Hervey, bereft of his own talents, was a man who distinguished himself by denigrating others. Having attached himself to Strongbow's court his sole purpose was to ingratiate himself with him. As his nephew, Strongbow felt obligated to accommodate him, but he was not popular in the camp. His sly ways became known, and he was regarded with suspicion. He spread a foul miasma in his wake.

'He's a coward,' Myler spat with a bitter venom. 'He's more guile than guts. He can't be trusted. He spills poison into Strongbow's ears. Be very wary of him, Aoife. We must be careful.'

I could see the worry in his handsome face.

We moved along the wall walk, and Myler spoke loudly now, more for the benefit of the prying eyes and listening ears than mine. 'As I was saying, m'lady, the Welsh longbow, in the hands of a practiced border man, can easily reach two hundred paces.' Pointing to the body of men under instruction in the buts below, he went on: 'That's Ewan Smith, with his son Robert beside him. Ewan is in charge of the archers. If there's a fight on, Strongbow takes Ewan with him.' Ewan was the centenar; he commanded the companies of Welsh bowmen who, Myler explained, were the backbone of Norman armies. Hunters and farmers by trade, they were trained from a young age to perfect their skills in archery. They were unequalled in their mastery of the bow; these skills had been recognised, perfected and put to devastating use by the Normans in battle. Welsh longbow archers could shoot volleys of bodkin-headed arrows with pinpoint accuracy that could penetrate all but the best armour.

'Watch this,' Myler said, as on his Ewan's command, Robert and a few dozen archers hauled the bowstrings and paused, holding the strained bowstaves still.

'Loose,' came the command, and a rush of arrows sped skyward, the fletching sparkling momentarily, caught by a hint of sunlight. The hooded crows scattered, startled by the noise and flashes as the arrows thumped with astonishing accuracy into the targets at two hundred paces. Each man had several arrows stuck into the ground in front of them, so after releasing, they quickly strung another arrow and let it fly with remarkable speed. The right side of each man's body seemed disfigured with the overdeveloped muscle that delivered the enormous strength required to continuously, and seemingly effortlessly, draw the bow. It barely took any time for these few archers to pour hundreds of arrows onto the targets. Myler explained that for added effect, the archers would stick the arrowheads into dung and filth before battle; that way, if the arrow didn't kill the man, the wound would most likely fester and putrefy from the foulness on the arrowhead.

'Lovely,' I said. 'Our hunting bows in Ireland couldn't shoot half that far.' I shook my head. 'They are only used at short distance. They've no accuracy at any kind of range.'

'I know,' Myler said. 'They are our secret weapon with the uninitiated. With enough of them, you can destroy half an army before you take your sword from its scabbard.'

Seeming pleased with the result, the young archer, Robert Smith, noticed Myler and I on the wall and waved. 'Morning, Myler. Nice to see you up so early,' he said, smiling cheekily at Myler. 'My lady.' He bowed to me with great diffidence.

'Smart bastard,' Myler said quietly, but grinning, he shouted down. 'Well, if that's what an early rise does for your aim, I hope all our battles are fought in the afternoon.' Myler laughed and led Aoife along the ramparts. 'He's a good friend of mine, Rob. He's the best archer I know, and he's very good with the men too. I'd be happy to have him with me any day in a fight. He's learned well from his father and has his own troop now.' He went on to tell me how he himself had been fostered into the care of Strongbow's father in the castle, where he had been reared alongside Rob and the other children of the household and staff. They roamed the castle and grounds in a pack, causing no end of mischief.

Rob's family had long been with the de Clares, one of the greatest baronial houses of the Normans. The name derived from the dynasty's administrative centre at the town of Clare in Suffolk in East Anglia. These lands had been granted to the family by William the Conqueror after the Battle of Hastings for the service of Strongbow's ancestor, Richard Fitz-Gilbert, Lord of Clare. Since those times, Rob's family played an important part of the household. In battle, his father had commanded the archers of Strongbow, as would be expected of Rob one day. His mother, Alice, organised the provisioning of the castle and oversaw the extensive kitchens which provided food for Strongbow's table and fed the multitudes who staffed the castle.

I had come to know Alice from my time around the kitchens, where I liked to lend a hand. Alice organised the butchering, storerooms and cooking. Forever busy, she rushed good-humouredly from task to task. While stern with the lads and girls whom she chased to their work, she had a maternal air about her and was well respected by all. She had taken it upon herself to care for my own mother, who had withdrawn into herself since our traumatic escape from Ferns.

My mother had taken the fate of Eanna very badly; closed in her room she wept from dawn till dawn and would speak to no one, despite my constant pleading. I was at my wits' end and feared for her. Alice, a kindly woman, nursed my mother. It was for her alone that my mother would sip meagerly at a broth Alice would prepare, her sole source of nourishment, sustaining her very life.

Alice had great sympathy for my mother's grief and worry at the loss of Eanna; some griefs can be understood only by those who have borne them. I shuddered at that appalling sight, seared into my memory, of when I had last seen Eanna under the sword of O'Rourke on the headland as we escaped from Bannow Bay, his distress exaggerated by tricks of the mind that tormented me from when I first awoke and rattled me mockingly as each day wore on. I could not imagine the horrors my mother endured.

'I've lost children myself, Aoife. Several,' Alice said one evening as we sat, her work done in the deep storeroom at the bottom of the dark stone corridor that led down from the kitchens. Tucked into the cooler depths of the castle, the food was preserved, and the wine kept longer there. It was her retreat, and I had become accustomed to spending many evenings there with her. 'Rob is my only remaining child. His father and I are very proud of him. But all children are precious to a mother, Aoife. Most women never get over the loss of a child. They learn the silent grind of daily grief. God forbid that happens to your brother. I fear your own mother will never recover. She grieves heavily his loss already.'

'She blames my father. I think she hates him,' I said. 'I don't think she ever really cared for him.' The gods knew my father was a vile man now. The burden of the throne did not sit well with him. He had been brutalised, his humanity trampled in the mud and blood of enemies and victims—betrayed friends and kinsmen alike. However, I remembered a time of a father's tender embrace, warm laughter, a considerate man. My childhood memories were of joy and freedom in the bustling town market of Ferns, the centre of my father's kingdom of Leinster. The seat of MacMurrough power, our royal residence was lavish, and we roamed the meadows, forests and rivers of its hinterland, looking forward to the homecoming of my father from his exploits throughout his and other kingdoms in Ireland. Now there was no hint or echo of affection between my parents. It was hard to believe it had ever been there.

'Aoife, girl. Love is not something I see a lot in the marriages of lords and ladies. I sometimes pity them, as at least I could choose my man.'

'As I can choose mine,' I said. 'It's our way in Ireland.'

'Hmm, so I have heard.' She raised an eyebrow. 'That's more than the ladies here can do. They are traded like cattle to suit the families' interests.' She paused now, turning her eyes on me. 'Aoife, be that the case—that you can choose your own husband—there are an awful lot of people far more interested in your marriage than there was in mine.' I could feel her penetrating gaze now. I avoided her eyes. I knew what she was hinting at—Myler. I felt she had been building up to some kind of a telling off over the last while. First, it was a gentle teasing about him, which then went on to a more nuanced comment or two about the two of us being noticed and commented on by the kitchen girls. I had ignored her well-intentioned ramblings—what business was it of hers? In Ireland, a woman had as much freedom as a man in these matters. Myler was more my age; He was also very handsome and had an earthly, uninhibited attractiveness about him.

As the silence deepened and I said nothing, like the clouds presage the storm, I could feel's Alice's disapproval brewing. After a while, she continued gently.

'Aoife, be more careful.'

'I understand my duty,' I snapped. 'I will marry Strongbow.'

'Good. I'm relieved, but that's not the impression you are giving around the castle with Myler.'

'Do you think this is easy for me!'

'No, I have no doubt, it's not. But you are being reckless, and it is not the way we do things here.'

The whites of my knuckles showed as I stared at my hands clasped tightly in my lap. I could feel the tears welling and showing on my cheeks. Alice leaned forward and gently placed her hand on mine. I saw a tear drop onto the back of her hand.

'Aoife, Strongbow is a good man. In time, a great respect can come between a man and a woman. Sometimes, even love will grow.'

'I know, I know,' I said shaking my head and wiping a tear. 'It's not that. I like and respect Strongbow. I know he is a good man.'

'What is it then?'

She listened, more with her eyes than her ears, as I told her of my sorrow. A sorrow that deepened in equal measure to the growth of my affection for Myler. But it was not that.

'If not that, then...what is it, Aoife?'

'Can't you see! Strongbow is nearly three times my age,' I complained. 'He's old. There's no joy in him. I know he's a good man, but . . .' I hesitated. 'I can't imagine, you know . . .' I looked to Alice pleadingly. 'You know . . .' After a long pause and no hint of understanding from Alice, I went on: 'Taking to the bed with him!'

Alice threw her head back and roared with laughter. 'Believe me, girl, there's a lot worse. I should know,' she said. Then, becoming serious again, she settled my ruffled skirts in a motherly way and said, 'Aoife, darling, you must never forget who you are. Others certainly won't. That royal blood that flows through your veins also determines the flow of your life. Even your marriage.' She sipped her wine thoughtfully.

I felt no comfort from her words. She saw the sad despair etched into my face. Was I condemned to a loveless life, devoid of the passion which burned in my every nerve and sinew? The goddess of life, yearning in my loins. She took my hands again and held my gaze intently.

'Aoife, listen. It's not the end. There is a way for love. God knows we all need love in our lives. When we are young, we need the passion that nourishes the sapling to blossom into the women we can become.' At this, Alice looked distantly into the guttering candle flame beside us, lost in some memory. A glow came to her thin, handsome face. She was an attractive full-bosomed woman with a fine well-proportioned figure. Closer to Strongbow's age, she turned many a man's head today and must have been some beauty in the prime of her youth. She smiled, as if chasing some memory, like a naughty child, back to her past, where it now belonged.

Returning to me again, she sighed and told me to drink some wine.

'You see, Aoife, I sometimes think love is like wine. You need to have tasted it to know its pleasures. Without it, we die a little. We grow like the tree that bears no flower or fruit. A grey, colourless pallor. Love can grow deeper roots in later life, but the sapling needs the water of passion, the girl needs the wine of love.'

Strongbow was no fool, she told me. He was a man who noticed things. She doubted that he wasn't already aware of my affection for Myler. After all, I was a real beauty and was bound to attract the attentions of men. I was blessed in that regard, and she told me to be thankful for it.

As for Myler, he was a dashing young man who caught the eye of all the girls. 'And quite a few of the women too,' she added, laughing wickedly. 'I can't say I haven't noticed myself.' She tittered. 'Sadly, he seems to reserve his affections for you, and you only, young lady. I can think of worse fates, girl.'

She rose and, taking the jug, tapped the large oak cask to release a stream of red heaven to fill us each another cup. 'Aoife, remember that Strongbow himself, for reasons of his position, must also commit to this marriage. Don't you think he has and has had other affections?' she asked. I didn't respond. I was sure he did, but he was very discreet about these liaisons; I appreciated that.

Alice looked at me knowingly. 'Exactly! You can be very sure he does. And just like him, you should be very discreet with your arrangements.' I searched her face to make sure I understood what she was suggesting. Was she telling me that I could fulfil my yearnings for Myler but discreetly, avoiding any embarrassment for Strongbow?

'Yes,' she nodded, quite animated now. 'That's exactly what I'm telling you. It's the way of things. Passions come and go. Particularly when we are young. Strongbow was also young once, don't forget.'

Alice relaxed. Sensing my understanding, she spoke more quietly now. 'Protect and respect each other with your discretion. That's what he expects of you, girl.' She finished and sat back and took a slow pull of the wine. She savoured it on her pallet and sighed deeply. 'You can forgive a man a lot if he brings you wine like this nectar of the gods of an evening.'

We both laughed, and it was as if a veil on an unfamiliar world had been lifted to give me a glimpse of understanding. I felt relief. I realised that just as these Normans had a lot to learn about Ireland, that applied in equal measure as to what we had yet to understand about them and their world.

AOIFE OF LEINSTER

THE LAST OF the day's light glowed red in the early summer warmth as I made my way down past the deserted kitchens to join Alice. The weak light from my lantern bounced against the walls and flickered into the dark alcoves brimming with stores. The shadows danced on the ceiling before me and seemed to chase menacingly behind, making me hurry down the broad flagstones, careful not to lose my footing on the uneven edges in the dim light.

The castle was still, with an end-of-day ease as man and beast rested from the strains of the day. The harvest was close and, gods willing, the weather would hold to allow good reaping. We needed a dry crop for the clean threshing and good storage of the hay. The grain stores had been cleaned, and the floors readied for the threshing. There was a constant hammering clamour from the forge as the blacksmiths replaced and repaired the iron-rimmed wheels on the rickety carts that would carry the earth's bounty from the harvest meadows spread far and wide across the castle estates. Finding Alice alone on these evenings, we would talk of our families, lives and hopes into the dusky early hours. She took time to explain the ways of the Normans, and I gradually became more comfortable in their world as my understanding of them grew.

Rounding the last corner in the ink-dark blackness, I raised my lantern to throw the dim light on the door to Alice's retreat. Something was different. I almost stumbled on the outstretched legs of a man sitting slumped against the wall, hidden in the shadow cast from the lantern. Lurching forward, I kicked a tankard of ale, sending it bouncing noisily across the stone floor, spilling the dark liquid widely. A curse and another large man rose heavily from a small stool placed in front of Alice's door. He staggered, drunkenly shielding his eyes and tipping the ale cup he held onto his breaches.

'Who goes there!' he slurred, swinging blindly at me with a short club he carried. 'Get lost, you've no business here.' He fell back against the door he was evidently meant to bar.

Recognising him as one of Sir Hervey's men, I heard the muffled sounds of tableware crashing to the floor behind the heavy oak door. Something thrown, smashing against the door, shattering across the floor inside. Then Alice cursing and screaming.

Before he could react, I threw the lantern into the face of the man barring the door. The oil spilled from the sump, splashing into his beard and across his tunic, and ignited. Panicked, he fled unsteadily down the corridor towards a water butt, beating widely at the flames dancing around him. A rancid smell filled the corridor. Just as well, I thought momentarily, he was too heavy for me to shift, sober or drunk.

Forcing the heavy cast-iron latch, I slammed my weight against the door and burst into the room. The door crashed against the wall and the sound boomed around the high stone-vaulted ceiling.

Rushing forward without breaking stride for, unarmed, surprise was my only weapon now, I saw Alice pinned by the arms to a long bench by Dwain, Sir Hervey's man, with her skirts around her hips. She spat, screaming viciously at Sir Hervey, kicking wildly when he approached..

I hesitated a heartbeat, not believing my eyes. Sir Hervey turned and looked at me with some surprise, then snorted dismissively. 'You again?' Then he struck Alice hard across the face, the force slamming her head against the bench with a loud, chilling crack. She was stunned by the blow. He sneered at me briefly. 'Hold her,' he snapped to his man.

Screaming, I threw myself at him. He was a light weasel

of a man but tall, and it was more the shock than the force of my weight that caused him to stumble and fall heavily to the floor.

In the confusion, Dwain released Alice, who gradually recovered her senses. Seeing me standing over Sir Hervey, she quickly grasped what was happening and, turning swiftly, lunged at Dwain. Her small butchering knife was quickly magicked from her skirts and pressed hard against his gullet. The slightest effort from her experienced hand at butchery would empty his veins.

'You bastard,' she seethed, blood trickling from her lip where Sir Hervey had struck her.

Somewhat dazed but recovering himself, Sir Hervey coldly turned on me. 'Bitch,' he snarled, and, picking up a heavy iron poker from the fire, he calmly rose to face me. I froze at the maddened hatred in his eyes, defenceless.

'If you touch her, I'll kill him,' Alice warned, pressing the blade deeper into Dwain's throat. Dwain whimpered.

'Do as you wish with him,' Sir Hervey said without even looking at her, and then he came at me, raising the iron.

Expecting the blow, I crouched, covering my head with my arms, trying to protect myself as best I could, but the blow never came. A sudden long silence and his heavy breathing. But nothing.

I opened my eyes. A sword reached over my shoulder, its sharp point touching Sir Hervey's throat. He stared open mouthed at the blade, still gripping the iron he held above his head, his rancid breath catching me. I could see his yellowed broken teeth. He yearned to deliver the blow. The sword slowly but forcibly increased in pressure, drawing a trickle of blood at its tip. Wincing, he slowly lowered the iron and dropped it to the floor, it's metallic fall reverberating around the cellar.

He casually settled his clothing. 'Well, well, Sir Myler.

What brings you here?' he said, backing away from the blade and sauntering to the table, collecting his cloak. 'Dwain, I think we've offered enough assistance to Alice this evening. Let us take our leave,' he said to his man and moved towards the door.

'Strongbow will hear of this,' Myler shouted, following Montmorency with his sword. 'You have no place in our cause. We shall be glad to see you gone, you bastard.'

Montmorency stopped. He turned slowly on Myler. 'Careful now, boy,' he said. Smiling derisively, he continued: 'Should Strongbow hear any false rumours about me,' he said with a sweeping gesture around the cellar, 'then'—pointing at Myler now, he continued with venom—'he will certainly hear of your dalliances with our little princess. I have witnesses! Did you enjoy your embrace in the forest on the hunt?' He looked at me contemptuously. 'I don't think he would be at all pleased. Do you, my dear Myler?' The shock of his knowing was clear on Myler's face, as was the fear. Sir Hervey grinned mockingly at his despair. 'You're out of your depth, boy,' he spat.

'Alice and I may have had a minor contretemps this evening—as is not unusual amongst people who hold each other in great affection.' He sneered and, turning to Alice, said, 'Wouldn't you agree, my dear Alice?'

'Bastard,' she snarled.

'Now, now, dear,' he said mockingly. 'Let's have no more of that. And do please spare Dwain any more anxiety and ease your knife from his throat. Balancing on his tiptoes was never his forte.'

He went on more menacingly now. 'So let me be perfectly clear, if Strongbow hears anything of this incident, I will immediately inform him about your behaviour in his forest.' We were stunned into silence. I said nothing, not trusting my words.

Pleased with the impact of his threats, he approached Myler, casually brushing his sword aside. 'You Geraldines have infected this camp. And I, for one, am deeply concerned that your ambitions and loyalty are more to your own family than to Strongbow, who, I might remind you, is my nephew.'

It was no doubt that the Geraldines made up a substantial part of the leadership of the campaign: Robert FitzStephen, Raymond Le Gros, Maurice FitzGerald, Myler, and even the archdeacon, Gerald de Barry. But their loyalty or motives had never been questioned. They needed the wealth and land that my father offered. However, Myler was now jeopardising their position, as blood ties ran deep in Norman families, and any rift with Strongbow would quickly spill into the broader family. I was keenly aware that without the support of the Geraldines, Strongbow would be greatly weakened, and it would, in all probability, bring an end to the planned campaign in Ireland. This would be disastrous for us all, not least for Eanna, who would not survive O'Rourke's cruelty should he learn of our failure to recruit Norman swords to our cause. Sir Hervey caught the look of concern that Myler and I exchanged.

'Excellent, I can see we all understand each other,' he sneered. 'So let this be the end of the matter. Shall we? Good evening,' he said, but before leaving he turned to Alice. 'It was almost a pleasure, my dear. But who knows what the future holds?' he finished chillingly before he turned and left.

THE SWALLOWS TOLERATED my presence as I strolled the walls, enjoying their warning chatter when I passed too close to their nests. Swarming from the walls, they sped between the men moving steadily with rhythmic movements, as if in a dance, cutting the hay for the winter fodder. My little escorts were fattening themselves for the coming winter, when they would leave us. The fishermen said they buried themselves in the mud flats, then emerged in the spring to return to their nesting grounds. Wherever they went, I would miss them and count the days till their return.

The autumn was no time to launch our campaign to return to Ireland in force. Restless autumnal winds and seas would keep sensible folk on land; abundant stores of summer food would dwindle quickly as the winter months dragged through the cold and rain. It was no time for armies.

Our departure had been delayed by the king of England, King Henry II. Relations remained strained, and although the king had given permission for his subjects to aid my father, he had made his opposition to Strongbow's involvement clear. To placate the king, he spent his time at court attending to the king's wishes. As a test of his loyalty, Strongbow had been tasked by the king to escort his daughter to Germany, where she was to marry the king of Saxony. With Strongbow away for several months, the plans for the invasion had been postponed, and the routine of the castle shifted to preparing the harvest and planning for the winter.

The early summer dawns rose quickly over the golden fields which swept from the castle; ripe, leaden crops swayed easily in the gentle winds. It would be a good harvest, and that meant an easy winter for man and beast. The rich fertility sprang from the ground and, from that growth, into the fattening animals and into the very blood of the men and women who flooded the fields and barns: mowing, loading, sorting and storing nature's bounty. The glistening bodies of the young men and women laboured in the joyous cauldron of summer heat as the Goddess smiled; there would be a good crop of babies next year too.

Time slowed in the warm, balmy evenings as everyone

gathered in the courtyard to be fed from the kitchens. Exhausted but content, strained muscles recovered, helped by the ales we served, rushing from table to table in an effort to satisfy the good-humoured demands of the thirsty masses.

Occasionally there would be calls for singers, and as the evening wore on into the quiet, dusky twilight, I would be asked to sing of Ireland. A respectful hush would descend on the merry crowd. I had been taught the many songs of our land at my mother's knee; I was of known good voice. The haunting, melodic sounds, intertwined with a druidic mysticism of our music, resonated in the castle courtyard in the still of the summer dusk. The flickering shadows seemed to dance to the slow, melancholic rhythms in the light of the torches and glowing fires. A trancelike hush gripped the stillness. Captivated, more enchanted than understanding, the people would plead for more and gathered silently to hear my stories of our land, loves and gods.

And it seems that this did not escape the archdeacon, who was none too pleased. For on one such evening, as I sang of the fertility granted by the earth mother, Danu, to our land, I could see Rob nudging Myler, nodding at the hurried arrival of the archdeacon in the courtyard. We were, as usual, sharing a bench, enjoying the close of the evening. Through Myler, Rob and I had also become good friends. Having finished my song, I pushed through the applause of the rowdy crowd to re-join them just as the archdeacon reached them.

'This should be good.' Rob sniggered into his cup. Myler elbowed him to keep quiet.

'Good evening, cousin. Will you sit and join us in a cup of ale?' Myler smiled, feigning surprise at his appearance.

'I won't, Myler,' he said, remaining standing with a thick manuscript wedged under his arm. He seemed flustered but eventually, plucking up his courage, he turned to me and continued rather formally.

'M'lady, I had heard of the goings-on here, and I am sad to say that the worst reports have just been confirmed.' He appeared exasperated. 'I must say, I think it most inappropriate of you to sing of false gods in the presence of good Christian souls. I must ask you to desist forthwith.' Agitated, some pages slipped from the manuscript.

'Yes, indeed, I must insist,' he continued, scrambling to retrieve the scattered pages. Rob couldn't contain himself and laughed as the flurry of pages scattered across the courtyard.

Myler's look warned Rob to stop larking as I helped the archdeacon gather his pages. That done, I half innocently asked the archdeacon, 'Which false gods might these be, Archbishop—sorry, Archdeacon?' Myler shook his head, pleading with me not to rile his cousin.

'There is only one God, our Lord God on high, who graces the heavens and rules the earth,' he rushed. 'Your pagan gods and their rituals must be washed from the memory of the people; they have no place. You imperil their very souls with such blasphemies.'

'Archdeacon, your god has been welcomed into our land in Ireland. But we have many gods. One more is no harm to us ... hopefully,' I replied. 'I think you well know that many of these *pagan* gods, as you refer to them, have been given a cloak of respectability by your church—a Christian cloak, so to speak.' I spoke quietly, for I liked Myler's cousin; he was a sincere man. 'And so be it, if that works for you, Archdeacon, but our gods remain with us nonetheless, and always will.'

'My lady,' he complained, half breathless. 'You cannot encourage unbelievers to ignore the word of the Gospels; it's just not right.'

'It would appear to me, Archdeacon, that you are the

unbeliever—or at least more of an unbeliever than I. I am willing to believe in all the gods . . . including yours if you so wish. Whereas you believe in just one. Does that not make you more of an unbeliever than I?' I teased and, taking his arm, gestured for him to join us, adding, 'So at least let us agree to differ agreeably.'

'I still think it most inappropriate,' he huffed, taking a seat and accepting the cup Rob offered. He was not an overbearing man.

'Archdeacon. Our gods are of the earth, rivers, sea and sky, men and women alike. With no disrespect, your god is of man and for men, and will pass when man's footsteps no longer dust the soil.' I continued, 'Like us, the gods should all learn to live with each other. We should demand that of them. After all, a god with no followers ceases to exist if he only exists in their minds. Is that not why some seek so many converts?' The archdeacon huffed his disapproval as Myler and Rob laughed and raised their cups to harmony amongst men and gods alike.

'No chance of that with the women,' Rob grinned. I managed to cuff his ear stoutly before he could duck.

And so we waited, my father's frustration growing by the day. His thirst for revenge dominated his every waking moment, obscuring whatever sense he had left; he threatened to return alone. Angrily, he cursed Donal and I when we spoke of the danger to Eanna. He had not been pleased that I had caused Strongbow to abandon the plan he and Sir Hervey had made for landing in Ireland. He called Donal a coward and spent more time in the company of Sir Hervey. We knew nothing of their schemes, but I feared their outcome.

Chapter Six
RASH DECISIONS

Chepstow Castle, Wales
Summer 1167

'I cannot wait any longer,' Diarmuit ranted. 'I have word that my enemies are busy with rebellion in the North. Now is the time.' He slammed his tankard on the table. 'And your ale is vile as well. I need to get out of here!' He rose and paced the length of the room before slumping back into his chair.

'Well, might I suggest you don't drink so much of it, Lord King,' Sir Hervey said, lifting the jug to replenish Diarmuit's tankard.

Eyeing him suspiciously, Diarmuit leaned forward with clenched fists. 'I will go alone, land from a small boat. I can reach Ferns unnoticed and gather some supporters to my side. That's what I'll do,' he said, and drank deeply, spilling more of the dark brown liquid down the front of his stained tunic.

Filling the tankard again, Montmorency continued quietly, 'I fully understand your frustration, Lord King. You have the ambition and decisiveness befitting your great position. Not matched by others in your family, I might add. But such a course of action would not be advised. It would be highly dangerous for you and a great loss to Ireland should its greatest king come to a sorry end.' He paused, watching MacMurrough, constantly amused at how this pitiful creature was so susceptible to flattery. He went on, 'It's not a risk we should take. However, I fully agree that you should return, and to do so, I might just have a suggestion.' He waited patiently for whatever trivial thoughts occupied MacMurrough to dissipate.

He had learned to despise MacMurrough; however, he had also learned that he was easily manipulated. If he returned alone, he would most likely be quickly apprehended, and God only knew what would happen then. He would be lucky to get away with his life, but certainly with his sight. The Irish had a barbaric practice of blinding their captives before releasing them to burden their families. They had a primitive belief that the fertility of their soil and health of their livestock were inextricably intertwined with that of their king. Physical impairment precluded a man from being king: lose an eye in battle, and the other will not see a throne again.

Montmorency knew that Strongbow could not send any of his followers without the king's permission. He alone, amongst Strongbow's men, had that permission, as did any other knight he could recruit to his cause. The king had granted him this when he placed him in Strongbow's court. However, this plan to return to Ireland now was fraught with danger; he would not take such risks. But MacMurrough would need some protection if there was to be any chance of him surviving unscathed, and there was nothing to prevent some impulsive young fool acting of his own accord.

Montmorency also knew that in returning, MacMurrough would certainly imperil his captive son, Eanna. But male heirs to the king of Leinster were an inconvenience as far as he was concerned. Any scheme that might rid the world of their presence was to be welcomed. And if MacMurrough returned with enough protection that he didn't get himself killed—not just yet, anyway—Montmorency thought he might just be able to put Diarmuit's other sons in harm's way in the process, just for good measure. So his scheme had its benefits. MacMurrough himself just had to survive long enough to marry his daughter to Strongbow. He had a plan.

'You will need a guard to ensure your safety. I assume Donal will accompany you, and could I also suggest you bring your youngest son, Conor,' he said.

MacMurrough nodded. He would bring him. It would be important to show confidence to the tribes if he was to gather their support. Bringing both Donal and Conor back made clear his confidence in regaining his kingdom; no potential heir would be hidden in a foreign land to preserve their bloodline should they fail. It spoke of his will and determination.

'Very wise, Lord King. In addition, his presence might encourage others to accompany you. Someone who could provide adequate protection for you in your endeavours.'

'Go on, I'm listening,' MacMurrough said, more thoughtful now.

As Sir Hervey replenished MacMurrough's tankard, he continued, 'I think we can create the conditions where some eager knight is keen to accompany you. And with that end in mind, with your permission, Lord King, I've asked the Princess Aoife and Sir Myler FitzHenry to join us later.'

Looking at him long and suspiciously with his sunken, dark eyes, MacMurrough scowled. 'What is this plan of yours, Montmorency?'

'Well, m'lord, before we get to that, I think you'd agree that in all my endeavours, I always have your best interests first and foremost in my thoughts.' He paused while Diarmuit wiped the ale from his beard on his tunic sleeve. 'As a great warrior king, I am only surprised by the modesty of your ambitions. Why limit yourself to Leinster when by right, the lordship of Ireland is your entitlement . . . and if I might say so, your destiny.' Montmorency almost laughed as he saw the lavish praise do its work on MacMurrough, who sat nodding and mumbling into his tankard. 'I am sure I can be of significant service to you in your just quest.'

MacMurrough stirred from his reverie of imagining himself on the throne of Ireland as *ard rí*, high king— O'Connor vanquished, O'Rourke dead. He turned on Montmorency and laughed, shaking his head.

'You? And what do you have to offer? You're useless in battle, so I hear. You've no army I can use. You talk a lot. What use is a man like you to me?' he spat, draining his ale, waving his hand dismissively.

Undeterred, as he had expected this from the brute, Montmorency smiled. 'Lord King. All great men of destiny require good and loyal counsel.' He went on. 'In particular, they need men knowledgeable in the affairs of their allies, who can look after their interests and keep them informed of matters which might otherwise escape their attention.' He scrutinised Diarmuit to make sure he understood what he was suggesting. Satisfied that he did, he continued, 'Working together, I can ensure you are kept fully informed. In addition, as Strongbow's uncle, I do have some considerable influence, which could, in the right circumstances, be used to your benefit.' He had gone far enough now. If word of this reached Strongbow, he would at best lose his position in the campaign, along with the spoils and wealth to be had should they be successful. Montmorency needed this.

His long career in the service of the king in France had not yielded him any great fortune. Landless and of no means, he had crossed the sea to enter the service of his nephew, Strongbow, having won the confidence of King Henry. Word of MacMurrough's pleading to the king and the spoils he promised had also reached Montmorency. Having no followers or reputation for military prowess, he had learned to use his guile and tongue in the courts of great men. Myler suspected the king had granted him permission to go on the understanding that he would be his eyes and ears in Strongbow's court.

MacMurrough stared moodily at him. Eventually, brushing his long, dank hair from his face, he said, 'I see, Sir Hervey. You will be my spy in this camp.'

Montmorency winced at this, but at least the man was not entirely a fool. He understood what he was offering. 'Well, I wouldn't entirely agree with your choice of words. But be that as it may, you must understand that things are not entirely as they seem here.'

'What do you mean?' MacMurrough asked, interested now.

'Well, one must be ever cautious about the motives of one's friends. This damn family, the Geraldines, have won the trust of Strongbow for now. But I, for one, am more than suspicious. They are far too many here, and I suspect that as soon as it suits their purposes, Strongbow's interests will be abandoned. You'll understand, Lord King, that this will put you in a perilous position, with their armies roaming your kingdom at will.'

Intrigued but worried by what he'd heard, MacMurrough rose and paced the room agitatedly.

Watching him, Montmorency went on to describe the power of the Geraldines and how their tentacles stretched deep into the court of King Henry. Their armies were feared by friends and enemies alike. They were an ambitious Norman dynasty without a land to claim as their own, and that should make any king very wary of their offers of help.

'So you see, Lord King, we must all be wary of the Geraldines. However, working together, looking after each other's interests, I'm confident we can overcome any threat they might pose and make use of them for as long as is necessary.'

'And what's in it for you, Sir Hervey? Why should I trust you?' MacMurrough asked.

'Indeed. Lord King, I am at the stage in life when I would benefit greatly from the wealth and security that good land affords. I understand there are vast tracts of such land in the southeast of your kingdom. In return for my services, you could grant me four cantreds. It would be a mere trifle to you,' he suggested.

'Four!' Diarmuit objected. 'Four hundred thousand acres! Your spying would not be worth that. I might pay a price of two cantreds to the man who arrives with an army on my shore. But not for mere spying.' He gestured dismissively.

Sir Hervey gave this some thought and then added quietly, 'Agreed. I'll take that. If I arrive with that army when you summon it, you will guarantee to me the grant of two cantreds. I think your offer is reasonable. So is that agreed, Lord King?' He offered Diarmuit his hand.

After some hesitation from MacMurrough, who feared trickery, Montmorency allayed his fears, and it was agreed. The two men gave their bond on the terms of the agreement, which were to remain known only to them.

Montmorency was pleased with the outcome. He would have accepted one cantred or less. Two hundred thousand acres would provide richly for his needs.

Drawing closer to the fire as the light faded, they discussed their plans. Montmorency drank the French wine of his own country, while MacMurrough drew heavily from the jug of ale. And while MacMurrough dreamed of his return and sweet revenge, Montmorency filled his head with the ambition of the high kingship of Ireland. He could see this toxic mix of greed, ambition and revenge for outrages suffered bubbling to a dangerous broth of conceited invincibility in MacMurrough. Sir Hervey would just have to make sure that the inevitable catastrophe which follows such hubris would be confined to MacMurrough and his family—an outcome that was eminently possible with such an imbecile.

※

THAT WAS how I found them—ensconced by the fire, deep in conversation which fell silent when we entered. My father's rooms were separate from those of the rest of the family, in a high tower in the southeast corner of the lower bailey. Treated as an honoured guest at the request of King Henry, Strongbow—forever trying to please the king—had made these privileged quarters available to my father. The thick walls and easterly facing orientation held the coolness, and the fires remained lit on the summer evenings to lighten the chill. Removed from the rest of the family, he often spent his evenings with Montmorency, who without doubt poured poison into his ears, inflating his fragile pride. That would not be difficult, and his sneering disdain told me as much when I unavoidably passed him while going about my business. I feared the ill-advised schemes he would concoct to tempt my father.

'Ah, here they are, together again,' Sir Hervey pointedly greeted Myler and me as we entered the dimly lit chamber, the last of the evening light lessening the gloom before the candles were lit.

'Thank you for coming. Your father and I wanted to discuss his frustration at the delay in returning to Ireland.' He rose and moved to arrange a chair for me, offering us some wine or refreshments.

'No, thank you.'

My father remained slumped in his chair, the toll of the ale telling in his manner, as was often the case more recently.

'Father,' I acknowledged him and was rewarded with a grunt of sorts. I continued, 'What is it you would like to discuss with us, Sir Hervey?'

'Straight to the matter in hand. Excellent!' He smiled, ignoring my hostility. 'Your father, in his wisdom, has kept a close eye on affairs as they have been developing in Ireland recently. The treacherous dogs, O'Connor and O'Rourke, are completely embroiled in a turmoil of their own making in the north of the country, Ulster. He believes they are fully occupied and seriously weakened by events. Consequently, and I have to say I think this is most perceptive of your father, he believes there is an opportunity to profit from their disadvantage.' I could feel a chilling fear rising in my chest, squeezing the breath from my lungs. Sir Hervey read my thoughts, writ large in the pale mask that drove the colour from my cheeks. Savouring it momentarily, he continued.

'So he has decided to act decisively and return to Ireland immediately. He will slip quietly into Glascarrig and proceed quickly to Ferns to gather the support of your people.' he said and sneered, relishing the impact of his words.

So this was it, the same stupid plan, except with no army this time. 'No!' I said. 'You cannot . . . What about Eanna? You know they could kill him unless we return in force. That's the only way they'll negotiate—if they are afraid of us.' I regarded my father coldly, standing over his slumped figure.

There was still some shame in the man, but it hadn't stopped him before.

He scowled into his tankard. 'I'm going,' he yelled, spitting ale through his thick black beard. 'And that's the end of it.'

'Strongbow has forbidden it,' I yelled. 'His decision was to land at Bannow Bay in force. This plan is madness.' I stood in front of him, demanding his attention. 'You know they will never willingly let us back. They will turn south to Leinster with a vastly superior force and destroy us.'

Nothing from him, no reaction, as he stared into the fire. I pleaded now. 'What about Eanna? You know what they will do.'

He gripped his tankard, mumbling and shaking his head. 'I'm going,' he said.

'No, Strongbow has forbidden it,' I repeated. 'You have no authority to do this!'

'Well, actually, m'lady, I think you'll find you are mistaken in that belief,' Sir Hervey interjected. 'You see, in his absence, Strongbow gave me, his uncle, full authority to act as I see fit to look after his interests in matters concerning our campaign in Ireland.'

I looked to Myler, who with a nod of his head confirmed this to be true. However, I had no doubt that Strongbow was set against any foolhardy foray with an unprepared force. But with Strongbow in Germany, Sir Hervey could work his mischief.

'It is my view that circumstances have changed considerably in Ireland, and I agree with your father's wise judgement that we should move quickly to take advantage of the situation,' he said.

'Donal agrees with me, this is madness,' I yelled, but I was fearful now. 'Please, father, please—you mustn't . . . please.'

'I'm going.' He stared sullenly into his tankard. 'Now get

out. Get out! Leave me!' He staggered to his feet, his chair clattering to the ground behind him.

Panicking now, I turned to Myler; he took my hand, trying to calm me, but he was powerless in this. Sir Hervey had the authority of Strongbow, and no one would challenge that.

Desperate for a way out, I thought if I couldn't persuade my father, I could scare him. Sober, he would understand that without a guard of Normans, he wouldn't last a week. Our own kinsmen would see the hopelessness of his cause; it would be perilous for anyone to support him. In all likelihood, they would capture him and deliver him to O'Connor to garner his favour.

'OK, go. Go to Ireland,' I screamed. 'But you can go alone, and you will be no threat to anyone. I can only hope they will take pity on you.' I tried scorn. 'Maybe they will put your eyes out and set you on the road, ridiculed and mocked by all.' That silenced him and he returned to his seat which Montmorency made a show of recovering for him.

Then, regarding me coldly, Sir Hervey put in, 'Ah, and that's where you are wrong, m'lady.' Moving to my father's side, placing his hand on his shoulder, he continued: 'Your father is planning to bring your younger brother Conor with him, to educate him in the ways of a king, I believe. Most admirable.' He smirked.

Myler steadied me as my breath shallowed to a quickened rasp. I gripped his arm for support, feeling my stomach lurch. What was happening? How could this be? I would lose Conor too. But I could see the sickening sense in it: with no army, he would use his son's life instead. Conor would be bargained, given hostage for support or to buy off an enemy, with little chance of surviving if his life depended on my father's word.

'No. No,' I whimpered quietly and fell to my knees. 'No. Please, no,' I said, pleading now.

Moving towards me, as if to assist, Sir Hervey said. 'Really, m'lady. I think you are overreacting...'

'Leave her,' Myler said angrily, almost pushing him away. He helped me to my feet, supporting me with his strong arm around my waist. I looked to my father and saw his silent intent, clouded with shame. Had he dispensed with the last vestiges of decency, of the love of a father, of the father's burning will, etched in our very core, to care for his child above all else? He remained silent. I watched as if the very humanity drained from the man, like the living blood, to soil the tiled floor of his chamber.

Conor would go, but if he must, so would I. And Donal would too. We would go to protect Conor. I told him this.

He didn't react at first but looked to Montmorency, who, appearing concerned, objected strongly, pointing out how dangerous it was for a woman. It was a plan fraught with risk, not least for my virtue should we be captured. And he, for one, would not wish that horrible fate upon me. The vile appetites of animals of men satisfied on such saintly, innocent flesh.

He looked me in the eye as he said this, both of us seeing him in the castle cellar assaulting Alice. I then understood how people could be driven to commit great cruelty on another human being. I shivered at what I was capable of at that moment.

'Strongbow's betrothed,' he continued, wringing his hands. Then he added, 'M'lady, you could not possibly go without a proper guard. I would not countenance it,' he objected. 'What can be done? Who could possibly protect you?' he finished and looked at Myler.

His intent was clear. He was manipulating Myler into accompanying us, thereby providing the necessary protection for my father. If it didn't end well, so be it. Myler's demise would mean one less troublesome Geraldine for him to worry about. I would discover in time his more depraved motivation for seeking to harm Myler.

For me, if Myler was to accompany us, it was welcome. My fondness for Myler had grown, and we drew ever closer with each day, tumbling headlong and willingly into each other's hearts. Despite the burden of loss which lingered ever present, ebbing and flowing through each day, my spirits lifted when I saw Myler. Without him, my thoughts would drift unbidden to him, lightening those moments with a ripple of pleasure that would sweep over me, gurgle away and then surge forward, washing my more sombre moods in a muted joy.

Myler stepped forward. 'I would consider it an honour to accompany you, Lord King, on your journey.' He understood Sir Hervey's intent, and while he despised the man, he knew this journey was perilous. The risk of ambush, betrayal or capture was real. He had little regard for my father; his concern was for me should we be attacked. He could not contemplate my death, but a worse fate would befall me if I fell into the hands of O'Rourke. He would not waste the opportunity of humiliating the daughter of Diarmuit MacMurrough.

'With an adequate body of men-at-arms which I can muster, I can ensure your safety, if you will permit me,' he said to my father. For his part, he looked to Sir Hervey for assurance on Myler's suggestion.

'An excellent suggestion, Sir Myler,' he said. 'I see no real objection.' Clearly having already considered Myler's use in this, he went on to explain how Myler would not be acting on Strongbow's instruction or with his knowledge. King Henry, who was not yet willing to let Strongbow sail to Ireland, had given his permission for others to offer assistance to my father, should they so wish. He could have no real objection to Myler going, who, although clearly in Strongbow's camp, was acting of his own accord. Strongbow's continued absence in Germany, at the wedding of Henry's daughter to the Saxon king, would provide him ample protection from the king's displeasure. He was very confident that Strongbow would have no objections, considering that the safety of the princess was also at stake.

'Indeed, it is most honourable of you, Sir Myler . . . selfless, I'd go so far as to say. Wouldn't you agree, m'lady?' he sneered, turning to me. 'Why hadn't I thought of that! An excellent suggestion.' He nodded to my father, who grunted his agreement.

However, my father insisted that Myler ready his men immediately. With the summer drawing to a close, the autumn seas would soon rise, and if he was to gather a force to his cause in Ireland, it must be done before the winter came. He would use the dead of winter to fortify his stronghold and ready them for war when the campaigning season began in the spring of next year.

Myler described how he would need at least three months to make the necessary arrangements, recruiting the knights, archers and foot soldiers. They would need to be provisioned and equipped with arms to carry them through to the spring, when they assumed the main force of Strongbow's army would land. An adequate force to mount a stout defence of Ferns would be wise in the meantime. Boats would also need to be requisitioned with trustworthy and tight-lipped sea masters who would not betray their plans to listening ears in the ports of Wales or Ireland. There was a lot to do.

'No!' my father yelled. 'We go now, before the end of the summer. I'm not waiting any longer.'

'Lord King,' Myler pleaded. 'I can't possibly assemble a force that could protect you for the winter in such a short time.' He looked to Sir Hervey, appealing for him to speak some sense to my father.

'No!' my father repeated. Sir Hervey remained silent, calculating.

'It's not possible, Lord King,' Myler insisted.

'You have one month,' Sir Hervey said.

'What? One month!' Myler rounded on Sir Hervey. 'You know damn well it's not possible.' He paused. Getting no reaction from Sir Hervey, he continued.

'In that time, I can barely assemble a bodyguard,' he said. Sir Hervey remained impassive.

'I'll have my own men with me,' my father said.

'Father, you know that won't be enough,' I pleaded.

'I will not be able to defend Ferns if we are attacked. I will not win a fight if we come up against any force at all. It's suicidal,' Myler said.

'So be it.' Sir Hervey shrugged. 'Sir Myler, if you are uncomfortable with undertaking the protection of the king and Princess Aoife, I'm sure we can find some other brave knight to accept the challenge?'

Myler, frustrated but outwitted by Sir Hervey, reluctantly agreed that he would muster what force he could in the time available. We would depart in mid-August 1167, a month from that day.

Part III

Impulse and Hate

Chapter Seven
THE RETURN TO IRELAND

August 1167

'All is ready, Aoife. You must be ready in two days.' Myler spoke softly, for there were ears that would be rewarded for passing word of our plans to return to Ireland. With such a small force, we could easily be taken upon landing. My pleadings with my father had fallen on stony ground—he was going. It was madness. Our only chance was to land undetected and to move quickly to Ferns and hope that we could persuade some of the old allies from our kinsmen to join my father's cause. Even then, I saw little hope of success.

The sun had crept higher that morning; the courtyard was coming alive with the bustle of men and the excited stamping and muttering of the horses in the courtyard below my open window. Le Gros shouted over the din, trying to put some order to things. Myler lay beside me, stretching in that last luxurious moment of fulfilled exhaustion before he would silently creep away, unseen, to join his uncles who were mounting jumpy stallions, ready to begin another gruelling day's practice.

Rising, he dressed quickly. I watched, relishing the beauty of the man whose warmth still clung to the bed beside me. Bringing me a mug of fresh water, he then sat wearily at the table away from the window, his shoulders slumped. He would normally bound through my door after the nights we snatched together.

'Aoife. Sit with me . . . we must talk.'

I rose and joined him, draping a light robe around my shoulders, comfortable in my near nakedness.

'There will be five knights in all, a score of archers and a body of foot soldiers,' he said, looking down at his large hands spread on the table between us. 'It's a small enough force but should be enough if they aren't waiting. Ferns is only a couple of hours march from the landing.' He did not look at me as he said this, and there was an unusual gloominess about him. The sigh of the wind through the open window deepened the silence that filled him. It was a silence I could not penetrate, and a darkness lurked in an arch of that gloom.

Our bodies had touched, merged. The rhythms of our breathing, our very heartbeats, coupling, unlocking a deep well of comfort, a precious pool of certainty in a raging sea. It was pure joy, sending waves of sensation through every sinew and nerve ending in my body while bathing my spirit in an unfamiliar restful calmness.

With Myler by my side, I felt that challenges could be faced and weathered, come what may. In that, I think there is the tender hand of the Goddess Danu, the earth goddess. The ancient Irish mother goddess from which all the Tuatha Dé Danann—the first Irish tribe—claimed descent. She was a triple Goddess—a concept borrowed by the Christian church—who controlled the rain, sunshine, and harvest; the health and fertility of man, women and beast. She had placed man and womankind at the heart of her earthly realm as her appointed custodians of the soil, the waters, the land's bounty and the beasts who roamed. A realm blessed and beset in equal measure, the universal balance of beauty and horror.

My feelings for Myler were such. I could not say I felt happiness, not with Eanna in captivity. Yet I knew I could face the challenges with him by my side. I felt a profound connection with him, a comfortable familiarity that was troubled by his bleak silence now.

His eyes found mine, and before he spoke again, I could see the sorrow in their depths. 'Aoife, I can't go,' he said softly. How I loved those soft eyes and the gentle tears now flowing, resting on his lips. Shaking his sunken head, he added, 'I'm sorry, so sorry.'

'But why? Why not? What's happened?' I pleaded, panicking now, for not to have him by my side in this was unthinkable.

Leaning forward, he took my hands in his and kissed them. I could feel his tears on my fingers and I buried my face in his thick, scented hair, so familiar now.

After a moment he straightened, looked at me and said, 'Please, Aoife, forgive me, but it's not possible.' The distress was etched into his face. He could barely speak. 'My uncles say the connection between our family and Strongbow is too strong. He couldn't credibly deny any knowledge of it if the king becomes aware.' He was silent for a while, as melancholy as I had ever seen him. 'So I can't, I just can't. Please forgive me. I love you so much.'

Shocked, crestfallen, no words would come. I sat there and looked at him, and he leant forward and kissed me. Our tears mingled on our lips as we sought each other. He rose and took me in his arms, folding me closer to still my trembling body. If only my life could be this: deep in the safety and warmth of his embrace. Damn them, but I knew what he said was true, and to press him to accompany me would be to ask him to betray everything he held dear. I gripped him, knowing I had to release him from the obligation he felt.

Eventually, easing myself from his embrace, I reached out and took his face in my hands, feeling the moist tenderness of his skin.

'Myler, *mo grá*. I see, I understand . . . it's just that I have come to rely on you, to need you.' I paused, seeing the pain pulsing through his eyes. I was despairing, but my words were hot irons in his heart. I had to stop. 'Myler, I know you love me. That will sustain me.' I smiled. 'I understand, I do . . . we both have our duties. Your uncles are right. If you came, it could ruin everything for us.'

'It won't be for long. I promise you, Aoife. As soon as I can, I will come to you,' he said, smiling gently now. 'And you will be in good hands in the meantime.'

'Yes,' I said. 'In this way maybe someday we can, somehow, be together.' I paused but did not have the strength to contain my sorrow any longer. 'I will miss you, miss you so much . . .' I wept bitterly now, clutching him tightly.

Releasing me, he gently stroked my hair, which hung loosely down my back. He went on to describe how we would be accompanied by Richard FitzGodebert and four other knights. He was a capable and trustworthy ally and could be relied upon. Of Flemish origin, he could not be easily connected to Strongbow. He had also asked his uncle, Raymond Le Gros, if Rob Smith could lead the archers and accompany the party. Permission was granted and Rob, as Myler's childhood friend, had readily agreed, as he wanted the experience of his first combat command without the oversight of his father. He had also given his word to Myler that he would protect me with his life.

Myler said he would remain at Chepstow and work with his uncles to prepare the army for when Strongbow secured the permission of the king to lead the support for my father to regain his crown and kingdom. I dearly hoped that would be soon, as our prospects in Ireland, a hostile land in turmoil with a perilously inadequate force, were none too good, to say the least.

WE EMBARKED for Ireland on an unseasonably cold day in August 1167. The light south-westerly wind would allow us easy passage to sail on a beam reach directly across the sea from St Davids at the westerly tip of Wales.

Our plan was to avoid the busy ports and docks and land at a quiet strand just south of the wooden pier at Glascarrig, the small port on the east coast that served Ferns. A day's ride north of the busy Norse walled city of Wexford with its bustling quays, our landing should go unnoticed by watchful eyes in the pay of O'Rourke for signs of the return of Diarmuit MacMurrough. He would hear of our landing as fast as a horse could travel after we beached our boat, but we should have reached Ferns by then. There, we hoped to quickly gather a force to discourage any early attempt to attack without a considerable force behind them, and that would take time to assemble.

Despite Myler's precautions to conceal the preparations for our return, the ports of Wales swarmed with all manner of people. Information was a valuable commodity there, and O'Rourke's spies would have paid well for news of our plans. Word would have reached them of my father's pleadings to King Henry for his assistance in regaining his crown. We were also sure they would be aware of our presence at Chepstow Castle as guests of Strongbow. That alone would signal my father's intent to gather Norman forces to his cause. They would be hungry to know as to when and how he would act.

All was made ready as the boat was held by its lines to the dock. Myler shouted a few last instructions to FitzGodebert and Rob and helped the dock men pull the gangplank. There could be no embrace; even our eyes could not betray our pain. We had tried to make up for what would be a season's worth of lost intimacy before he had left my room before dawn that morning; my body ached pleasantly from his urgent lovemaking.

There was ample room in the boat. No horses were to be taken, as Myler, with limited time, could not secure a barque with the harnesses to hold them suspended in the waist during the crossing. The Normans had perfected this way of transporting their valuable warhorses to avoid injury and panic in heavy seas. The heavy armour of the knights was to be distributed amongst their attendants to carry. The archers were laden with longbows and sheafs of arrows and, to my relief, were led by Rob Smith, as Myler had promised.

There was no better longbow man for this dangerous task, and he had also become a good friend. He was a light-hearted big-boned lad, with the biggest barrel of a chest I had seen on any man. He had the strength of a draft horse from his years of practice with the longbow. He was good company and seemed to be taking his promise to Myler as a sacred duty; he was forever in my wake.

There was nothing out of the ordinary about our vessel as we sailed for Glascarrig. A regular trading barque, its brown sail looked like any other which daily ploughed the coast and waters between the islands. It would raise no suspicions. But as the land drew steadily closer, we were wary that word of our coming had reached Ireland. There were many who would not welcome my father's return.

We had learned that Eanna remained unharmed and that he had been given as hostage to the rival king of the lands bordering western Leinster, Mac Giolla Patrick. He had long coveted our land and had been granted the western half of my father's kingdom of Leinster by Rory O'Connor, the high king, and his henchman, Tiarnan O'Rourke. O'Rourke was a cruel man and a sworn enemy of my father, and while I was happy to hear that Eanna was no longer in his hands, Mac Giolla Patrick was no better. However, Donal thought he had more interest in keeping Eanna from harm so as to have some leverage over our father should he return to reclaim his kingship.

The other half of my father's kingdom had been given to my father's brother Murchad, as was commonly the practice of the high king. His intention was to divide the family, weakening it as a combined force. A proven tactic, a defeated enemy's kingdom would be split between two rivals, who would inevitably weaken each other and any further threat to the high king.

In our case, Murchad would not oppose my father. He had remained loyal, and we hoped enough of our kinsmen would come to my father's side if he returned with a real prospect of regaining his throne, more from fear than from loyalty.

The bow of the boat dipped into the waves as the sail dropped. The gusts whipped the silver sands across the lonely strand as the oarsmen drove the boat onto the light shingle in a crunching, lurching halt. All was still. The grass dunes beyond the beach betrayed no sign of danger, with the birds drifting leisurely on the winds above. Watchful, Donal was pleased. The birds would have been screeching if there were strangers hidden there, watching us. Ever cautious, he set a small party to scout the area before we went ashore. We would be most vulnerable with our backs to the sea. If we were ambushed there, there would be little hope.

The scouts returned and, satisfied that all was clear, Donal ordered us out, and we jumped into the shallow rippling water. Picking our steps, we slowly waded to the beach. I carried Conor on my back and then set him on the soft sand, where he took off laughing at the joy of the clear day. The Normans were tense and readied themselves for a fight. Rob Smith arranged his archers behind the knights, ready to repel any attack as the foot soldiers quickly unloaded the boat. If there was an ambush waiting, it would be now. With the boat most vulnerable while lodged on the shingle, the shipmaster was eager to be gone and urged his crew to pass the arms and provisions ashore. Rob shouted angrily when a large sheaf of arrows was dropped, the soaked fletching on the arrows making them useless. Precious few had been brought, as with no packhorses, they were limited to what they could carry. Each archer hefted enormous burdens of bundled arrows onto their backs. That done, the shipmaster shouted his farewells, and the powerful strokes of the oarsmen pulled the boat slowly and then quickly into the swell of the bay.

The long waves brushed across the shingle behind us, sucking and gurgling noisily as they retreated to the sea. A tense stillness hung in the air. And then a sudden flurry of birds rose a screaming alarm from the dunes directly in front of us. The men dropped their loads and scrambled into a defensive semicircle formation around us. Unsheathing their longswords, the knights discarded the scabbards and spaced themselves in front of the foot soldiers, to afford them the space to work the swing of their swords. Standing behind the array of foot soldiers, the archers stuck their arrows into the sand, placing one in the bow, ready to loose a deadly volley at whatever emerged from those dunes.

'Hold steady, lads,' Rob ordered calmly. A scrambling noise rose from the dunes.

'Ready.' As one, the archers strained their bows, gauging the distance.

'Hold it. Here it comes!'

'Take your mark . . . on my word . . .'

Conor burst from the dunes in a cloud of sand as he rolled, laughing with the unrestrained joy of a child, down the sand slope. Jumping to his feet, he waved, 'Come on, Aoife, come on!'

In the confusion, I hadn't noticed him missing. He ran through the Normans, excitedly showing me his spoils: a few seashells and an old bone of some sort. I think the relief of the men overcame their anger. Laughing, Rob ruffled Conor's long golden hair, telling him he was the fiercest thing he'd ever seen, charging at him armed with deadly shells and pebbles.

I felt a bit sheepish. Donal was none too pleased with me, for Conor was my charge, and he hardly spoke to me as we gathered and set off from the strand towards Ferns, the seat of MacMurrough power in Leinster. From there, the place where our journey had started almost twelve months ago to the day, my father could claim some authority.

※

IT WAS clear as we approached the town that we were not expected. The few travellers we met on the road stood aside, regarding us curiously, with our hoods concealing our identities. I was worried that the distinctive V shape shaved into the back of the heads of the foot soldiers, who carried their helmets, would alert some observant eyes as to the presence of Normans. So we moved quickly from the coast, hoping to reach the town ahead of any news of our arrival.

The east gate was open as we emerged from the dark woodlands onto the expanse of sowing fields surrounding the wooden palisade walls. The scars from the fire which had engulfed the town when we fled a year past stained the walls at intervals. The blackened trunks of the oak trees marked the long, reddish-tinged walls like missing teeth. In some places, the stumps were all that remained, and I could see men labouring to repair one section close to the gate. I shuddered at the recollection of Conor sitting under the blade of the axeman in that very spot.

As an important trading centre, Ferns also hosted the large monastery, which my father had granted to the Augustinians to gain the favour of the church when he had need of it, which happened to be quite frequently in the past. The regular bustle of activity masked our approach as we passed through the gates. The damage wrought by the fire stunned us. Rows of houses and entire alleyways and streets lay in waste. The skeletal remains of the charred oak support beams of some stood derisively in places, mocking the expanse of what had been lost. The buildings on one side of the small square inside the gate still stood, somehow miraculously escaping the fire. The bright yellow of their fresh thatch shimmered in the heat; they had saved the houses by pulling down the old thatch to stop the flames leaping across the roofs in the gusting winds of that nightmare. An arid hint of ash caught the back of my throat; the light breeze still bore the trace of the inferno which had engulfed the town.

I shivered remembering the horror of that night when I had ridden headlong across that square to save Conor.

In the confusion of the bustling square, I could see Donal and the Normans quietly making their weapons ready. A guard who had been dozing in the heat roused himself. He shouted down from the fighting platform above the gate for us to identify ourselves.

He was shocked when my father threw off his cloak. Immediately recognisable, he was a huge man with long jet-black hair that merged into his thick beard. His voice, made harsh from the din of battle, boomed for all to hear; he, Diarmuit MacMurrough, as the only legitimate king of Leinster by blood right and the sword, had returned to reclaim his throne. It had been stolen by foul treachery, and he would avenge it in blood. Any man who opposed him would taste the steel of his revenge.

Squinting into the sunlight, the guard looked to the horn hung over the sharpened point of an oak trunk in the wall beside his spear. Seeing the armed men arrayed around the square, several archers with arrows in the bows, the guard, gauging his chances, sensibly did nothing. 'Lord King,' he said, with a bow of his head.

Donal ordered a few men to guard the gate, and we arranged ourselves with a vanguard and rear of men-at-arms and set off quickly towards the centre of the town, where our *caistéal*, or palace, stood.

Word of our return spread before us, rippling through the alleyways as we approached what had been our main hall. It was a large half-brick, half-timber cavernous room with a high beamed roof supported by thick oak trusses. At one end sat a raised dais, the throne chair from which my father oversaw official matters of the kingdom. The king would dine here on formal occasions, with the top table set on the dais facing the hall, as was also the custom in Chepstow when Strongbow entertained guests. The hall was built amongst an arrangement of smaller halls, some connected, which provided the extensive accommodation and living chambers for the family and guests of the king.

Ferns, with its royal palaces and residences, was the administrative centre of the most prosperous province in Ireland: Leinster. It was by far the largest Irish town in

Ireland—the coastal towns were controlled by the Norse—and could have been regarded as the capital. Although seeing the devastation that day, I doubted it could ever fully recover. It had been the venue for hosting vassal lords of the noble families of Leinster, foreign dignitaries, kings, and merchants, vying for the lucrative trading relationships that my father's kingdom offered. The extensive palace grounds were laid with paved-stone or raised-timber walkways, all set within an inner palisade within the town for added protection, but more to impress. Visitors would see the wealth and power of the king of Leinster in his stronghold.

As we approached, I could see that the palace bore little damage from the fire and was still largely intact. The east side of the town stretching down to the Bann—the small river that ran under the eastern wall—had suffered the worst of the fire as my father's men, escaping from the centre towards the east gate, had hurled their flaming torches from their horses, setting fires in their wake.

My uncle, Murchad, was plainly surprised to see us, particularly with the support of a band of well-armed Norman knights, foot soldiers and archers. He had had no word of our coming. Ever suspicious, my father had chosen not to test his brother's loyalty and risk our safety by alerting him of our plans. In the fickle, treacherous matters of the inheritance of kingdoms in Ireland, brothers were the least to be trusted.

The Normans were shocked by the venomous rivalries in the households of the royal families here. For them, it was the right of the first-born legitimate male child to inherit a father's lordship or kingdom. In that, there was a simplicity and certainty.

The long-established Irish custom meant it was possible for any warrior born of numerous royal families to emerge as king, providing he could win the support of enough noble families through alliances or threats. The crown was not any prince's right by inheritance. It had to be won, and many kings came to their throne with bloodied sword in hand over the corpses of their kinsmen. Hence, the main rivals for an aspiring young prince were, more often than not, those closest to him—and none more so than his own brothers. This left little room for love or loyalty. The passing of crowns in Ireland were bloody affairs indeed.

For now, my father's caution was unnecessary. Murchad was welcoming, having kept my father informed with secreted messages sent with loyal merchants to Chepstow. The loyalties of the kinsmen of the wider clan were far less certain.

The rise to win a crown in Ireland was built on the foundation of the family. First, a man would, through whatever means, take the leadership of his own family group as Ceann Finn (chieftain); these groups were bonded by family ties and common land ownership. Having achieved that, he would move to acquire the recognition of other families of his kin group in his region. My family, the MacMurroughs, were one of the most prominent royal houses of the most powerful clan in South Leinster, the Uí Chennselaig. As chieftain of the MacMurroughs, my father was accepted as head of the Uí Chennselaig clan, as had his father and his father's father and many more preceding.

My own father's rise to power had not left him with clean hands; he was well endowed with the ruthlessness required to gain a throne in Ireland. After his own father, Donough MacMurrough, had been killed by the Norsemen of Dublin in 1115, when my father was five years of age, the Norse had desecrated his body by burying him with a dog, the ultimate humiliation. My father's older brother, Eanna, had inherited the throne, being strong enough at the time to force the other dynastic families of Leinster into submission. When he died in 1126, these families, several with ambitions of their own to the throne, did not so easily agree to my father becoming king. There followed several years of bloody rivalry within Leinster, inflamed by the ambitions of other provincial kings, foremost of which were my father's bitter enemies of today, Rory O'Connor, Tiarnan O'Rourke and Domnall Mac Giolla Patrick.

At times, my father's cause appeared hopeless, but as with all who rise to great things, the path is seldom smooth and without moments of despair. An unreasonable persistence, when most would retire, and a resilience, when to continue appears futile, sustained him and gave him the most valuable of gifts: time. For in time fortune can turn, and so it did for my father. It eventually delivered the cream of the nobility of the rival Leinster dynasties into his hands. He murdered most and pierced the eyeballs of the others; thereby, in one fell night's gory work, he rid himself of any claimants to the throne of Leinster for a generation.

All bar one, his brother Murchad, who welcomed us to Ferns today. He was arguably my father's most potent rival; most aspiring princes to a throne in Ireland would have at least taken his eyes. I was to learn in time, when I came to understand my father better and measure his actions against the grim choices I myself would make, of his deep-seated humanity, not always apparent and often masked by a lesser cruelty. My father's affection for his brother, unusual in the times, had not let him sully his hands with such a barbarity. He would rule the Uí Chennselaig without the mutilation or slaughter of his own household on his conscience.

This, our clan, was dominant in South Leinster, part of one of the five provinces of Ireland: the kingdoms of the North, Leinster, Munster, Connaught and Meath. Each in turn was dominated by a clutch of family tuaths, one of which would emerge as dominant for periods, as fortune favoured, and provide the provincial kings. Our tuath, the Uí Chennselaig, had, through my family, sat on the throne of Leinster for more than three-quarters of a century.

However, even then, it was not a comfortable seat. The ambitions of the lesser families were little quenched, and a king's throne and life survived only by constant vigilance, as my father had explained to Strongbow on the evenings when we had dined together in the Great Tower at Chepstow.

'So, we cannot rely on the support of your own kinsfolk when we land?' Strongbow had asked my father on one such occasion. I learned as much as he did as my father explained the intricacies of power in Ireland; Strongbow took these opportunities to deepen his understanding of the land and people he would assail.

My father answered that truth with a smile, marvelling at the naivety. 'So has it ever been. The ties which bind a province in Ireland are weak and constantly strained. You see a clansman may give his life for his chieftain, but he has little notion of the province or a provincial king. Even less of a remote, rarely seen high king of Ireland—the ard rí.' He went on to explain how loyalty in Ireland was built on the practice of hostage taking. It was the accepted system of subjugation and enforcement of authority. By gathering the hostages of the noble dynasties of his province, a king could bend the families to his will. No one was bound by any higher sense of duty or loyalty. I was surprised when he quoted the Brehon law tract which cemented this practice, setting that expectation of a king: 'He is not a king who has not hostages in fetters.' I should not have been. My father was a man who had fought his way to a throne and held it for decades in the maelstrom that was Irish dynastic statecraft. He was well acquainted with its ways and what was required of a man to succeed.

He too had taken and given up hostages when necessary.

It was commonly the case that these hostages were treated as honoured guests, dining at the table of the king, their captor. It was equally common for their lives to be summarily forfeit by the axeman after some transgression by the head of their own family against their host.

'Listen, Pembroke.' My father addressed Strongbow in the familiar but formal use of his denied title, edging into flattery. 'Our land is best understood as a landscape of about one hundred and eighty-five clans of uncertain loyalties, some of whom are more commonly grouped together. You'll need to understand that. Aoife can help you with that,' he said, looking to me before continuing. 'The interests of these people do not stretch beyond the clan. Unless compelled to do otherwise, or they stand to gain, they will, at the very least, stand aloof from conflicts when they can.'

We listened as my father spoke with great authority on these occasions, and Strongbow's quiet concentration showed his respect for my father's knowledge and advice. It would be invaluable if he was to succeed in Ireland. He learned that this lack of cohesion at a level higher than the clan meant that the provinces, and to a greater extent the island of Ireland itself, could not mount an effective resistance to withstand invading forces. 'As the Norsemen found when they arrived a few centuries ago,' my father said. 'Having said that, it is because the tribes are difficult to unify that the land is near impossible to defeat, as the Norse also found. You see, there's no capital to capture, no single king's head which, when cleaved from his shoulders, would bring the rest of the land to heel.'

And while I learned much about the intricacies of the politics of power in Ireland on these evenings, I learned more of the man who had successfully navigated its treacherous waters for decades. He seemed to speak to me as much as he did to Strongbow. Back then I may have thought he was attempting to in some way explain his actions—his murderous cruelty, his fickle loyalties, his apparent lack of honour . . . his desertion of Eanna—an attempt to justify himself in my eyes. In time, as my life unfolded, I was to come to understand he was preparing me. The path he foresaw for our family, our clan, Leinster and ultimately Ireland would place me at its centre. With that faith would inevitably come unavoidable deeds, however unpalatable to those who wielded the knife.

'There's a mercurial nature to that island,' he had said, unconsciously leaning back and looking to the west, as if trying to grasp its essence from where he sat at Strongbow's table in Chepstow. 'It cannot be wholly grasped by man or God, as was also discovered by the Christian church.' He turned to the archdeacon, who had been invited to join us one evening.

He nodded his agreement to what my father had said and went on to express his exasperation at what he had learned of the Christian church in Ireland. 'It borders on heresy, m'lord,' he said to Strongbow, shaking his head. 'They recognise no central authority, barely acknowledging the existence of Rome. Their allegiance is local, to their local chieftains. There are multitudes of bishops, appointed at a whim. As they have no single king's authority by divine right, they have no accepted archbishop. It's ridiculous!' His frustration was obvious. 'I'd go so far as to say it's unchristian in its ways, almost pagan. They seem to have moulded more to these satanic practices than enlightened them with the grace of God. They have simply made their pagan feast days our saint's days, made their gods our saints. It's heretical!'

He explained how the Irish church had even gone as far as recognising that the dominant position of authority was with the abbess of Kildare. All other clergy, including the archbishop of Dublin, deferred to her—an abomination in the sight of the wider Christian church, which wisely confined female influence in the church to its rightful place. He looked to me as he said this. I remember thinking he would probably have phrased it differently had I not been present.

I knew his views on this matter, and he knew mine. He had been appalled at the authority of the abbess. Not long before, as we sat in the courtyard one evening with Myler, he became quite animated about it. Trying to justify his position, he had quoted some of the saints regarding the harsh attitude of his religion to women. Myler and I found it highly amusing as he shuffled through his manuscripts, eventually finding the authoritative scripts.

'Yes, here it is . . . "Woman is a misbegotten man and has a faulty and defective nature in comparison to his. What she cannot get, she seeks to obtain through lying and diabolical deceptions. And so, to put it kindly, one must be on one's guard with every woman, as if she were a poisonous snake and horned devil,"' he intoned loftily, although he did raise an eyebrow and seemed to lose a certain momentum as he finished. 'That was written by Saint Albertus Magnus, no less,' he said.

'Well, he must have met Agnes, the shepherd's daughter,' Rob chuckled as he joined us. Myler and I couldn't contain ourselves, and I felt for his uncle who, while earnest, didn't seem entirely convinced himself. But he persisted nonetheless.

'There's more . . . and we must respect the word of the saints.' He continued searching through his papers, finally producing a parchment with a flurry.

'These are from the writings of that great Christian scholar Origen of Alexandria, the third century I believe. What greater authority could we have: "'For it is improper for a woman to speak in an assembly, no matter what she says. Even if she says admirable things, or even saintly things, that is of little consequence, since that comes from the mouth of a woman.'"

He sat back, as if resting his case.

'I think it is indisputable that almost all of the most notable catastrophes in the world have been caused by women,' he insisted. 'It is the teaching of the church. Witness Mark Antony and Troy.' I had heard of this tragedy from my tutors in Ferns, where the great Roman general committed suicide on hearing of Cleopatra's own faked suicide.

'M'lady, are your own father's troubles not routed in the folly of his carnal desire for O'Rourke's wife, Dearbhail?' he said, almost pleading now, grasping that he was not winning his audience.

'I think you need another mug of ale, Archdeacon,' Rob said. 'And start using that head of yours, which Aoife's father certainly was not when he chased that man's wife, all his thinking that day done from below his belt.' He smiled.

In fairness and for all his seriousness, the archdeacon himself didn't sound convinced by his readings, but he had his duty.

'And could I suggest you be cautious about sharing those views with your mother . . . she may not entirely agree with you,' Myler said. The archdeacon's mother, Angharad, was Myler's aunt. Daughter of Nesta, the formidable Princess of Wales who spawned the Geraldine dynasty. Angharad had, by all accounts, inherited her mother's backbone. Myler's cousin avoided his eyes, giving the impression that the opportunity to raise the matter with his mother had not yet arisen and was unlikely to present itself anytime soon—on this side of the grave, to be more precise. We let the matter rest and enjoyed what was left of the evening's warmth in one another's company.

Having established ourselves without opposition in Ferns, my father instructed his kinsmen to be summoned to assemble there in three days. Murchad dispatched riders to the reaches of the province and openly acknowledged my father as king. As the clansmen began arriving on the appointed day, few would give any commitment and stayed aloof of my father, avoiding him. They would gauge the quality of the men who came and assess the likely strength of their numbers before they gave their oath to my father. The forces arrayed against them would be formidable, and unless they had a clear certainty in the success of my father's cause, they would quietly, but quickly, disappear back into the forests and, at the very least, stand aloof from the coming conflict. Some would certainly join O'Connor, hoping to profit from our destruction.

There was a tension in the hall on the third day when they finally gathered. Greetings were exchanged between allies, and sour words with rivals were avoided, with such family groups standing noticeably apart in the hall.

The murmured conversations stopped as my father entered and mounted the dais. With barely a passing observance to pleasantries, he turned quickly to his grievances. He complained bitterly of the treachery and injustice of the actions of Rory O'Connor, the high king, and his allies. An illegitimate curse on the land of Leinster he was, claiming any kingship here; his claim was a stain on the name Uí Chennselaig. He, Diarmuit MacMurrough, would stop at nothing to wash that shame from their land and clan. He went on to tell them how his just cause had the support of the king of England, Henry II, who had sent these fine Norman warriors as a taste of what was to come in the spring, when Norman armies would arrive to drive the usurpers from Leinster and restore him to his rightful place as king.

FitzGodebert, magnificent in full battle dress with his companions at his side, spoke of the truth in my father's words. He told of his king's revulsion at the treatment of the lawful king of Leinster and his fervent intention to ensure that right was restored to a fellow legitimate king. He paraded amongst the kinsmen arranged in family groupings around the hall, allowing them to examine his armour as Donal had suggested. The intricate work of the intertwining minute metal rings of his hauberk would not have been seen by most before. He explained how these chainmail shirts could withstand all but the most persistent thrust of a pointed blade. Worn over a padded overcoat, it could withstand heavy blows to the body. Over these, a coat of plate—a series of overlapping iron plates riveted to a fabric cover—allowed him unrestricted movement while providing the strongest protection to his upper body. FitzGodebert demonstrated to the captivated men how the coat was put on over the head and buckled securely at the back. Unlacing his cheek plates and taking off his helmet, they saw his coif of mail and the aventail chainmail scarf that protected his neck. A padded arming cap added some comfort for his head, but it was clear, these artefacts of war were primarily for the purpose of protecting the knight in battle. Designed from experience in combat over many centuries and built by skilled craftsmen, the kinsmen had not seen the likes in Ireland before.

FitzGodebert explained that the chainmail leggings—the chausses—were normally covered by leg armour, the parts of which one of his attendants showed to the ever-attentive kinsmen. They handled the well-worked shaped metal pieces with a quiet awe.

Donal waited until, having satisfied their curiosity, they

turned their attention to him. He could see that the display had had the desired effect. He began to speak.

The clansmen had heard of the prowess of the Normans in battle and listened intently as Donal spoke of what he had seen in Wales. He described their formidable weapons, horses and tactics. They heard the story of how a band of this warlike race had embarked from Norway under the leadership of Rollo in the year 911. These Vikings arrived in northern France and, within a hundred years, had secured the land as their own and named it Normandy in honour of their homeland. From there they had spread their dominion south through Italy, stretching to the Middle East and west to our neighbours, the land of the Britons. Now they were coming to Ireland. It was time for all men to choose sides wisely.

Donal was widely respected in the clan, more so than my father, who ruled more from fear than friendship. In many ways, Donal was his opposite: handsome, honourable, wise and trustworthy. He led our troops and cavalry, and men willingly followed him into battle. His words carried great weight with the clansmen, who nodded a murmured acceptance of the irresistible changes which would sweep through these lands. Whether it happened slowly or quickly, in time, fate would make itself known. Yet fate it was; it would happen.

For the clansmen, it made little difference who sat on the throne. Kings of other, faraway lands—Ulster, Connaught and Munster—had heretofore laid claim to and ruled these lands. Most of the clansmen were old enough to have lived under several such kings in their lives. They held their land at the pleasure of these kings, who could strip it from them at will. But these kings also needed their rents and support in times of conflict. If they abused these tightly interwoven family groups, they could quickly lose friends and make enemies in the process. Thus, if the clansmen paid their tributes and gave their support when required, they were left in relative peace.

So another king would not make much difference. In addition, if these Norman lords were as strong as Donal said, they could bring a peace that would allow them to tend to their lands and families without the incessant rivalries and war making which yearly laid waste to the land and cost dearly in the blood and freedom of their kin.

The Normans were also familiar to many who had known and traded with them. They came from the neighbouring Welsh land, as close as a short day's sail. Closer than the northern lands of Ulster or the western lands of Connaught, which would take many days to reach through the thick, dense forests and lawless broken roads of Ireland. And while the Normans were undoubtedly a formidable fighting force, they were great traders and builders. They never wrought destruction for its own sake, as they sought order and peace to create the foundation for prosperity and wealth in the lands they governed. Their written laws and courts gave men rights and some certainty in the vagaries of life. Donal told them how, many years previously, they had even outlawed slavery in their lands. This fate was a constant threat to the clansmen, who feared for their families.

In Ireland, it was routine for the defeated to be taken into a squalid slavery by their enemies or sold in the thriving slave markets of Dublin. The main source of food and wealth in Ireland derived from cattle. The vast herds required tending, and milking, churning, and cheesemaking was arduous, backbreaking work, carried out by an army of female slaves. Known as *cumals*, they were in constant demand; their importance was such that the term *cumal* was widely used as a unit of value for land or high-value goods.

The clansmen knew that the slave markets in Dublin, the

largest such markets in Europe, were an important source of slaves for the cold, ice-encrusted lands of the north and the sun-scorched shores of Africa. Slave traders came from far and wide to ply their trade there. Every man in my father's hall that day knew of people who had suffered that fate; they would never return. The people of Leinster would welcome being free of that fear.

I knew these men of our lands, and they knew me. They looked to me to speak when Donal stepped back. They listened as I spoke of the Norman practice of adopting the customs and traditions of the people they shared the land with. Even the local languages became their own in time, as it had in France and Britain. The clansmen would act as a body, seeking the strength of numbers. I could hear their muttering as they shuffled across the reed-lined floor of our gloomy hall seeking the views of their peers. Without the support of our own kinsmen upon which to build our army, we had no hope. Word of our return would quickly reach our enemies, if it hadn't already done so. How they reacted would depend on how they gauged our strength. If we could not rise our own kin now, we would be chased mercilessly from Ireland or to our deaths. I had little doubt that Eanna would not then survive the week.

Alternatively, if we were strong and threatened them, they would seek to negotiate. O'Connor and O'Rourke had created many enemies as they sought to subjugate the provinces. They would not seek to break or weaken their armies on a strong foe just now. However, if they sensed weakness, they would be swift and ruthless. This was why I had wanted to wait until the spring, when the large Norman force would be ready to accompany us. But for now, I desperately needed these men to come to my father's side today.

I could see that the clansmen knew the truth of what Donal and I had said. While suspicious of my father, they had some trust in us. They also knew it was vital to pick the winning side when these shifting tides of change swept across a land. That change would be driven by the force of the Normans, and it was my father who had them in his camp.

My father's hard and cruel face had watched each man sullenly as we spoke. They could feel the lust for revenge burning in his gaze and knew his axe would sweep widely and many would be caught in the arc his retribution would mark on this land.

'So, kinsmen, my victory is inevitable. I will regain all my lands,' he said through his thick dark beard. Then, pausing and coldly surveying the hall as if to speak directly to each man present, he continued, 'And with that will come a sharp vengeance . . . for all who have opposed me.' A longer pause now as he ran his hand down his long beard. 'Pay close heed to what I say now,' he said, and each man could see his doom in my father's face. 'I will spare no pain from those who fail in their duty to support me.' His menacing look and silence made his meaning clear: there would be no neutrals in this.

And so the clansmen, more from fear than out of commitment to my father, gave their support to our cause. After renewing their oaths, they set urgently to the task of preparing their followers for the campaign. My father hoped that the coming winter would deter O'Connor and O'Rourke from marching south against us until the spring. Donal doubted this would be the case and set about readying our force for the late autumn, when he thought they would come.

Chapter Eight
CILL OSNADH

Kellistown, Co. Carlow
August 1167

They were both wrong. A week after we arrived in Ferns, the scouts Donal had sent north brought word that the old alliance that had driven us from Ireland had re-formed. Rory O'Connor had joined forces with Tiarnan O'Rourke in North Leinster, and they were marching south from Wicklow. Mac Giolla Patrick, who had acquired half of my father's kingdom to the west, had marched to join them.

Hearing of the hurried arrival of the scouts, I rushed from the bright late-summer light into the dusky hall. As my eyes adjusted, I could see the war council gathered, with my father sitting on the dais, glaring at the exhausted young scout, who had ridden hard south to Ferns through Fid Dorcha (the Dark Wood). This forest spread across the land, from the high reaches of the mountains of South Wicklow to the rich fertile pastures surrounding Ferns. O'Connor had had his army cut a pass through this forest when he last drove us away. Its purpose was to give him quick access to our land should it prove troublesome again; he was making good use of it now. In Ireland, roads were narrow, pitiful tracks which did not allow armies to move quickly. It wasn't the mountains which hindered movement in Ireland but more the thick, impenetrable ancient forests of dark oak and towering yew trees which blanketed the lands. Closer to the settlements and towns, the people cleared land for grazing pastures. There were some areas around the larger towns where fields were made for the sowing of crops, but for the most part, the cleared land was used for grazing cattle and growing their winter fodder. Our lands hadn't been stripped bare of the forests for shipbuilding or crop fields, as I had seen in Britain.

'Mac Giolla Patrick will be with the high king by now,' the scout gasped as he gulped water from the cup he grasped.

'He's not the damn high king—he's the king of nothing here!' my father snarled, rising from his chair and moving towards the frightened lad.

'He meant nothing of it, father,' Donal intervened. 'Leave him be.' Replenishing the young scout's water from a jug, Donal said, 'You've done a great service to us, lad. Well done.' He smiled. 'Now tell me what you saw. How many are they, and how long before they march and reach Ferns?'

'Thank you, Donal.' He drank deeply and, recovering himself, looked up and continued. 'They are already moving. There must be at least two thousand. And that's before Mac Giolla Patrick joins them.' He gulped greedily from the cup again.

'Two thousand!' my father yelled, hurling his tankard at the scout. 'Why was I not told sooner?' he demanded. 'We can't fight them again. Get the men ready and bring all the livestock and food stocks into the town. We can hold out here until Strongbow arrives.'

Donal, stunned by the size of the approaching force, stated that he believed he could gather at most four hundred men to oppose them. 'But that's less than we had the last time they drove us from Ferns, is it not?' I asked.

There was a heavy silence before Donal eventually sighed, 'It is, Aoife. It is.' His despair weighed heavily on everyone. No one spoke. The state of disrepair of the walls from the damage of the fire ruled out any chance of holding the town against an army of that size. Given the winter, we could have strengthened the walls and dug the ditches; there was no time for that now.

'Well then, we must meet them in the Dark Wood again,' I said, breaking the silence. There was little enthusiasm for this either amongst the kinsmen. They were the lucky ones who had escaped the slaughter just twelve months ago in this very spot, facing the same enemies.

I didn't see that we had a choice. 'We can conceal our numbers from them there. Show them the Norman knights and make them believe we are many,' I insisted.

'But we can never win against a force this size,' Donal said, shaking his head.

'No, but we can sow enough doubt to bring them to negotiations. O'Connor doesn't want to weaken his army if he can avoid it.'

There was sense in what I said but even more in how I continued: 'There isn't any other choice. We can't meet them in the open field, and we can't defend Ferns against an army this size. The Dark Wood is our only choice.'

There was one last option, and I knew nearly every man in the room would be thinking it. We could abandon our cause and run for the coast and take a boat to Wales. How I wished that was possible. In doing so, we would be abandoning these kinsmen to their fate with our enemies. O'Connor would not look kindly on those who had declared for the MacMurroughs. An example would be made of some as a lesson to others who might oppose him here and in the other provinces of Ireland.

But our kinsmen would know they could gain O'Connor's favour if they were to seize and surrender us to him. Why wouldn't they, having come to my father's side and he then abandoning them? They would be rightly justified in doing so. They would have nothing to lose and everything to gain. Running to the coast was not an option.

Turning to the shaken young scout, I asked gently, 'How long do we have? When will they get here?'

'They're already on the move, so I'd say four days for the army. The scouts will be quicker; I'd reckon they'll be here in three.'

'OK, then. If this is to work, we have to be there, ready for them in two days.' I looked to Donal. 'Can you do that?'

Nodding, he straightened himself and replied, 'I don't see that we have a choice, sister.'

And so it was agreed, my father grunting his approval and shouting for the preparations to begin immediately.

※

THE SUMMER SHOWERS had been swept east by the light wind as our small army left in the cover of night. The stars shone weakly behind the bright moonlit sky. It would be a warm day, rising a ghostly haze to blanket the meadows and pastures which surrounded the long stretch of road to be crossed before the safe cover of the forest. We were wary of enemy scouts and spies.

I loved these mornings, but today a deep bleakness hung on me. I suspected Mac Giolla Patrick would bring Eanna, as he could prove useful to them in any bargaining that was to be done. Whatever purpose that served would probably not be good for Eanna. I longed to see him, but a chilling dread gripped me as to what I might find. Mac Giolla Patrick was known to parade his maimed hostages in front of his enemies to goad them.

I had been forbidden by my father from accompanying them as they set off to the northwest, with Donal in the vanguard with his mounted troop of cavalry. The only sound was the plodding of the horses' hooves and the muffled footfalls of Rob Smith's archers and the foot soldiers.

I remembered Chepstow, where the mounted Normans moved in a loud cacophony of clinking bridles and body armour jostling against an array of metal weaponry. Their heavy stallions, bred for their weight-bearing strength, stamped impatiently and snorted noisily. Their cavalry was not a stealth force used to surprise an enemy in silence. Fitz-Godebert and his companions had not brought their mounts to Ireland and walked alongside their men-at-arms.

In contrast, Donal's men rode quietly in the Irish fashion. Here we mostly used no saddles or spurs, using a short cropped stick to drive and guide the horse. The reins were formed from tightly wound rope to shape the headpiece—no bridle or bit. Our horses were trained to respond to the pressure from the rider's leg and thighs. The silence of the horses cloaked them in a ghostly gloom as they stretched away across the pastures towards the depths of the forest.

Later, having crossed the plains when the army was well enveloped by the stillness of the tress, I gently squeezed my legs around the horse's belly to ride abreast of Donal. Deep in thought, he was startled as I drew back the hood of my dark, heavy cloak.

'What!? What the hell are you doing here?' he said, but quietly, checking his horse. There was a low grumbling from the men following as they pulled up.

'I told you,' I whispered, 'I want to see Eanna. I wasn't going to stay behind.'

'Does father know you're here?' he said, looking over his shoulder. 'He will not be happy.'

'What does he care? And anyway it's done now. I'm here.'

'Christ, Aoife, you're a stubborn, wilful . . .' he searched for the words.

'Go on, what? What am I?'

'You're stupid, that's what you are,' he said, just as he noticed the handle of the battleaxe under my cloak. 'And what the hell is that? What are you going to do with that? You'll get yourself killed.'

I wheeled my horse away as he made a lunge for the axe. 'No, it's a spare one, just in case you drop yours.'

'Christ! Here, Rob, take that off her before she hurts herself,' he said to Rob Smith, who had appeared at my side. He seemed to shadow my every move these days.

I looked down at Rob, who looked hesitant. 'You can try, Rob, but I wouldn't recommend it.' He didn't seem at all keen to take me up on my offer.

'If you don't mind, I'll leave that in your capable hands, Donal.' He grinned and dropped back as Donal, exasperated, urged his horse forward and we crept silently, ever northward, through the forest.

THE BLUISH GREY of sparrow hawks flashed through the trees that skirted our path, pursuing the smaller birds we disturbed from their nests. The midday sun clung to the wind-sheltered forest trail, allowing no merciful cooling gusts to relieve the heat or clouds of flies which tormented the horses. By mid-afternoon we'd crested a low hill where the trail opened into a broad pasture surrounding a scattering of homesteads known as Cill Osnadh, Kellistown. A broad-winged eagle drifted patiently on the rising heat from the meadow but, disturbed by our appearance, turned east and, with a single, languid sweep of its white-tipped wings, headed for other hunting grounds. At least the hares would not die here today.

'Not here. We must find somewhere else to meet them. It can't be here,' my father said as we emerged into the sharp sunlight from the gloom of the forest.

'It was the best place then, and it remains so now,' Donal insisted and turned to Sir Richard FitzGodebert and Rob, who had joined us.

'You know this place?' Sir Richard asked. 'It's the best I've seen today for what we plan.'

'And it is the best we'll find,' Donal said and went on sombrely, 'and we have paid a heavy blood price in battle in this place not twelve months past.' He gazed across the meadow to the long mound of disturbed earth that betrayed the presence of the many graves of the kinsmen they had left here. He went on to describe how they had faced the same enemy at this very place in a decisive battle where betrayal by our own kinsmen of North Leinster resulted in the destruction of the power of the MacMurroughs. The bracken had run red with the blood of the elite veterans of my father's force, and the tattered remnants of our army had fled and limped back through the forests to Ferns.

'I would have won that battle but for their scheming treachery. The Uí Brian cowards deserted me here, and those dog shits, the Uí Failge, joined O'Connor and O'Rourke. The bastards led their vanguard against us here,' my father said.

'There isn't much loyalty amongst these lords,' Rob said, surprised by the squalid nature of how men readily broke loyalties and oaths here.

'And so has it ever been, Rob.' Donal nodded. 'A man's

loyalty is determined by his fear of retribution should he break his oath. And that's why today we must make them believe we are stronger than we are.'

The ground sloped gently from where we stood, down past the farmhouses, then onwards towards the opening in the forest in the middle distance. There the night-dark trees closed around the barely visible gap where the trail resumed its path north. Our chosen place was narrow enough to defend, with the trees closing on either side and the path at our back should we need it. The forest would protect our flanks and offer us some concealment. O'Connor would fear a trap and suspect the greater part of our forces lay hidden behind and around us. At least that's what we hoped. As we didn't have the forces to mount an ambush, we had to rely on deceit to force the negotiation. The armour of the Normans was to be spread amongst as many men as possible to give the impression of numbers.

'And no matter what happens, we don't want to get into a fight on the open ground. Stay up here, close to the trees,' Donal repeated. He sent two riders to the farmhouses to reassure them we meant no harm and to look for word of enemy scouts.

No sooner had the men begun arranging themselves when Rob shouted and pointed to two riders watching from the far opening of the forest trail, making no effort to conceal themselves. The sharp flicker of the afternoon sun on the metal of their battleaxes told us their purpose.

'So they're here,' I said.

'Yes, and they want us to know it. Their army won't be far behind now,' Donal replied, 'but we are as ready as we can be.'

'Good, Donal,' I said. 'We need to deal with this now, today. The more time they have, the more chance they'll discover how weak we are.'

He nodded, saying there was enough left of the day if they arrived soon.

They did. As we spoke, they began to trickle in, in twos and threes, and then poured from the pit of the forest. It must have taken two hours for the hoard to finally exhaust its flow and arrange itself in three massed bodies across the broad pasture. They flew no banners as the Normans did, so I couldn't tell the formations. However, Donal recognised O'Connor with the larger force on the higher ground to the right. O'Rourke was on the left flank, with Mac Giolla Patrick's forces occupying the centre.

'How many?' I asked.

'Doesn't matter. Too many . . . but I'd say two and a half thousand.' He turned to Rob. 'Can you hit them from here?'

'Not likely. That's seven hundred paces; we could do three and a half hundred at a stretch. They're on foot, so if they charge, we'll take down a good few, but no more than sixty, I'd say.'

'Not enough. We stick with the plan. They'll want to talk before the fight, but we have to meet them as far away from here as possible, down there,' he said, pointing towards their lines. 'I don't want them to see what we have here.'

※

Before long, a party rode slowly from the centre of their lines, which were by then arranged for battle. There were three of them, each carrying a branch of the willow, signifying a truce, as was customary.

'Three of them, so three of us. Donal and Sir Richard, come with me,' my father said. He still hadn't spoken to me since our vicious row when I refused to let him bring Conor on this errand. And he hadn't seemed surprised when he saw me on the trail in the forest today and simply ignored me. *Suits me*, I thought, as he passed.

'If they bring any more men, send an equal number of your men,' Donal shouted back to Rob Smith as they rode down. 'But hold back unless I call otherwise.' As he finished, I saw a fourth rider, nearly hidden behind the other three—a smaller figure on a pony whose lead rope was held by one of the men approaching us.

Unsure at first, but then the sun caught his flaming-red hair. I gasped. 'It's Eanna. I'm going,' I said, swinging myself onto my horse by grabbing a fistful of his mane in my left hand and urging him forward before anyone could stop me.

Drawing beside Donal, I could see the dread in his face that I felt in my heart. As we neared, I recognised Mac Giolla Patrick holding the rope, and I could see the pleasure he took in this cruel game on his hard, furrowed face. O'Connor, the high king, was mounted on a high black stallion which pawed the ground angrily. He wore an elaborate armour breast plate and a thick gold circlet around his neck. His greying hair matched his long-plated beard and reached down his back to his horse. He was at ease on the agitated animal, and he reassured it with his free hand after he had discarded the large willow branch. His deep-set eyes closely scrutinised each of us as we drew close to where they now stood.

We arrayed ourselves in front of them. It was the time for each to assess the confidence of the other, their willingness to fight, their unity, their command and their strength.

The horses stood in silence until each man, having taken his measure, moved his thoughts to battle. Sensing the change in mood, the animals shuffled, pawed and snorted impatiently. It did not bode well for us.

'You should not have returned, Diarmuit MacMurrough. You have no place here now,' O'Connor said calmly, keeping his horse in hand. 'Look at how this land welcomes you.' And he gestured at the armies arranged behind him. 'You had your chance to go; you should have taken it.'

Before my father could respond, O'Rourke urged his horse forward and pointed his finger in my father's face. 'We fertilised this soil with the slaughtered guts and blood of your kinsmen. I watched their heads spit and sizzle in my fire to keep their godforsaken spirits from poisoning the land,' he snarled.

Spitting fury through his teeth, my father pulled the head of his horse around to drive O'Rourke back, and both men made to arm themselves before Donal lunged forward, grabbing my father's reins. O'Connor also moved quickly, forcing his horse between them, telling O'Rourke to calm himself and observe the honour of the truce.

'I'll have my revenge on that bastard,' O'Rourke yelled.

'You were never man enough for her,' my father laughed, wheeling his horse around to stand beside us.

'Father! Stop it. Control yourself,' I shouted at him.

'You'll taste your own balls before I'm finished with you,' O'Rourke said, smiling grimly through thin lips, showing his broken teeth.

O'Rourke had just cause for his venomous hatred of my father, a hatred which was far greater than the normal enmity between rival kings. Not fifteen years previously, my father had been allied with the high king, the same who faced us today, against O'Rourke. Defeated, O'Rourke had been forced to part with a substantial part of his kingdom of Bréifne, which lay north of our lands in Leinster. However, my father had gone further: he had sought to humiliate O'Rourke by abducting his wife, Derbhail. To be defeated in battle was not necessarily shameful, as many a brave warrior could testify, but to have your wife taken to satisfy the carnal desires of your enemy was utter humiliation for O'Rourke.

Even in the dizzying, shifting sands of fickle alliances and treachery of the Irish nobility, Diarmuit's actions were unprecedented and had sent shock waves of revulsion throughout the land. Soon after, Derbhail had fled to the safety of her own father, who was the powerful king of Meath, which lay further to the north.

'You broke the agreement. I had withdrawn to Ferns as agreed,' my father addressed O'Connor, calmer now. 'After you returned to Connaught,' he continued, 'he came back with that bastard and attacked us.' He gestured angrily at Mac Giolla Patrick, who was grinning broadly, enjoying the vicious spat between my father and O'Rourke.

'Well, you haven't exactly made a lot of friends around here, have you.' Mac Giolla Patrick sneered. 'I won half your lands'—he reached and pulled the pony around—'and this.' And there was Eanna. His beautiful pale blue eyes, quietly pleading through his tears.

I went to move my horse forward to go to him, but Mac Giolla Patrick wrenched the rope, jolting Eanna unsteadily. 'Careful now, Lady Aoife. Or he might get hurt.'

I remained still and silent, but my relief and joy at seeing him well pushed my tears to flow into my smile. I strained to pour my love through my locked gaze with his innocent eyes.

'So let's make sure everyone behaves themselves, shall we?' O'Rourke laughed now.

All the while this played out, O'Connor had shifted his attention to FitzGodebert, who stood beside Donal. He was resplendent in the full battle dress of a Norman knight, not previously seen on the battlefields of Ireland. With the visor of his helmet raised, his full coat of polished plate reflected the afternoon sun and extended down to cover the chausses, the thick chainmail leggings protecting his legs. His surcoat was emblazoned with a bright red heraldic coat of arms, gripped by a thick decorated leather belt buckled over it. His long sword hung heavily in a gold-laced, fleece-lined scabbard.

Seeing his gaze, Donal gestured towards FitzGodebert. 'Please let me introduce Sir Richard FitzGodebert.' He paused to let them dwell on Sir Richard, knowing each of them would be assessing the effectiveness of his battledress.

'Sir Richard is a Flemish knight in the service of the Earl of Pembroke, Sir Richard de Clare, also known as Strongbow. The earl has been charged by Henry, King of England, Duke of Normandy and Aquitaine, and Count of Angevin, to offer every assistance in righting the grievous wrong done to my father, Diarmuit MacMurrough, the rightful king of Leinster. As an acknowledged ally and fellow legitimate king, Henry sees it as his sacred duty, supported by a papal bull, to do all in his power to restore my father to his throne in Ireland.' He paused now.

I had prepared this for Donal, drawing on my conversations with Myler. We had rehearsed it repeatedly, and I was impressed by his delivery. It had the desired impact, judging by the long silence as they scrutinised Sir Richard, who bowed his head slightly.

However, it was not entirely true. The English king remained wary of Strongbow, and while he had granted permission for his subjects to assist Diarmuit, he continued to refuse to grant Strongbow leave to muster his forces and depart for Ireland. He remained bitter over Strongbow's support for the rival camp before he came to the throne. Strongbow and his followers, wealthy Marcher lords such as the Geraldines, were a formidable force, and he could not risk them establishing a kingdom in Ireland beyond his writ, which could, in due course, become a powerful threat to his crown. He had enough trouble with threats to his lands in the east in France without a troublesome lord establishing himself to his west.

'Sir Richard has joined us to lead the first army which has accompanied us to Ireland,' Donal finished, as a stirring in the ranks of O'Connor's Connaughtmen caught their attention.

'That may well be the case,' O'Connor said, sounding unconvinced as he turned his shrewd eyes to take in the meagre ranks of our men arrayed on the slope behind us, 'but it would be far better for you if that great army you speak of was behind you today.' He turned to watch the growing clamour from the ranks of his men. A body of horsemen had come through the front rank, pacing their excited animals alongside the jeering foot soldiers who began to raise a slow rhythmic pulse of spear on shield. They could see that the small army of Leinster would be easily overrun, and just as fear dissipates from men facing death, bloodlust quickly deafens all else. More riders poured forward as the dull thump of weapons on willow shields steadily rose to fill the valley.

O'Connor struggled to keep his prancing stallion in hand as he shouted above the rising din, 'As you can see, my men see no reason to talk. They are eager for a fight.' Wheeling his horse around, he shouted with an added urgency now, for once started, battles had a life of their own. The one thing you can't do with spears is sit on them, and he knew things would get out of hand here quickly. 'You must submit now, and I will treat you fairly. You had no cause to bring the foreigners to our land, Diarmuit MacMurrough.'

But my father could scarcely hear and was watching the clustered horsemen who had started moving slowly forward towards our battle line over to our right. I squeezed my horse forward to get closer to O'Connor, being careful not to get too close to his sweating stallion, which could lash out at either me or my horse.

'There are indeed many foreigners here today,' I shouted

as he looked down at me. My mare shied away from his stallion, but I wheeled her back. 'But the only uninvited foreigners in our land, Leinster, are you and your army!'

Surprised, he gazed fixedly at me, keeping a firm grip on his reins. Then he laughed loudly before his horse reared, spooked by the deafening roar sounded by his army as the horsemen rushed forwards.

'Hold those fools,' he roared, and gestured for O'Rourke to stay the main army from moving forward. But it was too late for the troop of horses, which gathered pace and rushed up the slight rise towards our right flank. There were easily enough to break our thin line, and the jeering army clearly expected the line to flee in the face of the coming onslaught. We watched, helpless, as the Connaught cavalry bore down, expecting the worst. But nothing seemed to move. I could see Rob, standing with his archers behind the Norman knights, mouthing orders. In unison, like dancers, they seemed to move. Placing an arrow on the bowstave, nocking it, hauling the cord and holding impassively for the order from Rob to release.

At what seemed an impossible distance, we saw the bowstaves snap forward and the volley of arrows shoot skywards, soaring through the air before gracefully curving, dipping and smashing into the leading horsemen. Without armour, the broadhead arrows sliced easily through the flesh of man and beast. The struck horses that did not fall thrashed about in a frenzied agony, driving the broadheads deeper into muscles and arteries. As the main body of horsemen continued surging up the hill, the archers maintained a rain of arrows with astonishing speed. Each man seemed to move with a rhythmic fluidity: release, place, nock, haul, release, place, nock, haul . . . As fast as you could say it, it was done.

The jeering from the army began to fade as the devastation on their cavalry became clear. The gentle hill was littered with fallen horses and men. A few crazed horses crashed back through their lines. The jeering was gradually replaced by the spine-crushing cries of wounded men and the screeching of horses. In silence the army watched the remainder of the cavalry reach the thin line of our flank. As they approached at speed, the Norman knights stepped forward and arrayed themselves. Heavily armoured and carrying no shield, they each seemed to crouch side-on towards the approaching horsemen. Holding their longswords two handed over their left shoulder, they waited. I had seen them practice these techniques over and over at Chepstow. Their armour could withstand the first blows of a rider's weapon; their aim was to unseat the man.

Deftly sidestepping at the last moment, they slashed their swords across the horse's front legs or swivelled and cut the back legs from under it. Either way, each knight felled a man in the first assault. Even at this distance it was shocking to see the efficiency with which each stepped forward and casually dispatched the fallen rider.

The remaining horsemen, having witnessed the fate of their companions and still suffering the rain of arrows from the archers, turned and fled. A heavy silence engulfed their army now. I could see that O'Connor was taken aback, but he also knew that if he unleashed his army, he would certainly win the day. The sheer weight of numbers would eventually prevail, but at what cost to his army. And he had other more pressing needs for his army, what with the trouble brewing in Munster.

'That was none of our doing, Ard Rí,' Donal said, purposefully addressing him as high king. 'We can discuss terms and avoid further unnecessary killing.' Donal knew O'Connor would be reluctant to fight if it could be avoided. Unnecessary slaughter was not the Irish way, and we had to do anything to survive this day. We would not win this battle. But now O'Connor knew he would pay a heavy price in men and horses.

He nodded. I looked to my father to agree, but he was no longer with us. As we had turned our attention to the unfolding drama not three hundred paces to our right, my father, unnoticed in the confusion, had spurred his horse back up the hill to rejoin our men who stood on the far flank.

'Donal! Look! Father!' I said, pointing to the hilltop where we could see him ordering the men to mount up. A few dozen gathered in a body around him. We could see him mouthing orders, gesticulating towards the surviving Connaught horsemen retreating down the slope. I could not believe what he was doing.

'The fool!' Donal shouted. 'What's he doing? He has no chance. We have to stop him!' He turned to O'Connor, who by now realised my father was gone and was mustering our cavalry for a charge down the slope in pursuit of the retreating Connaughtmen.

'We have no part in this, Ard Rí,' he said, raising his voice over the rising snorting and stamping of the excited horses. 'I will stop this madness!' he shouted over his shoulder as he wheeled his horse and made to speed up the slope to intercept my father.

I struggled to hold my mare in hand and she reared, screaming her objection to being held as Donal passed. I only managed to put a hand to his reins and stop him by good fortune as I turned and landed in his path. I barely remained on her back by grabbing her mane, my hand slipping on the rising froth on her neck as her excitement grew. It was too late to stop my father now. I knew the fate of those horsemen was decided before they suddenly broke down the slope with my father at their head. If Donal tried to intervene now, I doubted he would see the sunset.

Initially they caught the remnants of the retreating Connaught cavalry and cut them down, driving their spears into their exposed backs.

But as sure as the swallow returns in the spring, what then happened was unavoidable. That certainty made it harrowing to watch.

O'Rourke, seeing my father coming down the slope with the pursuing horsemen, hefted his battleaxe and, circling his horse in front of his men, who had remained in battle order, screamed his war cry and charged. His army surged forward, gathering pace as they rode hard up the slope. They parted to let their own men pass, and I could see the hesitation in my father and the Uí Chennselaig horsemen when they realised O'Rourke's calvary was upon them. It was too late. They were quickly engulfed. Surrounded on all sides, they disappeared into the mass of enemy riders. The Norman archers stood there, watching helplessly, unwilling to shoot their arrows into a fight where the arrows would not tell friend from foe.

I could see my friends and kinsmen being surrounded, hopelessly wheeling their horses, trying to fend off the spear thrusts. They were easily picked off, dragged from their horses; I could hear the battleaxes shattering skulls and ribcages. And just as quickly there was a quietness, only the sound of horses snorting and prancing excitedly. I saw O'Rourke take the head of a young lad I knew with a savage blow, almost casually. I knew he was an only son, and his death would shatter his mother. O'Rourke made sure there were no wounded to fill the valley with their pain. Only one man was left alive, and he was now kneeling at his feet. My father.

We had stood with O'Connor, watching helplessly. He glanced up the hill to where the Norman knights stood impassively with the remains of our men. Following his gaze, I knew he was thinking he could beat us a little easier now.

'It's not worth it,' I said pushing through his guard. 'You saw what they can do. They have not lost more than a man or two.' His eyes showed a calmness as he considered his options. This man could be reasoned with, I thought. 'You have beaten us now. Give us reasonable terms, and my father will submit to you as ard rí. There is no need for more killing.'

He seemed to nod and, looking at me, said, 'Let's see what he has to say, shall we?' His bodyguard had arrived, and turning to the man, he told him to tell O'Rourke to keep my father alive. 'You'd better be quick. The only reason he's still alive is O'Rourke wants to kill him slowly.'

The vicious grin on O'Rourke's bloodied face as he stood over my father was telling. Here was his most bitter enemy, on his knees before him. The pox-ridden dog that had humiliated him by stealing and abusing his wife, Dearbhail, almost fifteen years ago was at his mercy. He had waited a long time to exact his revenge for all the kingdoms to see and have his honour restored.

'You're going to taste your balls first,' he spat into my father's face as we approached. 'Get me a sharp knife,' he yelled to his men and levelled a forceful kick into my father's stomach, forcing him to the ground. 'Tie his hands.'

'Tiarnan,' O'Connor called to him as we pulled up. 'Tiarnan. He's less trouble to us alive now than he is dead,' he said. But O'Rourke looked beyond reason, and with spittle running into his beard, he levelled a vicious kick into my father's face. O'Connor persisted, 'Tiarnan, listen to me now. Alive, he'll keep the other young bucks who are chasing his crown in control. Kill him and they'll squabble for it, and we'll get dragged into it. We have Munster to deal with, and there's richer spoils there.' I could see the raw anger in O'Rourke, but he hesitated now.

O'Connor went on to tell him how diminished a creature my father was compared to him. He, O'Rourke, was now a great king through his alliance with O'Connor, the high king. He had gone from strength to strength with ever increasing wealth and fame throughout the land, far beyond his own kingdom of Bréifne. And look at my father, vomiting in the mud before him. He was nothing now.

O'Rourke knew he was right. He would not get his blood revenge, but MacMurrough would pay a heavy price. He growled his frustration and slammed his boot into my father's face again.

'Leave him now,' O'Connor said with an authority that let O'Rourke know the discussion was over. 'Pick him up and bring him here.' He had my father unbound and ordered a man to clean the mud and blood from the beating he had received.

I know I should have felt for him now, but my bitter anger at him left me torn between wanting him dead and knowing that keeping him alive was our best chance of surviving until Strongbow could come to out aid.

Leaning forward and resting his hands on his horse's neck, O'Connor spoke loudly for all to hear, 'MacMurrough, I'm giving you a chance to live. These are my terms. They are non-negotiable.' He went on to describe how Diarmuit would be stripped of the bulk of his lands apart from Ferns and a reasonable portion in the far southeast, around Wexford. The Normans would return to Wales, and my father would submit and recognise him as the ard rí.

Even then I wasn't sure what my father would do. The terms were more generous than I had expected, but O'Connor was a man with good judgement. He knew to strip a man completely of his dignity was folly, and in truth I was relieved that O'Connor hadn't demanded that one condition I feared most. But then it came.

'And you will deliver to me your young son, Conor, to be held as surety to make sure you observe the terms. Where is he?' he asked.

As my father was about to speak, I quickly interrupted, 'He's in Wales. He did not accompany us.' O'Connor looked unconvinced, so I continued. 'I will go in his place.' Now he appeared surprised, and placing a hand on his hip, he laughed.

'You, *mo chailín*, are best placed at your father's side with your older brother Donal. He grinned. 'He has a need of wise heads around him. Believe me.'

And so it was agreed that he would take seven other hostages instead, and my father accepted the terms and bent his knee, the customary act of submission to a higher king.

'It's still too good for him,' O'Rourke growled. 'His father's fate is what he deserves.' We all knew how my grandfather had been murdered by the Norse of Dublin over fifty years ago. He had suffered the ultimate humiliation of being buried with the corpse of a dog.

'No, Tiarnan,' O'Connor said firmly. 'That's settled. He will not die today. His crimes are a matter for the law now. We will summon the Brehon, Cormac, and he will decide.'

A commotion at the rear of the assembled crowd caught everyone's attention before O'Rourke could continue complaining. The assembled warriors turned and parted as a tall, clean-shaven man strode purposefully forward into the circle. Older than most, probably beyond sixty, he moved with surprising ease and quickly surveyed the group with his one good eye. His woven long cloak bore the braided green hem of a Brehon, while the large gold broach fastened at his right shoulder denoted his seniority in this cast of law keepers.

'Cormac, we were just going to call for your help,' O'Connor said, dismounting, as did everyone as a mark of respect for one of the most senior and respected Brehons in the land.

'Yes, I was aware,' he said, looking around. 'Isn't there somewhere to sit? It's been a long walk. I'll never get used to those dammed horses.' There was a flurry of activity as a small stool was brought up and arranged to his satisfaction, upon which he eventually placed himself heavily. 'There now, that's better,' he said, settling his cloak. 'Now, what seems to be the problem here?' He beamed, taking a draught from a water pouch he carried.

O'Rourke, unable to contain himself, poured forth his grievance. Barely stopping for breath, he paced, shouted and gesticulated angrily at my father, who I could see was surprisingly calm. 'I want justice. I want his head.'

This took quite some time, and all the while Cormac watched him carefully. I'd swear he could see more with that one eye than an army of men with two. When O'Rourke had finally exhausted himself, Cormac sat, silently observing him. Eventually he spoke.

'Justice. You want justice.' He paused nodding. 'And justice you will have, Tiarnan.' A longer pause now, and he rose easily from his stool, making me think his show of sitting earlier had been just that, a performance to get the full attention of everyone. 'But Tiarnan, justice is not a solitary creature. It must live amongst us, long after the punishment is felt.'

He paced slowly around the gathered circle who had come to witness his judgement. Brehon law was a code of conduct for everyday life that developed over the centuries in Ireland, even before the Celts arrived. First collected by a great Brehon, Ollamh Fódha, a thousand years before the birth of the Christian God, it dealt with every aspect of our lives from land disputes, to marriage and divorce, to recompense for theft or violence, even the rights of animals and the care of trees. Men and women were regarded equally in these laws and were equally subject to it. Even a king in Ireland was subject to the law. I look back across the long years and sometimes think that this was perhaps what we really had in common with Strongbow and the Geraldines: they resented the right of the English king to make the law and impose it upon them. Maybe our way, the Irish way, was why they stayed and readily became one with us.

'Gentlemen,' Cormac beckoned to the men gathered around him. 'Come closer. Let those at the back hear what I have to say. I am a Brehon, a keeper of the laws.' The men shuffled closer as he continued. 'As you know, as a Brehon, I have an obligation to you all to explain my judgement. So please come close, put your weapons away for today and you might just learn something useful.' The two armies gathered closely around to hear Cormac now; there would be no more bloodshed today in his presence.

'So there must be fairness,' he continued when a quietness settled, 'but above all else it must bring us back to harmony.' And raising his voice to reach those at the back, he became more animated, almost pleading. 'Tell me, what earthly good does it do to kill a criminal who has killed another man?' He paused. 'How does that benefit the grieving wife or the children left fatherless and penniless?' A longer pause. 'Anyone?'

Almost chastising now, he continued, 'No one? Exactly, because it won't. And will the executed man's kin simply thank you for your kind service in lopping his head off and wander off home?' Moving slowly around the closed circle now, the men in the front rows avoided his fierce gaze. 'They won't! It will be a blood feud. And you will all be seeing a lot more of me, doing just this, deciding the law,' he shouted, seeming exasperated at the futility of it all. I remember

AOIFE OF LEINSTER

thinking it was a masterly performance with a great purpose: to teach the law.

'And if we were to apply the barbaric "eye for an eye" principle used in other lands in this case, do you, Tiarnan, want to have your way with MacMurrough's wife?' he asked, not expecting O'Rourke to answer, but when he saw that Tiarnan was about to speak, he quickly interrupted him. 'Be careful now, Tiarnan. You know well that under Brehon law it is an offence to insult a woman. An offence which carries a heavy éineach fine. So now is one of those moments in life when a wise man, which I know you are, does not miss the opportunity to say nothing!' He finished, and O'Rourke, knowing the truth of this, stayed silent.

Slowly he returned to the stool in the center of the crowd and settled himself with a heavy air of responsibility. 'So, Tiarnan, there will be no more killing. I know it will satisfy your thirst for revenge, and that, I do understand.' He shook his head as if in despair at the folly of human nature. 'But it will not serve you or our people well, and that is precisely why our laws push firmly in the other direction. An eye for an eye and a tooth for a tooth is not the way of our laws. That is futile, and these ancient laws have served us well.'

O'Rourke dropped his head, spitting fury but knowing the Brehon's word was law.

Turning to my father, Cormac regarded him coldly. What he had done was well known to everyone. It was not a question of his guilt. 'Diarmuit MacMurrough. You were once a great king, and heavy is the fall under that great weight, is it not? What do you say to these charges against you?'

'I did not abduct his wife, Dearbhail,' he said, and turning to O'Rourke, he continued, 'she came willingly.'

O'Rourke rose to the provocation and, cursing, made to rush at my father before he was restrained by the men standing around.

'Tóg go bog é, Tiarnan. Don't rise to it. We must hear him,' Cormac said, settling things. Then he proceeded to question my father as to how bringing an army into O'Rourke's kingdom of Bréifne and subsequently leaving with his wife and considerable spoils could in any way be considered a form of courting.

'You have a strange way of wooing a lady, Diarmuit MacMurrough.' There was a muted laugh from the crowd. 'Furthermore, the Senchus Mór, the Great Ancient Law, contains clear laws allowing a wife to divorce her husband and leave with her fair portion of their wealth. She can leave him for many reasons.' He was addressing the crowd now. 'Including obesity or if he is unarmed . . . and by that I mean, for the slow amongst you, not being able to get your cock up.' The crowd roared with laughter now. Shaking his head, he asked, 'Given that, Diarmuit MacMurrough, your account of events seems to me like a strange way for her to go about leaving him, does it not?'

'That bastard forcefully abducted my good wife and abused her against her will,' O'Rourke shouted, now almost weeping at the horrors that had been inflicted upon his Dearbhail.

'Indeed, Tiarnan.' Cormac raised the eyebrow over his one good eye and slowly approached him. 'And where is she now? Has she returned to you?' The question was met with a telling silence from O'Rourke. He stood stony-faced, avoiding Cormac's eye. There was a lot which was not said. This had all happened before I was born. Had she really been abducted by my father, or had she willingly fled O'Rourke? Considering she had brought all her wealth with her, it must have been planned. What's more, not long after her arrival in Ferns with my father, she had freely returned to her own father in Meath. It did not sound like an abduction.

Cormac let the silence hang, scanning the onlookers,

inviting them to draw their own conclusions. Then, grunting contentedly, having made his point without uttering a word, he left it there and didn't pursue it with O'Rourke, who remained silent now, seemingly happy not to dwell on the circumstances in which his wife, Dearbhail, had left him.

'Does anyone else have anything to say on these matters?' Cormac addressed the wide gathering.

'There is another grave matter for which he must be held to account,' O'Connor spoke up, stepping forward. Pointing to my father, he went on accusingly, 'Diarmuit MacMurrough has committed a great wrong by bringing armed foreigners to our land. This can bring no good. It must be stopped, and he must suffer punishment for this to discourage other foreigners from coming here.'

Cormac sighed, a slight exasperation creasing his brow. With a shake of his sunken head, he asked, 'Foreigners? Indeed, Rory, foreigners.' Lifting his gaze with a puzzled expression. 'And who exactly are these foreigners you're referring to, Rory?'

O'Connor gestured towards the Normans, who, remaining cautious and not fully understanding what was happening, stood apart from the general gathering. 'These men, the English. They have come armed for war with ill intent into our land.'

'The English . . . is that what they are?' Cormac said, looking up the hill to where Rob, FitzGodebert and the rest of the Normans watched the proceedings. 'Let me see . . .' He made a show of straining his one eye to survey the group.

'From what I see from here, that one is Flemish,' he said, pointing to FitzGodebert. 'As are those few. That man with the longbow is Welsh, and I'd venture that all his companions are also Welsh. I see several very well-dressed Frenchmen, and . . . I might be wrong here, not being blessed with the second eye, but I don't actually see one Englishman amongst them.' He finished and turned to O'Connor with a baffled look.

'Well, call them what you wish, Cormac,' O'Connor said, 'the foreigners should not have been brought here to the land of the Gaels by MacMurrough.'

'Foreigners . . . the land of the Gaels.' Cormac slowly paced the circle, hand rubbing his chin as if struggling to grasp the issue raised by O'Connor. He stopped and turned to a very tall warrior standing close to O'Rourke.

'Well, you're a fine strappin' lad. What's your name?'

'Conor O'Ronáin,' he replied, hesitating, a bit uncomfortable with the attention he was getting.

'A fine Gaelic name. From the kingdom of Bréifne, I'd venture?' Cormac asked, and the warrior nodded.

'I thought so. That's a fine head of golden hair and beard you have, you should be proud of it,' Cormac observed, and the lad relaxed a bit, pleased with the compliment from the Brehon in front of his companions.

'But the Gaels were a smaller race, with a darker skin and hair,' Cormac said. 'Either that or flaming red, like many amongst us today.' And he invited the men gathered to look around them.

'So you, Conor, either have known Norse blood in you or your mother had an unknown Norseman in her . . . unbeknownst to your father!' The men laughed and goaded the lad, who suddenly deflated, flushed with embarrassment.

'In fact, there's a good smattering of very tall Norse-looking lads standing around here today, bearing proud Gaelic names coming from proud Gaelic kingdoms.' Turning to the wider gathering, he drew their attention to the fact that the Norsemen of Dublin who had joined O'Connor's army today did not look much different from the rest of the Irish army. It was impossible to tell them apart.

'My point, Rory, is that I don't see an army of pure Gaels

standing behind you here today. I see a mix of two fine peoples, blending to one.'

O'Connor acknowledged Cormac's point. However, he suggested that the Norsemen had come to the island of Ireland over four hundred years ago and had now become established and accepted.

'Exactly. When they came, they brought their ships, tools, weapons . . .' He pointed to a large twin-bladed battleaxe. And their blood.' He swivelled dramatically to single out Conor again. 'And from what I see, we are all the better for it all.' He opened his arms as if to embrace the entire assemblage.

'That may well be true, Cormac, but we Gaels have welcomed enough foreigners to our land now.'

'Foreigners? Rory, before the Norsemen, do you know who the first foreigners were to come to this land?' Cormac asked.

Receiving no response, he continued. 'No? Well, you weren't paying attention to your seanchaí when you were a garsún. So let me tell you now. Pay attention this time.' Although a Brehon specialising in the law, he had a deep knowledge of our history. Traditionally, each king would have his appointed bard, skilled in poetry, music, history and the law. As these areas became more specialised, there emerged the seanchaí who would learn and recount the history. The Brehons specialised in the law, and poets and musicians developed their own skills. However, the Brehons, in particular, would be well versed in aspects of each discipline and were the most respected of all. Cormac, in teaching mode now, showed his deep knowledge of the happenings lost to many in the mists of time in our land.

He agreed that Rory was indeed correct. The Norsemen first arrived on our shores about four hundred ago. However, before them, in a timeframe not too dissimilar to that, the Gaels themselves had arrived in Ireland from the land known as Iberia. They had not been welcomed by the Tuatha Dé Danann, the tribes whose land they coveted here. Ultimately, they had come to an agreement to divide the kingdom between the two races. The Gaels would take the world above, and the Tuatha Dé Danann would take the world below, the otherworld.

'Now I might be going out on a limb here, but I know which side of that bargain I'd prefer.' Cormac mischievously raised the eyebrow over his remaining eye. 'What I mean is, *world below* sounds a bit vague to me, so let me be more specific . . . six feet below!' The men laughed. They would have heard the myths. Cormac's interpretation seemed to fit a lot more closely with their experience of the world. It was why he was known and held in such respect across every meadow, stream and forest of this island.

'That's the Gaels for you, Rory, the first foreigners to come here. Like the Norse, they blended and became one with those who were here before. They adopted the law, probably improved it. This place has a way of getting under your skin. You might come here, but it conquers you in the end.'

He continued to tell how the Gaels, who today seemed to be objecting to foreigners, were no angels themselves in this regard. These Irish Gaels, known as the Scoti to the Romans, had driven the Picts from the north of Britain to become the Scottish people that we know today.

'You see, Rory, as some wise person said, or will eventually get around to saying at some time: *when races are strong, they are not always just, and when they wish to be just, they are not always strong!* He paused, inviting O'Connor to draw the parallels himself.

Hearing Cormac telling—no, performing—the story of our land, I came to understand the seamless blending of men over time, a garnish over the sensitive skin of the Goddess Danu, the earth, who lent her name to the first tribes, the Tuatha Dé Danann. From another goddess, Éiru, and the Norse word *land,* the very name of our island was a mix of two races—Ireland.

'Before me today I do not see one race. I see a people, a strong people who are layered like the rings of a tree, building, becoming ever stronger with time as it grows out. The Tuatha Dé Danann first—and only the Gods know who was before them—then blending with the Gaels to form yet a stronger core. In turn, then, absorbing the Norse to become stronger still . . . and so it will continue,' Cormac said.

'Rory,' he said gently, 'if you'll forgive me, that's a fairly high horse you sit on, but don't let it obscure your view.'

I was glad when he finished by reminding O'Connor that since the first Gaels had arrived, there had been five kingdoms on the island. As far as he was aware, where we were gathered today was Leinster, not Connaught, where O'Connor was king, and as such, he was pushing it a bit expecting a Brehon to chastise a king for inviting whomsoever he wished into his own kingdom. Particularly at the behest of another king who himself seemed to be trespassing. O'Connor wisely stayed silent.

'Fine,' Cormac continued. 'Now, as I was saying, does anyone have anything *relevant* to say on these matters before I pronounce judgement?'

Finding no response, he paused to gather himself. Then, straightening his back and holding his long staff horizontally between his hands to signify the judgement of the ancient law was to be made, his voice boomed formally, 'With the authority of the Brehon, as keeper of the laws of the Senchus Mór, as bequeathed in me by the people, I decree that you, Diarmuit MacMurrough, have committed an offence and broken the law of Cáin Lánamna. That law decrees that should a man rape or steal the wife of a high noble or king, the full honour price of the husband is owed by the perpetrator.' He paused here for breath, and the crowd murmured a whispered approval. They had expected this. Brehon law relied on a clearly defined set of fines for nearly all crimes. The status of the victim was used to set the fine; that status was given a value known as the honour price, and only a brehon could set a person's honour price. It carried great weight in society; men and women would measure their worth against others with it.

These fines would affect the kinsmen of an offender, as they would be expected to contribute should the offender not have the means to pay it himself. In this way, the Brehon law encouraged the wider tribe to temper any bad behaviour of their own kinsmen. An expectant hush held the air still as the Brehon was about to set O'Rourke's price.

'In recognition of the grave wrong, and the manner of its doing, I am setting Tiarnan O'Rourke's honour price at five times that of Diarmuit MacMurrough.' My father visibly staggered at this, but Cormac continued. 'I am doing this because a man more often assesses his worth against that of his rivals. And this I think will be the most difficult part of the punishment for you, Diarmuit MacMurrough, your value as set against his.' He gestured to O'Rourke. 'So your honour price I set at twenty ounces of gold.' There was a gasp from the crowd. 'And you will pay, as éineach fine, one hundred ounces of gold to Tiarnan O'Rourke.'

This was a masterly twist by Cormac. It had not been necessary to set my father's honour price in his judgement, but by doing so he knew O'Rourke would be more than pleased.

O'Rourke was also shocked at the sum. But it wasn't that which had him grinning; it was the humiliation of my father by the staggering difference in their honour prices. It was the worth of a man. This would reverberate throughout the land and be seen as a crushing humiliation for my father and a full and remarkable retribution for him.

My father's clouded face showed the same. It was an enormous sum, even for him, but it was the shame. I think he would have preferred death to this, but it was done now. The law was made. He would live and we would pay. And, as no king had done previously in Irish history, no future king would abduct and abuse the wife of another. But not from fear of his enemy. His own kin would forbid it.

Chapter Nine
A BLEAK WINTER

Ferns
Winter 1167

Winter can be bleak in Ireland, and this one certainly was. It was as if the gods had abandoned us. Low grey clouds hung in a stifling thick sky before being swept away by angry winds that veered endlessly from north to south, east to west, throughout the day. It was impossible to get good shelter. Incessant sheets of rain swept level across the sodden ground, leaking under the doors and rising through the sunken floors. We stayed indoors but shivered in the dull, damp foul-smelling gloom of the few rooms the monks had made available to us in the Augustinian monastery in Ferns. The food the monks served seemed to taste of the mud that was everywhere.

It was a dreary place. I was sure in time it would become something like the fine monasteries I had seen in Wales, with their stone buildings and churches, rich lands, full barns and meadows bulging with cattle and sheep. That winter, it was a poor place, with the monks housed in wood-built hovels, no better than the animal house and grain stores.

The winter had been spent in the painful task of gathering the éineach fine which my father had had to pay to O'Rourke. My father had demanded that our kinfolk pay a heavy part of it, as was his right in Brehon law. There were bitter men and women who had surrendered long-hoarded coin and heirloom necklaces and broaches to pay for his stupidity. There would now be many of our own kin who would be more than happy to see the end of Diarmuit MacMurrough, so we were safer in the relative obscurity of the monastery, where would-be assassins would be reluctant to violate sacred ground. But that wasn't our biggest worry.

While O'Connor and O'Rourke were occupied with the suppression of Munster, we had some hope of being left alone. However, sooner or later they would come, and as winter moved through spring and into summer, there was still no news from Wales. We worried and wondered if Strongbow would come at all. Since FitzGodebert had returned there with his followers after our defeat at Cill Osnadh, we had heard nothing. Only Rob Smith had insisted on remaining behind when they left, having given his oath to Myler to protect me. Myler had in turn sworn that he would come no matter what came to pass.

But as the year darkened, I could see Rob, with no word coming from Myler, brooding over the gruel we ate from coarse wooden bowls. Like me, he was beginning to doubt if we would ever see them; we also knew it was dangerous for messengers, as spies were watching the ports to make sure there was no sign of the Normans returning.

Rob had kept himself occupied by adopting a group of strong young lads to train in the skills and practice of longbow archery. I accompanied them as they went into the forest to select the yew trees from which he taught them to make the bowstaves. The tall trunks of the trees were cut into man-sized sections, the length of the longbow. Rob showed how the bowstaves were cut from the band where the hard inner core, the heartwood, merged into the softer outer layers of the tree. In that way, the bowstave was softer on the inner side, which was drawn towards the archer. The stiffer outer side was then straining to right itself and would snap powerfully to the vertical again once the archer released the bowstring. It was this tension that gave the longbow its formidable power. Too much softwood and there would be no power; too much hardwood and no archer would have the strength to draw the bow.

Carving small notched endpieces from cow horn, he fitted them to the tips of the dried, smooth bowstaves. 'This is where we loop the bowstrings,' he said, attaching the hemp cord which he had looped at both ends. 'But don't do it until you're ready to use the bow, or it'll take on the bend and lose power.' Stringing the bow at one end, he braced it against his foot and bent the bowstave to loop the other end. None of the others had the strength to bend the bowstaves to attach the cord, and it was funny to see the staves flying, catching one or two in places where it hurt.

'You're more danger to yourselves than anyone else.' Rob laughed. 'But it'll come in time. Practice and eat your gruel,' he chided them. But they did get better, and soon most of them could string their bows without too much difficulty. 'Well, it's a start,' Rob said, 'but remember to keep your bowstrings dry. If they get wet, they're useless.' He was serious now. 'Archers don't wear armour; we need to be nimble and quick. And we're also useless with swords because we spend all our time using this.' He held up his own magnificent longbow. 'So that's what your hat's for. Not to keep your stupid heads dry'—he took off his hat to reveal a couple of bowstrings—'but to keep your strings dry.'

'Now listen to me. If there's a lad on a horse waving a sword about and coming for you, this is what you do.' Rob turned to Padraig, one of the young lads who stood with the others.

'What do you call an arsehole around here?' he asked.

'A what?' Padraig responded, smirking.

'An arsehole! You arsehole! You're one, most of the time.'

'Oh. Well, that'd be a *thóin*,' Padraig answered sullenly, bridling at the goading in front of his friends.

'As in *Póg mo thóin?*' Rob looked perplexed. 'I thought that meant *Yes, sir.*' The bunch of young lads sniggered at Rob's gullibility. They had been using it with Rob when he berated them in the archery drills.

'Oh . . . I see now. Well, aren't you a bunch of jokers,' he shouted. 'Well, stop your sniggering and pay attention, this is important. It could save your arseholes.' He was serious now. 'If there's a horseman coming at you and you've no arrow in your bow—this is the drill.' The lads knew their lives could depend on this and stopped their messing.

'Hold the bow out level in front of you, like this.' Rob crouched down onto his hunkers, and the boys followed, concentrating. 'Keep your feet planted square.' They all shifted their weight to ground themselves solidly. 'Good, now watch the horse, and when he's no more than three or four strides out . . .' Rob stood and examined their positions. 'Very good. Now here he comes . . . now quickly drop your heads as low as you can between your knees.' Their heads dropped, and now a long pause from Rob. The lads strained to hold the awkward position. 'And kiss your thóin goodbye.' He collapsed against the wall, roaring with laughter.

But not for long. Grasping that they had been had and feeling the safety in their numbers, they went for Rob, who, not fancying the odds, took off across the paddock. Still shaking with laughter, he was barely able to run. They caught him easily and hoisted him to the deep mill pond and fired him in.

'You're only a bunch of *thóin mórs*,' he roared, surfacing and spitting water. 'You see, Aoife, I'm learning the lingo,' he shouted to me but disappeared again under a hail of potatoes from his laughing apprentices.

There was considerable commotion when the abbot's ceremonial embroidered cloak was stolen. Suspicion was firmly placed on us, the newly arrived guests, and my father ordered that the culprit should immediately return the vestment and there would be no more made of it. Miraculously, the garment was discovered in the far dairy the following day, but devoid of a large silk embroidered hem, which had skirted the lower part. I remember the abbot looking rather foolish with his spindly legs showing when he wore the garment after that. It was a mystery as to what had happened.

Coincidentally, it was around then that Rob happened to come into a good source of silk thread for fletching the arrows. 'We could use gut, but God had been good to us and decided, in his infinite wisdom, to bestow us with good silk for his own divine purposes.' He winked at the lads, mimicking the high-pitched voice of the abbot. Carefully he wound the delicate silk thread around the three goose feathers he attached to each of the long ash shafts. He coated the shaft between the fletch with a beeswax and pine resin mixture to bind it firmly in place. Finally, he glued the forged arrowheads he had brought from Wales to the tapered ends of the shaft using animal tallow boiled from the hoof of a cow.

'This long sharp one is called a bodkin,' he said, holding up two arrows with different arrowheads attached. 'It can cut the best armour at one hundred and fifty paces like it was butter. Lethal! This one is the broadhead,' he said, indicating a flatter head with slightly barbed points at the edges. 'That

I'd use for hunting or horses. It buries deep, won't come out easily, and cuts the innards to shreds if the beast runs or thrashes about.'

I suppose it was the first masterclass in war bows that the Irish had ever received, and the lads learned quickly, as Rob spent his days drilling them in the meadow outside the monastery. He was very happy with this, as he could avoid the monks, who, he said, stank worse than the latrine outhouse.

And that was why I was surprised to see him one July day as I walked among the swooping swallows as they harvested the flies on a gentle breeze, chattering joyously. I loved these graceful, beautiful creatures. They always seemed on hand to comfort me in my sorrows and share excitedly in my joys. Rob beckoned me into the thicket; I could see a tall, hooded monk standing behind him.

'Aoife,' he said, almost whispering. 'Aoife, are you alone?' He scanned the meadow leading across to the monastery. 'No one else around?' I could see his excitement and joy. 'Quickly!' He bundled me deep into the dense darkness of the willow trees, thrusting me in his haste into the body of the hooded monk. And even in the transparent gloom of the thicket, as sure as the swallow finds its nest, I knew it was him.

Tearing the hood from his head, our eyes barely met before our lips. Seasons of tension and yearning released in a kiss of joyful pleasure, tasting of flowing salty tears that reached his neck as I hungrily kissed his skin. I needed his taste. This happiness was all I wanted, this feeling to go on forever as I felt the familiar strength of his embrace. Oh, please let it never stop.

'Don't mind me, then.' Rob coughed. 'You two just carry right on there.' As if dragged back to this world, Myler and I burst into laughter at our loyal friend's feigned indignation.

He had travelled alone, disguised as a Frankish monk. Crossing from Wales a week ago on a small fishing barque, hiding in the forests and avoiding the roads, he made his way from the coast to Ferns, where he had learned of our whereabouts. In Chepstow, word of the defeat at Cill Osnadh had reached Strongbow; he was furious that Diarmuit had been so foolish in leaving for Ireland unprepared. He had agreed to Myler's request to travel in disguise to seek news of our welfare and prospects.

'Aoife, Strongbow has not yet been granted the permission of the king to land in Ireland. He is frustrated but more hesitant now after the mess your father has made of it. He's now less sure of the success of the venture,' Myler went on.

'Myler, it's almost autumn now,' I pleaded. 'We won't last much longer. If you don't come next spring when the weather allows, it'll be too late.' I went on to tell him how O'Connor and O'Rourke and their allies were laying waste to the country, invading the kingdoms of Munster and Ulster. When they were firmly under O'Connor's heel, they would turn to us again. They would not leave the thorn of my father alone to come back to prick them. More importantly, as soon as they set their eyes on Leinster again, Mac Giolla Patrick would see no reason to treat Eanna with anything but vengeful brutality.

'If that happens, we have no hope, and Strongbow's plans to come to Ireland to escape from under King Henry will end,' I said. 'None of us will survive.'

Myler grimaced at this. 'Then you must come to Chepstow to explain to Strongbow, Aoife.' He gripped my hands. 'He respects you, above all else. He will listen to you.' Lowering his head, I sensed his sadness as he continued. 'I think he has a great affection for you, Aoife.' Folding me into his arms, we both knew that what we did could ensure we would never be together and I would then be wedded to Strongbow.

Myler stayed in the dense willow ticket, away from the curious eyes of the monks, who would easily recognise him as an impostor; we were not sure they could be trusted. My father agreed that I would return with Myler, and to encourage Strongbow, he produced letters for me to carry offering land and wealth to any man who came to our aid to restore the fallen king of Leinster. For if Strongbow would not come soon, he would offer the rewards to others.

> *If anyone wishes to have land or money,*
> *horses, equipment or chargers,*
> *gold or silver, I will give him*
> *very generous payments;*
> *if anyone wants land or pasture,*
> *I will enfeoff him generously:*
> *I will also give him plenty of*
> *Livestock and a rich fife.*

How a shelter of trees in a hollow of ground beside a slow flowing stream could soothe the soul of worries. I whispered the dogs to rest as I stole barefoot from the abbey in the still blanket of the night. A family of rabbits, startled from their play, bolted to earth, little knowing the vixen was almost upon them. She skulked brazenly across my path, irked her hunt was disturbed. Disappearing over the rise, a silhouette chiselled in the sharp moonlight, she paused in a final search for her prey and was gone.

We wrapped ourselves in the heavy blankets, our bodies exhausted, breathless. Our mingled sweat sent stabbing shivers through my body, cold rivulets on my burning skin, between my breasts, like a nail drawn along my naked back. The fire bounced warm on glistening skin and his sleepy, sated eyes. Sweet-scented smoke of crackling, summer-parched willow quivered into the night. The vixen screamed, more distant now; a fish dropped into the pool of the rippling river.

Slowly, through my nose, I inhaled nature's intoxicating broth: damp riverbank earth, fire smoke, night air laden with the harvest and a lover's musk. My naked limbs were on warm earth; our breathing grew settled.

'We must go soon, Aoife,' Myler said. 'The sea will become more restless shortly.'

I leant back, relaxing against his chest as he folded the grey blanket around us. It was made of a coarse flaxen material, produced by the monks and used as bedding and cover. I had secreted several, unnoticed, to Myler in the thicket.

He told me how Strongbow was spending nearly all his time at the king's court, trying to please Henry. He was hardly at Chepstow, and when last there he had expressed great reservations about the probable success of the plan to come to Ireland.

'That's why I think he is trying ever harder to find favour with Henry,' he said. 'I fear he thinks his future may be in Britain, under Henry, now that such a mess has been made of our plans to come to Ireland.'

He explained how Strongbow believed it was Sir Robert FitzStephen and Myler's other uncles, the Geraldines, who had encouraged my father to return, departing from the plan agreed upon before he left for Germany. It was the only plan that would have ever worked—to return in force.

'But that's untrue. I was there . . . so were you. It was Sir Hervey who did it; it was always madness,' I objected, turning to face him.

'I know. It was Sir Hervey who placed the blame on my uncles. I was there, the bastard.' He paused and then continued. 'Strongbow was dismayed. He believed in the sound judgement of my uncles. Now he doubts them, Aoife.'

'I don't understand. Why didn't you tell him what happened?' I asked.

Hesitating, he lifted his head to look at me. 'He threatened me, Aoife. He knows about us. He says he has witnesses, several from the castle who will attest to it.' Shaking his head, he continued, 'He may be hated, but he has his ways of coercing people. I don't doubt it.'

He explained how Montmorency had warned him against informing Strongbow of the circumstances of our return to Ireland. As a consequence, Strongbow had lost faith in Myler's uncles and placed all his trust in Montmorency. He alone had his ear and was given sole authority in his absence. He had advised Strongbow not to confront his uncles, as this could alienate them and bring an end to any hope of gathering the required forces to mount a successful campaign in Ireland.

Instead, he had assured Strongbow that with him in charge as a steady hand, he could keep a watchful eye on things and make sure no further rash decisions were made; after all, he was, he had said, the only blood relation of Strongbow in the camp. Myler was furious but helpless, and his uncles could not understand Strongbow's sudden shift in favour to Montmorency.

'So, you see, Aoife, you must come and convince Strongbow. Right now, the only one he is listening to is Sir Hervey, and I've no idea what that bastard is up to.' A haze of moths danced in the glimmer, occasionally landing in my hair. *How the swallows would feast here if they hunted by night,* I thought. Myler brushed a moth aside; I felt his fingers running over my skin.

'At least, I will see a lot more of you for a while.' He smiled.

So we stole quietly, on a still dark night, from the willow thicket. On foot, we were a few short hours from the coast which we would reach before dawn. It would have been easy enough to find a trading boat sailing for Bristol or St Davids from Wexford, once we had the coin to pay a shipmaster for the passage. However, silence was harder to come by, so we would sail from Glascarrig, the small port that served Ferns. Amlaib, the old Norse shipmaster who had stood at his oak tiller under a cloud of O'Rourke's arrows on the night we escaped from Bannow Bay, would meet us at the quay there. We would arrive to catch the ebbing tide and make once again for Wales.

I insisted on bringing Conor against Myler's objections that he would slow us down. He relented when I told him that was up to him, as he would be carrying him, and anyhow, I would not leave him in my father's care. Rob, having fulfilled his promise to Myler, came with us, and he talked incessantly about seeing his mother, Alice, back at Chepstow as the four of us set off towards the slivered hint of dawn in the eastern sky.

Part IV

Return and Understanding

Chapter Ten
THE PRICE FOR AN ARMY

Chepstow Castle, Wales
August 1168

The sails were set as we left the quay at Glascarrig on a southeasterly course. Amlaib pointed the bow for the mouth of the Severn, and not a sheet was touched until we rounded St Govan's Head in Wales as dawn broke the following day. The steady south-westerly wind and a mild swell made for a comfortable crossing.

The favourable weather put the crew in good spirits. We sat sheltered under the raised deck in the stern of the boat and ate the bread and cheese I had stolen from the barren kitchens of the monastery. There would be no hot broth to warm us on Amlaib's boat.

Wisely, he would allow no flame over the gunnel. His cargoes were more often than not flammable, and he had given up trying to discourage his crew from bringing ale in their water casks. Ale, flame, sheep's wool and a rocking boat did not mix well.

We were content with our lot beneath the stern deck,

listening to the song and banter of the sailors as the dusk rose from the east across the cloudless sky. A star-speckled blackness followed, gradually layering to a graded turquoise as the moonlight danced on the waves breaking on the curved bow and parted in our wake.

With little work, the men sat comfortably amongst the bundles of hides packed into the belly of the barque—a cargo from Wexford Amlaib would deliver to a merchant in Bristol. There he would collect another cargo for the return journey. His services were much in demand, and he plied the sea route between the islands constantly. The merchants favoured the rates his deep bellied barque could offer, particularly for Wexford-bound goods. There, the wide and shallow bay was notoriously fickle, with the ever-shifting sandbars bedevilling the outer estuary, grounding many unwary helmsmen.

The town of Wexford sat on the southern shore of the Slaney, a fast-flowing river that rushed from an inner estuary through a narrow channel and scoured the deep channel where the early Norse raiders chose to anchor their boats.

They had built their first longphort here. It was a timber semi-defensible structure where they would overwinter, having spent the spring and summer months raiding the monasteries and settlements of the Gaels. In time, this temporary refuge had become permanent and developed over the centuries into the walled town of Wexford.

Just beyond the town, the bay quickly widened into a shallow broad estuary, and the fast-moving waters slowed rapidly. Buffeted by wind and tide, they deposited their burdens of sand and silt, seemingly at random, around the estuary. However, there was a pattern to be discerned, and it was the exclusive preserve of seasoned and local shipmasters like Amlaib to know on a day where the sandbars lay and where the safe channel was to be found. Such knowledge was worth the value of a cargo to merchants, the knowledge gap between riches and ruin.

The wind remained steady as we rounded the headland at the mouth of the Severn in Wales. The sailors adjusted the sheets to gather the wind as Amlaib first set the course more easterly across the bay and then northerly into the narrowing mouth of the Severn, the longest river in Britain. We passed the bustling quays of Bristol to the east, and soon after, Amlaib called for reduced sail as he eased the tiller to guide us westward into the mouth of the Wye River.

Chepstow was not two miles upstream, and I knew we would soon see the busy quays before the castle itself would come into view around a westward bend in the river, standing high on the cliffs towering over the town.

'It might look like it's very high now,' Amlaib said as we rounded the bend. It was a majestic sight. Built to impress, it towered over the river and surrounding landscape. The sails were dropped, and the oars readied. 'Give it a few hours and the tide rises so much that I could nearly drop you over the walls.' He laughed. We had arrived at low tide, and I remembered the extraordinary change in the river level between the tides.

'I reckon it's the height of forty men, at least,' he said. 'I've never seen the likes of it.' Manoeuvring the boat and seeing none of the deepwater quays free, he told us he couldn't wait for higher water, as he had to make Bristol by noon to deliver his cargo.

A boat was summoned from the shore, and as we took our leave, my eye was caught by a figure in a dark cloak, arms buried in the long sleeves against the brisk morning chill. He stood on the small terrace, where Strongbow and I had spent many pleasant evenings two years previously.

His sour gaze caught my eye, held it.

Expressionless.

Montmorency.

❦

My joy and tears at seeing Alice, my friend, were short lived. Releasing me from her embrace, I could see the dread in her handsome face, lines of worry etched into her brow. My mother had not taken our departure to Ireland well, she told me. Alone, with all her children gone from her, she had withdrawn further into herself. Alice had watched as her body faded with her spirit, consuming itself before her eyes.

'She's withering quickly now, Aoife. I fear her strength can't last. She has clung to life in the hope you'd return.' Alice's eyes glistened. 'Brace yourself, Aoife,' she said, as she took my hand and led me to my mother's chambers in the east tower.

'She hasn't taken food this past week. I wet her lips to stop her thirst, but she hasn't spoken in days except to call your names.' She stopped before the low conical door frame.

'She has not long, Aoife. A slow death is cruel to the body. Now, there is no greater joy for her than to see you before she dies. Remember her as she was before.' I nodded as she eased the door open.

The rank air hung stagnant in the gloom of the room. Flickering light was thrown from the fire burning behind the shuttered windows.

I did not recognise the skeletal figure lying prone on the bed, shivering continuously, wracked with shuddering convulsions that arched her body, shoulder to heel, from the bed; a grimace of pain momentarily gripped the sunken, collapsed face. A wafer-thin layer of translucent skin clung to her skull, her teeth were bared.

Revolted, I turned to Alice, confused. Who was this? It

couldn't be. Grasping my arm, she nodded and gently guided me to the bed and whispered into my mother's ear.

'Mór, listen to me, Mór. It's Aoife, Aoife is here. She's come to you.' The figure on the bed stiffened, a stab of pain from deep within. Settling slowly as if preparing for the next, the rasping breath rattled and faded.

Motioning me forward, Alice could see my shock; she pleaded now, 'Speak to her, Aoife; she must hear your voice. Now, Aoife, or I fear she will go.'

I could not.

'Aoife, you must speak to her.' Louder now, Alice grasped my hand from my face.

'Now!' Alice demanded.

'Mother,' I whispered. 'Mother, it's me, Aoife.' Moving closer, I lifted her hand, feeling the chill on her skin and the bones underneath. I was startled when the hand tightly gripped mine.

The laboured breathing stopped abruptly. The sunken eyes flashed open over a rush of colour that swept into her face, lifting the deathly pallor. A brightness took her eyes, and a smile shaped her lips. I could see my mother now.

Overcome, I kissed her lips, my tears running into her eyes, which seemed to glisten all the more. My tears in her eyes—I would cry for her now, for ever more.

Her breathing deepened. The shivering stopped. Her body calling on its final reserves of strength to allow a mother a farewell to her child. She smiled.

'Aoife, *mo ghra sa*, my love.'

I strained to hear her.

'*Máthair, mo ghra. Máthair.*' I could not be strong. My grief welling from within, I wept. She smiled, gripping my hand now, my heart forever.

'Conor is returned with me. Shall I fetch him?' I asked, sensing there was not long.

She nodded. 'And your father?' she asked.

'He's still in Ferns, mother. Where he can stay.' I stopped, not wanting to distress her now.

Her head fell to the side, searching for my gaze. 'Aoife, tell me. Tell me everything, please.'

I remained silent. I would not trouble her with life's torments now. They would be nothing to her soon.

'Aoife, please. Quickly now, please,' she pleaded, an urgency in her faint voice.

Seeing she wanted to know, her need to know, I started. I told her of our arrival at Glascarrig. She laughed quietly at Conor's bursting from the dunes on the beach and the startled Normans. She raised an eyebrow that our kinsfolk of the Uí Chennselaig had agreed to support her husband again. She shook her head at the inevitable defeat at Cill Osnadh. I stopped there.

Her head lay to one side, looking at me. She could always know my thoughts, or at least that something troubled me, something I was not saying.

'Aoife?' she said, smiling. 'Aoife . . . tell me.'

I looked to Alice. She probably knew nothing of the ruinous éineach fine that had been placed upon my father by the Brehon, Cormac, in the aftermath of the battle. However, now was a time for truth. A time—the final time—when the happenings in the lives of two people must be spoken of, for whatever purpose, or forever they will live on, unresolved, while the people die.

Alice nodded, so I told my mother of the fine, hoping that would satisfy her.

My mother held my gaze, questioning. I had never spoken to her of the abduction of O'Rourke's wife, Dearbhail, by my father. I had long wondered as to the circumstances but knew it was a subject not to be raised. Any mention of her had always been met with a burning glare from my father or an abrupt departure by my mother.

'What is it, Aoife? Why such a heavy fine?' she asked.

When I didn't respond, she squeezed my hand. Alice nodded more urgently now. Reluctantly, slowly, I recounted what had happened—how my father had been found guilty by the Brehon of breaking the law of Cáin Lánamna, the law that decrees that should a man rape or steal the wife of a high noble or king, the full honour price of the husband is owed by the perpetrator. It pained me to have to remind my mother of how my father had betrayed her, despite him denying the abduction.

She remained silent. I thought I could feel her shame and humiliation. I hated him all the more for being the cause of this distress to my mother in her final moments.

'I'll fetch Conor,' I said, rising to break the tension and hoping to offer her some relief with his joy.

'No, Aoife, sit.' She gripped my hand tightly. 'I must tell you something first.' She strained to lift herself to hold me with her. 'Sit, please.'

She settled as I sat on the bed, holding her hand. Her breathing steadied again. I gently raised her head and pressed some water to her lips. She drank deeply, steeling herself to her task.

'Aoife, a great wrong has been done your father,' she said. 'He speaks the truth—he did not abduct Dearbhail. She came willingly.' As she spoke, the tension eased from her strained features. Her grip lessened, and as she relaxed, I could see the echo of her youthful beauty. Strange, with death so close, how the pulses of memory and form move through us.

Transported to that time, soon after her marriage to my father, it was as if she relived the painful events but, and in some way, reconciled and forgave. She spoke.

Theirs had been a marriage of two dynastic families of

Leinster, the MacMurroughs and her family, the Ni Tuathail. She had not known my father but had consented to the marriage nonetheless. Indeed, her affections lay elsewhere in her youth. Lifting her eyes to me, she continued.

'Aoife, although we women have our rights, you will find that your blood is the tide on which your life must travel . . . not your desires.'

Alice caught my look of alarm that my mother could know of Myler. She shook her head vigorously—she had not betrayed me.

My mother went on to tell me how she had learnt in time how my father had, in his youth, fallen in love with a beautiful young princess of north Leinster, Dearbhail Ni Maeleachlainn. From a noble family of royal lineage, she was descended from Ireland's greatest ard rí, Brian Boru.

It was a genuine affection between my father and Dearbhail, my mother whispered, not driven by dynastic ambitions. A youthful love, which is no more resistible than the rising of the sun, and should not be so. A love that was shattered as my father's fortunes waned and a marriage was hastily arranged for Dearbhail with an ambitious neighbouring king, Tiarnan O'Rourke. A marriage made necessary for the safety of her family to appease the warmongering of O'Rourke. It was the reason Dearbhail had agreed to the marriage.

My father had been distraught. All the more so when, almost immediately, O'Rourke resumed hostilities against Dearbhail's father, Murchad Ua Maeleachlainn, king of Meath. Dearbhail suffered greatly as a consequence.

Dearbhail was of a delicate nature, more saintly than worldly . . . nearly angelic, my father had told my mother as events unfolded back then. Consumed with the Christian God, he suspected she was not suited for this world. He was pained by O'Rourke's mistreatment of her, and he shuddered at the memories.

Fearing she would leave him, as was her right, O'Rourke had imprisoned Dearbhail on an island in a lake in his kingdom of Bréifne, but not before her virtue had suffered his abuse. Throughout this time my father had, through his spies, maintained a secret communication with her. With each letter my father received, his anguish increased as he learned of the depravation and torment the sweet girl suffered. He felt her withering as the years passed and knew her kindly soul would not leave that island in bodily form as things stood.

With my mother's knowledge and more from pity for the sufferings of one he had held dear, he took the opportunity of an unfavourable turn in fortune for O'Rourke to mount a foray into Bréifne to rescue Dearbhail from the island.

Enraged, O'Rourke had let it be known that my father had forcibly abducted his wife and imprisoned her in Ferns, where she suffered terrible abuses in his bed. Nothing could have been further from the truth, my mother said. Dearbhail was a broken, enfeebled woman when she had welcomed her into her house. She herself had cared for her, and my father had shown great kindness as she was nursed back to health over the months. He had not countered the lies O'Rourke had spread about the circumstances of Dearbhail leaving him. To do so would have brought the wrath of O'Rourke and O'Connor onto Dearbhail's family in Meath. He would suffer the wrath of the nobility, the church, and the Brehons, each outraged at his perceived misdeeds and abuse of the law.

'Don't judge him so harshly, Aoife,' she said, her voice weakening from the strain of talking.

I pressed a damp cloth to her dry lips; it dribbled down her cheek. Or were these her tears now. She went on to tell me how when Dearbhail had recovered her strength, she had returned to her father in Meath, the threat from O'Rourke having dissipated. He was occupied elsewhere.

'That poor girl never recovered from her ordeal in O'Rourke's hands. She buried herself in her religion like many broken souls do, seeking solace and certainty in a magical world from the pain and uncertainty of this earth.' She stopped. Her body arched, wracked with pain. She gave a soft, barely audible cry. Then looked at me, almost pleading.

'Please, can it stop, Aoife, *mo ghra sa?*' Her voice trailed and her breath slowed to a rattle in her throat. Holding my gaze, she smiled as her eyes closed slowly over the fading spark of life.

'*Mo ghra sa.*' A final whisper from a slight tremor of her lips. A mother's love. I kissed her. Her hand slackened in mine, and she was gone.

I DISLIKED THE HOODED CROWS, but they were suited to this place. They deepened my gloom, their black caps sitting on what looked like the grey chainmail aventails the Norman knights wore to protect their necks and shoulders, watching. They were killers and would have taken the chicks of the swallows were their nests not cleverly tucked under the castle eaves. They seemed to revel in the blustering autumnal winds that heralded the coming of winter.

My swallows had departed. The small delicate nests were silent now of the chattering clutches. They had gathered in their family groups, their tribes, in the kalends of September. Unusually quiet, they perched in the rims of the small turrets on the walls. Within reach, they sat silently, like spirits, watching me. Used to my presence, as if contemplating their journey, they looked forlorn, mourning the passing of the summer, or mourning with me the loss of mother, as I liked to think.

Then, one wispy morning with a glimmering sun, they had gathered on the roof ridge of the Great Tower. A couple, then more, took flight. Swooping and calling, enticing the younger ones. It was time to go. I watched as a last bird was berated from the ridge, the flight now impatient to take their leave.

A rush of wind felt in my hair. Another. An excited chatter flashed past my ear. And another. Many more, like a swarm of flies around a horse's head on a windless hot summer's day. A joyous, noisy farewell from my friends, wishing me well and lifting my spirits. The revolving circle of the dance of life would go on; we would meet again next year.

There was a sullen atmosphere in the castle. Strongbow had not yet returned to Chepstow. He was ever at the king's side, doing his bidding in his efforts to regain his confidence. There was some hope now the king would relent and give his permission for the campaign in Ireland. To that end, Myler and his uncles had been called to Strongbow's side to quell some unrest in Northumbria. Merciless to his enemies and unforgiving to recalcitrant lords, the king would extract a heavy price from Strongbow for his forgiveness.

I felt Myler's absence. Montmorency oversaw the affairs of the castle with the rest of the knights away with Strongbow. He was insufferable. I avoided him as best I could. Apart from passing encounters in the courtyard, our paths seldom crossed. I would keep it that way. Alice warned me to be on my guard – he had abused some of the kitchen girls and seemed to take pleasure in the violence and reluctance of his victims.

But with the king's ear, he was the key to unlocking the Norman army I needed to reach Eanna. His influence could sway the king to let Strongbow sail for Ireland with his followers. They all needed Montmorency as much as I did. Although I despised the man, I had to tread carefully with him.

My only solace was with Alice. Her kindness after my mother's death sustained me. As the dreary winter evenings drew ever darker in the draughty rooms of the castle, we took to spending our evenings in her warm cellar, down the broad flagstone steps from the roaring fires of the kitchen. On occasions, she would have a large, copper bath filled from the water boiling cauldrons of the kitchen. I would luxuriate in the soothing warmth, my spirits lifting with the steam swirling into the stone vaulted roof.

On one such evening, drifting from a deep reverie, I heard the click of the door latch behind me as Alice returned. I had not noticed the water had cooled, and I rose, asking her to pass me my robe, which lay on the chair across the room. I could feel the warmth from the fire before me on my naked body sharpening the chill on my back from where she had closed the door on the cold corridor.

The click of the lock snapping into place startled me. I turned.

Montmorency.

He secreted the key into the pockets of his cloak, surveying my nakedness.

'What are you doing?' Standing in the high-sided bath, I could not move quickly to grab my robe. Gauging my thoughts, he did just that.

'Oh, no need for such modesty, m'lady. I believe there are those who have already taken their pleasure on your intimate delicacies.'

'Get out!' I shouted, hoping Alice would hear.

'The kitchens are empty, m'lady. Do not strain yourself. You are alone now.' Placing the robe in the far corner of the room, he moved closer. Walking slowly around the bath, his breathing quickened. His eyes burned into my body, defiling. The cellar was deep, isolated. I felt something brush my rump. I turned, slapping at his hand, but he had withdrawn.

'Apologies, m'Lady. A slip of the hand,' he smiled.

'I will tell Strongbow of this.'

'Oh, spare me, m'lady,' he said casually. 'You won't . . . and we both know why.'

I hesitated.

'Exactly." He resumed his slow walk around me. 'M'Lady, you and I should be more friendly. We have a lot in common, don't you see.' There was almost a pleading tone to his voice. 'For our own reasons, we both want to bring an army to Ireland. However, I think you have more of a pressing need than I do, if I'm not mistaken. Happily, I can help you with that with my relationship with the king. I think we can help each other.'

I felt the chill creeping up my back, over my shoulders. I said nothing.

Watching my reaction, he continued slowly. 'I see you agree,' he nodded. 'I, for my part, would be delighted to help.' Then weaving his fingers and purposefully turning his focus to my body. 'On your part...' he hesitated, 'if only we could be a bit more intimate.' He stopped.

'Get out! Never. I would rather die.

He sighed as if dealing with a wayward child who would, in the end, succumb to the way of things.

'That, m'Lady, would be an awful tragedy. An outcome none of us would wish for. But without our army, I fear it would be inevitable.' He held my gaze. 'Worse still, your brother Eanna would perish, along with your other brothers, your father...your entire family, possibly.'

I knew the brutal truth in what he said. No member of the MacMurrough family would survive if our enemies secured their hold on our kingdom; alive, we would forever be a threat.

'And the saddest thing of all, m'Lady, is that it is completely avoidable. If you could only see your way to being more…cooperative.'

Gathering my robe and handing it to me he said. 'However, this time, I do understand that you need to reflect on things. I would not want any reluctance when we eventually come to an understanding.'

I took the robe and covered myself quickly. 'Can you leave now…please.' I said, turning my back on him.

'Certainly, m'Lady. Good evening.'

Chapter Eleven
REVEALING THE EARL

Chepstow Castle, Wales
October 1168

As the winter gripped the sodden land, autumn leaves in her wake, the campaign season ended. Armies could not march on mud. Horses needed fodder, men their meals. When the Goddess withdraws from the dance of life to rejuvenate in the warmth of the earth's core, winter's barren lands could provide neither. Soldiers retreated behind well-provisioned palisades or turned their faces homeward. Cold earth was seldom doused with the warm blood of battle. Men preferred to kill and die in the sun.

Myler and his uncles, the Geraldines, had appeared one evening as the early dusk settled on the castle. Riding from the northwest, I saw their silhouettes sharp against the fading glow of the sunset. They seemed to pause there. The lights of the town glimmered, dominated by the flaring torches of the castle courtyard, the swaying lanterns placed at regular intervals along the battlements. I made regular use of their light to stroll the walls in the evenings and early mornings.

Beyond earshot, I saw them break forward down the gentle slope towards the castle dell, the deep ravine which ran the length of the southern curtain wall of the castle. It provided a natural defensive feature to complement the sheer, unassailable drop from the northern wall into the River Wye. The turf scattered from the pounding hooves, splashing skyward. The gradual rise of the drumbeat was followed by the rhythmic snorting of galloping horses, needing little urging from their riders—a horse knows its home. The men laughed, shouted and cursed in their banter. A race home.

They jostled for position as they rounded the southeast tower and charged for the gates. Although large by any measure for a castle, the gates could not accommodate two charging Norman warhorses. I could hear Le Gros shouting for everyone to pull up; at least someone was sensible. When Myler and others did, he paused . . . then charged forward, iron-shod hooves skidding on the cobbled stone under the arched portcullis. Galloping into the courtyard of the lower bailey, he turned, performed a flamboyant bow and declared himself the winner. The faux outrage of the others could not stem their laughter.

It had been a successful campaign, hence their good spirits. The king had expressed his thanks to Strongbow for their service in restoring the peace in Northumbria. He was grateful, and Myler sensed their fortunes were turning with the improved favour of the king. This was good news for everyone. There was real hope that the king would now let them sail for Ireland.

However, there was doubt in Strongbow's mind as to the wisdom of risking his armies in Ireland. The disaster of my father's early return to Ireland had infuriated him. The chances of success were now significantly diminished, with the element of surprise wasted. Added to this, his improved relations with the king meant that his prospects here in Britain were now more favourable.

I had spoken to Myler's uncles of my father's renewed offers of land and wealth to any man-at-arms who would come to his aid. From that, I knew they remained eager that Strongbow should stay committed to his plan to come to Ireland. Myler explained that this would remain the case, as Britain was not a land short of Norman knights with little prospects and less opportunity.

Nonetheless, despite all this, they would not act without Strongbow. He would need to be persuaded first.

'So I must speak to him, Myler,' I said. 'Where is he?'

'He turned for Pembroke on our way.' He paused. 'I believe he will return to Chepstow in a few weeks.'

Pembroke was another significant castle held by Strongbow, several days ride to the west of Chepstow. Strongbow visited it frequently, tending to the affairs of his lands, I had presumed. I never had cause to visit the place.

'Myler, we don't have that time. If we are to go in force in the spring, we must begin the preparations now. Time is short,' I insisted. 'I will ride to Pembroke and talk to him. He is reasonable; I can persuade him.'

Knowing Myler as I did now, I could tell he was uncomfortable, uncertain.

'Have you spoken to Alice of Pembroke?' he asked, avoiding my eyes.

'Alice? Why?'

He stayed silent.

'Myler?'

'You must speak to Alice, Aoife.'

'What?' I tried to catch his gaze. 'Myler!' I sought his eyes.

Exasperated, he threw his hands into the air. 'OK, OK . . .

sit down, Aoife.' He guided me to a small bench and sat beside me, holding my hand.

'And swear to me, Aoife, you will never tell anyone where you heard this . . . particularly not Strongbow.'

I looked at him quizzically. What was all this about?

'Swear,' he insisted.

'I promise.'

And he told me.

Apparently, there was more than administrative affairs to occupy Strongbow's attention at Pembroke Castle. There was also his mistress. She had lived there as long as Myler could remember, and although he visited her frequently, she had never come to Chepstow, and Myler had never met her. As his mistress, Strongbow respected the etiquette of these matters rigorously. She would not have any formal place by his side.

I had known that Strongbow most probably had such connections, but hearing it for the first time was not easy. Such a long-standing arrangement was also not unusual. The higher Norman lords would marry for dynastic purposes. A wife must bring wealth or prospects to advance their fortune and that of their followers. Consequently, these types of arrangements were common before and after marriage. I had not expected anything much different. After all, in Ireland, a man could take two wives and more concubines. However there, a wife could easily divorce her husband and take an equal share in the wealth, more if she had brought the bulk of it to the marriage. Women could also take lovers, and Brehon law allowed for these arrangements with or without the consent of her family, the law always seeking the moderating balance. The ways of the Normans gave women no such rights.

Myler scrutinised me, gauging the impact of this revelation. His kindness would not have wished me distress.

Probabilities become realities; when thoughts are articulated, they seem to take on a shape that must be seen. Words put edges on thoughts that throw shadows and can be felt on the skin. They become real.

I would have preferred it otherwise. An image of a man, a husband, devoted to his young wife, who might in time turn her loving gaze towards him. Childish notions of a young girl. I laughed inwardly at my hypocrisy. I knew the way of things. More glaringly, lofty virtuous ways had been readily abandoned with my robes for the man who now held my hand.

'I see,' I said. Then I continued. 'It's fine, Myler, it's the way of things. In fact, I'm no angel myself in these matters, as you may have noticed.' I smiled at him. Surprisingly, he remained glum.

'There's more, Aoife. There's a child. A daughter, not much younger than you, I believe. Aline, Aline de Clare. She also lives there.'

I must have shown my shock. Looking back, I should not have been surprised. These things could be avoided, but they happened. I stood and paced. Surprised at my own reaction, my sudden venom for a girl I had never known. I had always easily befriended people, but here I felt an unfamiliar loathing. A visceral fear of a threat, an unfamiliar feeling borne from deep within, from the blood, my blood . . . royal blood.

'I feared as much. The child will make things difficult in the future. Any children I might bear for Strongbow would have to contend with the child,'

Myler looked perplexed. 'What do you mean?' he asked. 'She will have no rights. She is illegitimate.'

It was now my turn to struggle to understand. 'Illegitimate? What do you mean?' For in Ireland, under Brehon law, there was no notion of illegitimacy. Whether born in or out of marriage, it was of no consequence in law or attitude. The distinction was truly a foreign concept. Indeed, there were many such children as the first year of marriage was seen as a trial period for each to assess the suitability of their chosen partner for a life together. If either party decided to end the relationship, it was done on a no-fault basis, and the law clearly set the responsibilities of the father and mother in respect of any resulting children. These children had equal rights to succession to any subsequent children of their parents.

'How can a child be illegitimate, *outside* the law?' I asked. 'Whose law? How can a born child be illegal?' It was a ridiculous notion to me, near comical.

Myler went on to explain how every monarch's crown could only be fully legitimised by a coronation approved by the pope. So, kings and queens were very attentive to the whims of the church. They enforced Christian ways on their people. Particularly the laws surrounding marriage and inheritance where a man could only have one wife. The children of that marriage could inherit whereas any children outside of the marriage could not legitimately inherit a title and the wealth that came with it—they were considered illegitimate.

Grasping his meaning, I sensed my hostility to Strongbow's child abating remarkably quickly. I was a bit ashamed of how easily I had been willing to trample upon the interests of an innocent girl when my own were threatened.

However, such is life. As Alice had repeatedly told me, it was my blood that would shape the course of my life; there was a lot more at stake than my own innocent girlish notions. Against this, I started to get a different sense of my father and what he had done. If I could stand over an injustice against an innocent girl, what leap was necessary to let harm come to someone I knew, and then to kin, beyond that to a brother, even a son or daughter?

Would I find the reasons to justify abandoning them if the time came? Would I leave a child under the swing of an axeman to die, knowing only by doing so could my other children survive? Could I also murder and pierce the eyeballs of my kin, knowing not to do so would condemn my own children to the same fate? I shuddered at the thought of it. I preferred to think I wouldn't, but I wasn't so sure now.

I could feel the pulse of that royal blood in my thoughts, washing away a childish innocence, loosening my hand on simplistic certainties and noble principles. My grip would ease further as the inescapable current of life swept me on.

The choices my father made, although repugnant, could be understood. Was that what Strongbow had meant when he suggested that he would not have done much differently? Would I?

For now, I was relieved that the girl would pose no threat. I must have shown my delight, for when I turned to Myler I could see the anguish etched into his handsome face. A fathomed sadness in his dark eyes seeing my future, the children I would bear for another man. A man he too loved like a father.

His agony jolted me back to my own sorrow for this loss. The sacrifice I would also make. Life tends to tinge every joy with a shadow of sorrow, but then again, our trials are also often lightened with a wisp of promise. The world would not let me forget my blood, as Alice had told me . . . but nor would my very blood itself. I could see now how it must be. I would do my duty by my family and do whatever was required to protect them and further our interests. It was either that or perish.

I moved to close the heavy shutters on the window which overlooked the lower bailey of the castle courtyard. My chamber was visible to prying eyes from the ramparts on the south wall on the opposite side. The castle was alive with the return of the Geraldines and their following men-at-arms and archers who ambled through the gates. The horses whinnied their joy at their return over the shouting men and wagons clambering over the cobblestones. We would not be missed for a while. Barring the door, I returned to hold his sunken head in my hands where he sat on my bed. The rich, silky thickness of his long hair was scented with rose oil. I had not seen him in weeks. I missed his tenderness. Opening my robe to expose my breasts, I pulled his lips to my nipple and felt his tongue circle, his hands moving from my thighs, fingertips down my spine to firmly clasp my rump. A heightening of the noise outside caused us both to look to the barred windows. The confusion continued; I held his head to my breast, we had only moments. Pushing him back I went to him. Rhythmic thrusts, mingled breath, lost in each other; the quick thrust of seed, a rush of relief, mixed in the cacophony of noise rising from the courtyard muted in the moment's reverie. Then the pounding, becoming real, clear, the pounding on the door; Alice's urgent shout:

'It's Strongbow. Strongbow is returned! Aoife, he is coming!'

Chapter Twelve
PAYING THE PRICE

Chepstow Castle, Wales
Winter 1168

Strongbow had not gone to Pembroke; he had unexpectedly followed the Geraldines to Chepstow. Receiving word that a messenger from the king would arrive at the castle, he had turned this way.

'M'lord,' I heard Alice say in the corridor approaching my chamber. 'It's a pleasure to see you returned safely.'

'Alice, I'm glad you are well,' he said. 'Is the princess in her chamber? I'd like to speak with her immediately.'

There was no hiding place. My chamber, while large, was uncomplicated. The windows overlooked the busy courtyard, but even if they hadn't, Myler would not survive an escape from the second floor unscathed.

Closing my robe, I motioned for him to be silent. I moved quietly to the door making sure it was barred.

'I trust you had a successful campaign in the north,' Alice said, raising her voice to ensure I was aware that Strongbow stood outside my chamber door.

There was a moment's hesitation, in which I could sense his impatience with Alice. 'It was Alice. Now please open the door and inform the princess I'll speak to her now,' he said.

Myler rose and made for the window. Brushing against the table, he knocked a pewter water pitcher to the floor. It crashed noisily on the flagstone.

'Alice,' I called loudly. 'Alice, are you there? Could you bring me another jug of hot water for my bath? It's getting a bit cold. Alice?' I waited, hoping Alice would quickly grasp my ruse.

'Certainly, m'lady,' she responded after an unnerving delay. 'I was conversing with Strongbow, who has just returned. I was just about to explain to him that you were in your bath and could not entertain him right now.' She was in her stride now. 'Can I suggest you join him in the Great Tower momentarily?'

Thank you, Alice, I thought. 'I'd be delighted. Please tell him I'll be there presently.'

With that, I heard the sound of him retreating down the corridor. The ashen look on Myler's face did not lessen for a week.

As the news spread of the visit of the king's messenger, there was considerable excitement in the castle that Strongbow's fortunes had been revived. There was great hope that the king's favour would be fully restored and Strongbow's titles reinstated. Until now, the king had refused to recognise him as the Earl of Pembroke, a punishment that had brought great anguish and shame. With the king's favour restored, it was expected that permission to undertake the campaign in Ireland would also be granted.

Strongbow looked in high spirits as I walked the length of the Great Tower, keeping my winter cloak clasped against the chill of the room. The fire in the large open hearth on the north wall had not yet taken, and the dry oak logs cracked noisily as they settled into the rising flames. Although early afternoon, the pallid greyish winter light from the high windows could not lift the gloom of the cavernous room. The heat and pleasant waft of burning firewood would eventually banish Autumn's musky dampness from the hall, which had lain idle in Strongbow's absence. Servants rushed about, shielding tapers to light the candles.

I was not happy to see Montmorency there. I had hoped to speak to him alone or at the least with Myler's uncles present to lend their support. Ever gracious, Strongbow rose and placed a kiss on my hand, bowing.

'It's lovely to see you, m'lady. I'm so glad you have managed to return safely.'

Offering him a courtesy, I returned the compliment and expressed my delight in the success of his campaign in Northumbria in the king's service.

'Thank you. We fulfilled our duty admirably, and I am now very hopeful that the king's messenger bears good news." He smiled and, turning to a tray a servant brought, offered me a glass of his fine burgundy, remarking, 'I believe we both developed a liking for this one during our most enjoyable evenings on the river terrace these two years past.'

Tasting the wine, it reminded me of the man's warmth and sincerity. I remembered I had grown quite fond of him and had enjoyed our conversations on those warm balmy summer evenings, sitting on the small private castellated terrace, which captured the last of the evening sun before it dipped below the westerly rise.

'However, I believe you had a fraught time in Ireland,' he said, more serious now. 'I was dismayed to hear your father discarded our plan and sailed for Ireland.' He looked at me searchingly, but before I could speak, Montmorency intervened.

'Indeed, m'lord. As I said, it was most unwise. I did everything in my power to dissuade him from this reckless course, but . . .' he hesitated. He took on a pained expression, as if continuing with great reluctance:

'M'lord, you will be well aware I am loath to offer criticism of my comrades, but there were those imprudent voices in our camp who planted this rash idea with him.' He shook his head, a sad disappointment in one who has been let down.

I was seething at the duplicity of the man.

'I fear the Geraldines have again shown very poor judgement in these matters,' he continued. 'As we have discussed, m'lord, we must be ever more cautious in future in whose advice we seek.'

'I agree, Sir Hervey. And again, thank you for your sound judgement in the entire affair; it has been most unfortunate. At least I have you to rely on.'

Montmorency brazenly held my gaze, the hint of a sneer in the twist of his mouth. Daring me to speak, knowing I would not, my silence adding weight to his lies.

Strongbow stood in the well of one of the high narrow windows, his silhouette framed against the light, watching me. Leaving a silence for me to fill. If there was anything to say to counter Montmorency's account, this was the time. He was giving me the opportunity.

I said nothing.

The silence hung heavily in the gloom.

Eventually, he sighed, my silence confirming Montmorency's account.

There was a melancholy about him now, as if he too was saddened by a betrayal of trust. I could see his thoughts, poisoned by Montmorency. How could he have misjudged these men—men he had fought beside and relied upon? It was inexplicable to him.

He spoke of how the entire campaign was now highly

precarious. My father's actions had forfeited the element of surprise. Our enemies were alerted to the threat, my father having told them explicitly at Cill Osnadh that more Norman forces would follow. They would be ever watchful and ready to react quickly and in force to any incursion. Surprise was lost and the chances of success of the expedition significantly diminished as a consequence.

'M'lady. This was your own warning to me when we first met in this room two years ago,' he said, almost apologetically. 'You were right in your assessment of the situation then . . . and that remains the case today, I am afraid.'

My own words, which had, I thought, avoided disaster back then. Were they now to decide Eanna's fate? It was the prospect of further Norman armies arriving in Ireland which kept him alive. His life could be used to threaten and bargain should that come to pass. As soon as Mac Giolla Patrick and O'Rourke no longer feared a Norman army would stand behind my father, he would die.

This and my own childish passion for Myler forced me to hold my tongue against Montmorency's lies. Why was I so foolish to indulge a girlish urge for romance, for passion? Whatever satisfaction I had carried a heavy price now. The distrust in Strongbow's camp, which I had caused, was adding to his misgivings.

Was I to be the cause of Eanna's death? I felt panic.

'I agree, m'lord. We have indeed lost the advantage of surprise,' I said. 'However, I was at Cill Osnadh that day. We were vastly outnumbered and did not want to fight. I think you may have heard what happened from Sir Richard Fitz-Godebert?' I asked. I didn't want to recall the stupidity of my father when he had unnecessarily dragged our cavalry into a hopeless fight.

Strongbow nodded. He had indeed spoken to FitzGodebert soon after he returned from Ireland. He had recounted the events of that disastrous day in detail. Most notably, he had described the Irish army. It was the first time a Norman force had encountered the Irish on a field of battle in Ireland. What he saw did not impress him.

He reported how the Irish were poorly disciplined and badly armed. Although fine horsemen, they rode in the Irish style, without saddles or leather bridles. With no body armour, they were vulnerable to every cut and arrow, as were their horses. For the most part, they carried short spears, which they would throw, largely inaccurately. They could use them quite effectively in close order, in a thrusting manner from behind small round shields. Some carried the large twin-bladed axe, a practice they gained from the Norse on the island. They were nimble in the saddle and on foot, but against this, the Norman battledress of chain mail and armour was wholly effective. The Irish would have difficulty disabling a Norman knight with a first thrust; they were then very vulnerable to the superior Norman weaponry of the mace and longsword.

He went on to report that the Irish were poorly trained and seemed to arrange themselves as groups of smaller armies rather than as one whole force. There were no effective archers to speak of. Those they possessed used a common hunting bow, with limited range and accuracy. The arrowheads were broad, effective at close range in bringing down an animal or a man. However, they were useless against armour at any distance, not being narrow and heavy like the armour-piercing bodkin arrowheads the Normans had designed for that purpose.

'Yes, I have talked in detail with FitzGodebert of what happened and what he saw. It was, indeed, most instructive.' He went on to tell of his belief, based on FitzGodebert's report, that a Norman force could prevail against a much larger Irish army. And in that, there was hope. There remained a realistic possibility of success. So all was not yet lost.

He approached me and took my hand.

'Anyhow, Aoife, there has been enough procrastination. We all need to know our future paths.' He smiled. "You, me, my followers . . . everyone. We must decide.'

He faced into the framed light of the window, his shoulders rising with his breathing, arranging his thoughts. Was it a draught in his hair, or did I detect a hint of a shake of his head?

Turning to me, he looked saddened.

'Aoife, I remain very unsure. It is so fraught with risk now.' He paused. I knew he did not want to speak of his improved prospects in Britain as the favour of the king was restored. He now had less need of Ireland.

'However, I must decide. I will meet the king's messenger and dine with him this evening,' he said. 'I will make my final decision tomorrow morning.'

Then, turning to Montmorency, he continued. 'Sir Hervey, above all others I value your opinion in this. Your judgment has proven sound. What is your advice, Do we go to Ireland?'

Montmorency briefly caught my eye.

'I'm flattered, m'lord. You do me a great honour,' he said. His flickering eyes seeing his scheme. 'Indeed, these are momentous decisions . . . which must not be taken in haste, as has happened previously.' He nodded knowingly. 'If I could, m'lord, I would like to glean the full facts from the princess before I give you my recommendation.'

Strongbow agreed. Being very reflective himself, he valued those who, armed with the facts, gave reasoned thought to their advice.

Embodldened, Montmorency continued.

'Could I suggest I give the matter my full attention, in

private, with the princess this evening while you are entertaining the king's messenger? When I am fully satisfied'—he paused, looking me straight in the eye—'then I will give you my advice . . . in the morning.' He smiled.

'Excellent, thank you, Sir Hervey. I will make my decision then.'

We walked the length of the hall towards the large studded oak doors. When we were safely out of earshot, Montmorency whispered, 'Come to my chambers this evening when Strongbow is at dining. Come appropriately dressed and scented . . . I prefer lavender.'

<hr />

I COULD HEAR the echo of voices and laughter as I turned from the kitchens down the wide stone stairs that led to Alice's cellar, ducking to avoid the stone arch which had given many rushed kitchen lads a nasty surprise. Rob sat with his father, Ewan, by the fire, while Alice busied herself amongst the flaxen sacks of the stored provisions and raised side-on casks of ale and wine. The seeping fire smoke mingled with the heady musk of the tinder-dried spices arrayed on the shelves—arriving from near and far, the sharp smell of cloves, ginger, cinnamon and more. Since returning from Ireland, Rob had been inseparable from his father. As often happens, the taste of the unknown and our own deeds drive us homeward to the people and places we know.

Seeing the anguish in my face as I pushed open the door, Alice immediately turned to her two men.

'You two have a lot to do, so off with you now.'

'No, we're fine, Mam,' Rob said. 'All finished for the day.' He sat back contented, musing into his mug of ale.

Ewan looked at his wife, feeling the instant change of atmosphere in the cosy cellar as only a husband can after years of marriage, as if the window had been thrown open to a sharp frost. Following Alice's eyes over his shoulder, he saw me.

'Oh,' he said. 'You're right, Alice, I just remembered.' He stood up.

'What?' Rob objected. 'Well, not me. I'm fine here.'

'Rob! We're busy . . . get off your arse. Let's go. Now!' Ewan made himself clear with a hint of the sergeant's authority in his tone. That did it instantly. Rob jumped to his feet and obediently followed his father out, looking puzzled.

Alice closed the door behind them and turned to me. Holding me at arm's length, she took a moment to sense the depth of my pain.

'Sit down.' She led me to the cushioned high-backed chair Rob had vacated near the fire. Taking my cloak, she fetched me a cup of diluted wine and waited for me to calm myself. I could see the circular ripples on the surface of the transparent ruby liquid caused by the shaking of my hand.

'Take your time, Aoife. Drink slowly . . . breathe deeply.'

I gripped the cup tightly with both hands, the ripples heightening. A slight heave as a sob rose from my belly, through my arms, rattling my grip, spilling the wine on my skirt. Alice gently took the cup from my trembling hands, placed it on the table, looked at me hard. Then she swallowed me in her deep embrace. I wept.

After a time, when I had exhausted myself in her warmth, she softly released her grip, as if having squeezed the pain from my body.

'There now, girl.' She looked into my eyes, searching for a hint of my grief. 'What is it? Tell me now.'

My own distress did not lessen as I recounted my torment. If anything, the agony reflected in her kind face increased the hollowing misery I felt from the base of my tongue to my loins. I would not unsee in a hurry the violation I would endure. I suffered the indignity long, and many times, in that moment. How our minds can punish us like nothing else can. This pain before the deed. What pain would I endure after it was done?

I vomited suddenly, arching forward, one violent retch, the splash rebounding from the hard stone floor to catch the hem of Alice's dress, the reddish tinge of the wine staining the linen.

Calmly she rose, and after handing me a cup of fresh water, she wiped my face clean with a soft rose-scented cloth. I felt it's cool chill on my burning skin.

She filled a pail with sawdust from the barrel in the corner kept for the many spills which occurred in the kitchens and cellars. Scattering it around our feet, silently we watched the white purity of the sawdust darken from within, a spreading pink tinge deepening to the red.

We remained silent.

Eventually, in almost a whisper, I said, 'If I say anything, they will kill Montmorency . . . but then Eanna will also die, and we will lose everything'

Alice, still staring at the damp sawdust, simply nodded her head.

'What do I do?'

Alice offered nothing. When she did lift her head and turn to me, I could see the tears in her eyes.

'Aoife,' she said, and gripped my two hands. 'I cannot advise you on this.' She shook her head. 'This decision must be yours . . . and yours alone. You will live with it, and its consequences, either way for the rest of your life.' Letting go of my hands, she rose and stood by the fire hearth.

In that room, warmed by the glowing, summer-seasoned logs, with the woman who had become my dearest friend, almost a mother to me now, I had never felt so alone. It was the dawning of the darkness that is the solitude of life.

She slowly resumed her seat beside me and draped her arm around my hunched shoulders. My clenched hands loosened to ease a flow of colour to my fingers.

'Aoife, only you can decide; your blood will present you with many unpalatable choices in life. However, whatever you decide will be the right thing for you to do.'

Then, wishing to ease my anguish a little, she continued.

'For what it's worth, there are those in priestly robes who will say that a woman's virtue should never be willingly compromised . . . a sin of the highest order, they will say.' She paused now.

'If they have stood over their child's grave, as I have, I will listen. If not, they should wrap their certainties in their priestly garbs and, how do I put this politely, depart . . . they know not of what they speak.'

That faint light which lit one path offered some guidance as to what I already knew I must do.

'Alice. I need lavender scent.'

However, I also knew that one day I would murder Montmorency. I needed him now to make sure that army came to Ireland to save Eanna. That done, I would kill him.

❦

I NEVER SPOKE AGAIN before I left my chamber to go to his quarters. Alice had knocked on my door and entered silently. Never catching my eye, she washed me from a large pail of lukewarm water she carried from the cauldron in the kitchen. Steering me to the small, cushioned stool by the fire, she stood behind me, combing my hair. The slow rhythmic pull of the comb and her fingertips caressing my scalp produced a soothing trancelike calm.

I stood naked and she caressed the lavender scent along my neck, over my shoulders, between my breasts. Raising my arms, summoning a childhood memory evoked by the smothering motherly care, she draped a beautiful ankle-length muslin chemise over my shoulders, lacing the short ribbons at my neck. Wordlessly.

Producing a damask gown with ornate embroidery, discarded by some noble lady visitor to the castle or a mistress Strongbow, she turned me and laced the cords at the small of my back.

'You will wear these garments once and only once. You will return directly to my cellar when it is over. There I will bathe you and we will burn these and all they are in the fire. It will be done then.' Again, she would not catch my eye.

Fetching a pair of bright yellow slippers, she knelt and slipped them onto my feet. I steadied myself with my hand on her shoulder.

She rose and busied herself with her boxes. 'Strongbow is now with the king's messenger. They are dining in the hall above the kitchens.' She paused, caught my gaze briefly before turning quickly away. 'It is time.' She sat on the stool, almost with her back to me, stony-faced. She would not be the one to weaken my resolve. I knew she felt the revulsion as much as, if not more than, I.

Tightly clasping my long cloak to my neck against the wintry chill and pulling the hood, I lifted the latch and left.

※

THE WIND HELD Strongbow's swallow-tailed banners pointing south. I hugged the north wall of the middle bailey against the intermittent flurries of rain, which pounced every time I lifted my head. I could feel the pebbles through the thin soles of Alice's parlour slippers.

I hurried, not wanting to meet anyone. My long cloak hid my dress and slippers, hardly appropriate for the battlements, but nothing could mask my dread to any but the blind.

The hooded crows screeched mockingly, unseen from the heights of the Great Tower as I passed from the courtyard, through the arched gate and into the narrow gallery that ran along its north side. The torchlight reflected from the stone arch as I approached, heightening the blackness beyond. A large crow, taken by the wind, almost caught my hood before recovering itself and squawking noisily, careening skyward. There were no chattering swallows to guide my path on this dark winter's evening. I would walk this path alone.

The long arcaded gallery was unlit. Connecting the upper and middle baileys of the castle, the weakly pointed openings overlooking the river took little light from the night. Through the open door at the far end, I could see the well-lit courtyard beyond, along with the winch for the stone cistern that stood at the base of the cliff. The cistern had been built above the high-tide waterline to catch the fresh water flowing from a vigorous spring. Lack of water being the greatest threat to the defenders of a castle under siege, it readily provided a secure supply for the garrison's needs.

Sharply framed in the light of the doorway, I could see the large bucket used to carry the water dangling there, buffeted by the wind, sounding a hollow thump against the timber frame. A recurring, rhythmic drumbeat accompanying my slowing footsteps, my sinking heart.

I sensed a presence in the impenetrable darkness of the corridor. Turning from the river, it was upon me before I knew, the scarce light catching a buckle, a touch of skin. Moving towards me, with the advantage of the light, the bulk reached out. I recoiled and almost stumbled against the wall. I felt hands grip my shoulders.

'M'lady. Forgive me, I startled you.'

Strongbow said this with an even voice, but whether it

was a trick of the moving light and shadow or something else, his eyes blazed with a depth of anger over a hard-set grimace I had not seen before. His tight grip betrayed the intensity within. I saw an acidity in that anger, a threatening bitterness of barely suppressed violence. His grip tightened, his eyes flickering amongst options. I braced myself.

He loosened his grip.

'Aoife, I'm glad you're here . . . and now.'

He took me by the arm and led me through the doorway into the light of the courtyard, out of earshot form the Great Tower and any guards who might be lurking in the shadows. Satisfied we were alone, he turned to me.

'I had to leave the table. I couldn't contain my anger. However, I couldn't show it either.' He paced before me; suppressing the venom in his voice to a whisper, he told me of the king's continuing animosity towards him. In spite of his having spent the greater part of the previous year escorting the king's daughter to her marriage to the king of Saxony, or of his constant presence at court to do the king's bidding, or of his having brought his followers to Northumbria to suppress some recalcitrant nobles, the king steadfastly refused to relinquish his enmity towards him. It was impossible.

The king, through his messenger, had again refused to recognise his title as Earl of Pembroke and, outrageously, had openly spoken of his musings on granting the title and lands to more favoured lords in his court. The atmosphere at the table in the dining hall was tense. Sir Raymond Le Gros, Sir Robert FitzStephen and Sir Maurice FitzGerald were all present. They had come in hope of a truly deserved return to favour for Strongbow, which would revive the prospects for our entire camp. They now sat, stony-faced to the last, appalled by the maddening stubbornness of the king, whose bitterness was destroying any prospects for a revival for any of their fortunes. After many years of such ill treatment by the king, if their loyalty was to be forever spurned, what was the point in it?

'I know exactly what they are all thinking in there.' Strongbow's frustration was evident.

'One wrong word from me, and it will be open rebellion. That bastard lackey of the king, who seems to be enjoying this, will be sucking his balls for dessert if he's not careful.'

Recovering himself, he continued. 'Sorry, Aoife, forgive me. I shouldn't use such intemperate language with a lady.'

'I have heard worse, m'lord.' I smiled.

Pausing, he turned to me, regarding me closely, then he laughed. A gentleness returned to his face as he approached and, smiling, took my hands.

'Aoife, when I first met you over two years ago, you were a child. Before me now, I see a woman. A woman of great beauty with greater depth in your eyes. You have a strength I have not seen before.' He paused now, as if measuring each of his next words. He was a man of great honour, and once his word was given, it would never be retracted.

'Aoife. I will come to Ireland. On that, you have my word. I will be honoured . . . privileged that you will be my wife. Together we will build a kingdom. But for now, I must go back to this king's bastard and feign loyalty. That I must do until the time is right.'

And with that he was gone from the light of the courtyard, back through the door leading through the gallery to the middle bailey.

I stood alone, numbed, staring at his receding silhouette passing through the long dark corridor. A drop, another, a patter, then a loud crack of thunder and a deluge poured from unseen clouds in the ink-black sky. I was instantly drenched in its intensity. Throwing back my hood, I craned my neck to feel the force of the heavy drops hitting my face, my lips, my eyelids, rivulets filling my ears and streaming chillingly yet refreshingly down my neck, around my breasts, over my belly, my loins, down my legs. I looked down to see the delicate yellow slippers filled with the stream of water, lavender-fragranced water, washed, cleaned from my body into the earth. I would detest the smell of that flower for as long as I lived.

Inhaling deeply of the rich earthly dampness a rainfall rises, my eye caught a dark form standing in the grey shadows on the wooden landing at the top of the stairs. Montmorency stood watching me. How long he had been there and what he had heard, I did not know. Pausing for a moment more, he turned and was briefly framed in the doorway by the light from the fire within before he was gone.

I burst through the door of Alice's cellar, trailing a stream of water, and threw myself into her arms. Eventually calming me and extracting the course of events since I had left her not long before, she was overjoyed. We first cried and then laughed. We laughed more and celebrated my good fortune, that lucky turn of fate. When Rob and Ewan returned, Myler was with them. Seeing me there, they at first moved to leave immediately, but Alice happily insisted they remain and join us in some ale and wine to see the evening out.

Our high spirits sustained us throughout the evening and into the early hours. We sang and joked and recounted tall tales, hidden from the castle in the depth of the cellar. I could see the men looking quizzically at one another as the evening wore on, Ewan shaking his head knowingly at the two younger men: you could never fathom a woman.

Chapter Thirteen
PREPARING FOR WAR

Chepstow Castle, Wales
Early 1169

Preparations began immediately. Strongbow had convened his war council the following day, after the king's messenger had departed. The sullen faces gathered around the long table in the Great Tower transformed instantly in a surge of excitement when Strongbow disclosed his intentions. True to his word, he had invited me to attend; with my father and Donal in Ireland, I would be a valuable source of local knowledge. Sitting at the table, it seemed more like a family gathering of the Geraldines, with Robert FitzStephen, Maurice FitzGerald, Raymond Le Gros and Myler. Montmorency, sullen for once, was also present. He avoided my eyes.

While it would be impossible to hide their preparations for war, they could disguise their intent. Word would be put out that Strongbow was preparing a smaller force to be available to do the king's bidding, as he had informed his messenger the evening before. The Geraldines had been dismayed to hear this; they saw little point in expending further energies in the cause of an ungrateful king.

Now, understanding Strongbow's ruse, they sat forward, their smiles and nodding heads eagerly anticipating the campaign plans. They knew Strongbow was not one for haste and would only have acted as he did with well-formed plans. They were not disappointed.

There would be two phases to the landing. This suited the time available and the scrutiny his actions would attract from the king and his spies. In the first phase, a small force would depart in late spring, when the weather was favourable and adequate preparations were complete. This would be a force of approximately six hundred men in total. It would be led by Sir Robert FitzStephen, who would be accompanied by Myler, his cousins Miles FitzWilliam and Robert de Barry, the archdeacon's brother. Three ships would sail from St Davids, and two from Milford. Dividing the preparations between the two ports would attract less attention. Maurice de Prendergast, a Flemish lord from Rhos in South Wales and a close ally of Stronbow, would sail from Milford.

Like me, the men around the table were taken aback by the extent of Strongbow's planning. This had not been conceived overnight. Having listened to FitzGodebert's account of the battle at Cill Osnadh, he believed the force would require approximately five hundred Welsh longbow men, forty knights and sixty men-at-arms, some mounted and some on foot, as well as two ships capable of transporting approximately twenty horses each. These vessels would need to be acquired and adapted for these purposes. Much discretion was required in this task, and for this reason Strongbow turned to Myler and, asking his forgiveness for identifying him as a junior member of his followers, asked him to source these ships and to see to their preparation. He would attract less attention in the ports than his uncles, who were more widely known as his men.

Maurice FitzGerald and Raymond Le Gros would assist in the preparation for the first expedition and the wider planning for the second, which would follow with a more considerable force as soon as possible, but probably not until the Spring of the following year. Strongbow would accompany this second force.

'In the meantime, I will do everything I can to cajole the king into giving me permission to sail. However, once I sail, you will all understand . . .' He did not finish the sentence.

The consequences for Strongbow were clear to everyone in the room. Open defiance of the king would mean he would forfeit his lands and titles. There were many ambitious lords in the king's court only too willing to accept the grant of his ancestral lands from the king. If the campaign in Ireland was not successful, there would be no home to retreat to in Wales for any of them.

If it was successful, it would at the very least mean banishment in Ireland. Most probably, the king would not be willing to tolerate a defiant lord of growing power and wealth on the western edge of his most precious kingdom, Britain. A rebellious lord could embolden others. The more successful he became in Ireland, the more certain would be the king's arrival with a formidable army to crush him. The whole venture was a huge gamble. The only possibility of a good outcome for them would be for their success to be of such magnitude that the king would be reluctant to do battle with a sizeable, well-prepared force on unfamiliar ground. In those circumstances, he would calculate it best to reach an accommodation with Strongbow. This would require significant sacrifices of the gains they would make to the king, but it could work. Although Henry was ruthless, as all great kings must be, he was no fool.

'Gentlemen, now you understand my full intent. Each man who commits to accompany me must do so in the full knowledge of the consequences.' Strongbow paused, looking around the table at each man in turn for their understanding; one by one they nodded their heads.

'Thank you,' he continued. 'Now I am asking each of you for an oath of silence and your steadfast commitment to the end.'

A longer pause now. Then he looked at me and said, 'M'lady, you have mine. I will see this venture through to the end, whatever that may be.'

The room was silent when he finished. The men present understood the magnitude of the decision they were making. It had far-reaching consequences for them and their families. If their mission failed, those who sailed would not survive the king's wrath if they did not die in Ireland. Their families would be impoverished if they lived, and their name would forever be tainted with the stain of treachery—an offence this king would never forgive, as his treatment of Strongbow had shown.

Nonetheless, their minds were clear. Norman blood ran rich with ambition. Bred for battle, they could not be idle. A king who would disrespect their family name, who would deny them their birthright, who would wilfully deprive them of the opportunity to acquire land and wealth, who would in fact threaten the confiscation of what they possessed, was not a king who deserved their following. The heavy silence in the room did not betray an unwillingness; rather, it held the weight of the implications of the decision they would make. It was Maurice FitzGerald who broke the silence. He was a man of few words, more inclined to action, but his judgement was highly respected by all. He spoke slowly but deliberately.

'M'lord.' All eyes turned to him. 'This English king does

AOIFE OF LEINSTER

not regard us as one of his kind. An Irish king has requested our help against invaders who have unjustly stolen his kingdom and are laying waste to the entire island. We are unwelcome in the kingdom of the English king and can help undo an injustice in Ireland. I say we go to Ireland and make common cause and our futures amongst them.'

Rising, he placed his right hand to his chest and pledged his sword to Strongbow. Then, each man present rose in turn and made his own oath.

The crack as Strongbow slammed his hand on the table shook me. He laughed loudly and shouted for wine, embracing each of them in turn. He seemed invigorated by the decision.

Raising his cup, he urged them all to drink deeply, for from this moment forward there would be little rest until they achieved their aims in Ireland and settled terms with the king of England.

'To Ireland.'

THE EARLY MONTHS of the year were cold but dry as the castle bustled with activity. In the meadows outside the walls, the comforting quiet before each dawn was replaced with the harsh cursing of the sergeants and the pounding of hooves as the drilling intensified. The clamour spoiled those stolen moments I had enjoyed each morning before the farrier stoked his furnace and bawled his threats at the stable lads to awaken them from their sluggish ramblings. I suffered this gladly.

The sheltered dell outside the south curtain wall of the castle whistled with arrows. The archers had set their butts to the west end. I watched them pacing the distances and gauging the accuracy of their shots in the changing winds, leaving as little as possible to chance, their deadly skills honed daily. One consolation was the discontent of the hooded crows, disturbed by the constant flights of arrows. To no avail, they bawled their complaints loudly from their eyries on the roof of the Great Tower.

I watched the entirety of it all as the weeks passed, the detailed planning, the exhaustive preparations, the constant drilling, the weaponry skills, the hammering from the forge. Body armour, lances, swords, flails, battleaxes, war hammers—our armies would never best these Normans in the field of battle. From what I saw, the small force of six hundred that was planned for the first landing would probably prevail against any Irish army. A force of many thousands, which Strongbow told me King Henry would someday bring to Ireland, would easily devastate and subjugate the entire island.

I knew we had a lot to learn, and quickly, if we were to be prepared to defend ourselves against the king's ambitions. However, the more I saw, the more certain I was our men could never beat them in the field; they could only be brought to our ways by our women in their beds. Let our men learn the skills of weaponry and battle from them, while our women marry them and bear their children. After all, it is women, for the most part, who teach children the ways of the land—language, customs, even the law itself. Tumbling from these beds, I imagined these children would fare well in this uncertain world.

There was some unwelcome news when Myler told me Montmorency would accompany us. He was surprised at this as Montmorency was not a man who could be relied upon in battle and avoided placing himself in any danger. However, Montmorency was very keen to go and persuaded Strongbow saying he alone had explicit permission from the king to go to Ireland and that his inclusion gave the campaign some legitimacy. Strongbow agreed and had even given him some authority in the affair. Myler was certain he had also sown doubt in Strongbow's mind about the trustworthiness of the Geraldines. Myler's uncles were not pleased.

Regardless, Myler had quickly sourced two large trading barques with sufficiently low draughts that would beach on the sands at Bannow Island. We would not be disembarking at the deep-water quay in the bay from where we had fled, as it was too vulnerable to attack; we would land on the island instead.

Docked at the quays beneath the castle on the Wye, work commenced immediately to adapt the two boats to carry the horses. In centuries of warfare in the lands around the Mediterranean, the Norman's had perfected the techniques for transporting horses by sea. The bellies of the boats were stripped and the planking above the hull was strengthened to take the weight of the horses. Their iron shoes were to be removed for the journey to take the force from their kicks, which could damage the hull and other horses. Heavy iron rings were secured into each side of the hull and to the supporting joists of the deck above the horses.

At over thirteen hands, they were large animals compared to those we had in Ireland. Understanding the importance of horse breeding to their success in warfare, the Normans had taken the bloodstock from southern European lands, particularly the Iberian breeds, and produced larger, more powerful animals capable of carrying a fully armoured knight while also having the dexterity and bravery required in battle. In Ireland and Britain, the knowledge of horse breeding had not developed as we fought our battles on foot, simply using horses as a means of transport to a battlefield. As in all times, it is the needs of war which accelerate the perfection of the means—in this case, the horses.

The Norman horses used in battle were known as coursers. They were not their heaviest horses, which were destriers, used mostly for jousting. Strongbow possessed several such animals in his stables. I saw one giant of an animal which stood at fifteen hands.

Though lighter, the coursers were very fast and strong. Being highly bred, they were full-blooded, hard to handle and stallions for the most part. They did not geld these animals as the knights used their fierce temperament to charge down shield walls bristling with spears, kicking and biting as they went. I had seen one animal rip the muscle clean from a man's arm. It was not a pleasant sight. I was wary of these beasts.

Keeping the stallions under control during the sea journey was essential. Too close, and they would fight savagely, causing injuries, and they were too valuable for that. More importantly, if the weight of twenty heavy animals shifted awkwardly in a shallow-bottomed boat with a low keel, it could easily capsize.

As the work progressed, Myler showed me how each animal was separated by a wooden stall. Their head collars were attached face-on to the hull over a food trough, keeping their powerful hind legs away from the timbers of the boat. A kick from one of these animals could knock a plank and hole the boat. Canvas slings were attached to the iron rings on either side of the hull. When the horses were loaded, the slings were passed under their bellies, and they were were hoisted. Suspended in this way, just above the deck, the horses were surprisingly calm. Even in this, the Normans left nothing to chance. With the work on the boats complete and the time for our departure approaching, the horses were walked daily to the boats, loaded and hoisted. They were then fed. Each animal was assigned a stall with familiar travelling companions on either side. Horses, like humans, have their likes and dislikes. An ill-chosen neighbour would provoke a vicious fight between two high-blooded stallions—something best avoided in the confined space of a ship's hull. The horses became quickly used to the routine, and eager for their food, they strained on their lead ropes to mount the gangplanks, dragging their handlers to their stalls.

With some reluctance Strongbow agreed that I would accompany the first expedition, bringing Conor with me. He did so on the condition that upon arriving in Ireland, I would retreat to the safety of Ferns and remain there. I never explicitly agreed to do this, although I admit, he would be forgiven for believing otherwise.

Myler was delighted that our friend Rob Smith had been given charge of the archers. His father, Ewan, who had always led the archers on campaigns with Strongbow, would travel with the main force next year. Rob was cock-a-hoop and strode about the castle with an exaggerated sense of self-importance. Myler took every opportunity to disavow him of this, much to everyone's amusement.

Towards the end of April, all was ready; Strongbow convened one final war council, a long, tedious affair in which each detail of the preparations was examined exhaustively. Not without justification, I must say, for several matters were rightly not to Strongbow's satisfaction and were rectified. Myler himself attracted his displeasure for provisioning the horse transports with just two days' fodder and water. Strongbow insisted on four, and the departure for St Davids was delayed for a day while Myler saw to it.

Finally, the day came, and the empty boats sailed for St Davids. We would bring the horses overland through Chepstow and meet them on the quay there. We said our farewells. It was a bittersweet moment with Alice, my friend. She assured me she would be accompanying Strongbow next year, but for now, I would miss her. I seemed to be forever weeping in her arms.

We filed through the gates of the gate towers. I had taught my mare to trust me with no saddle. Strongbow had given her to me for the return to Ireland. She was a beautiful chestnut-coloured animal with a lovely temperament. I had named her Millie, from my own language, for her gentleness and strength.

Initially she was uncomfortable with the feel of my thighs on her back and my legs around her belly, but she gradually settled, becoming more confident that I would not be unseated—that I knew what I was doing. There was a bond that sometimes developed between a human and a horse, an understanding of mutual respect and care in which the animal would slowly come to know its rider and understand that it would not be set to any task beyond it. Each would know the other's mind, almost rendering the reins or legs unnecessary. In return for this care, the horse would do all it could to protect its rider. Even when startled, it would move in a way to keep them seated.

And so it happened. In the confines of the gate towers, in the last week of April, Millie spooked sharply, shifting suddenly to the left, but she moved quicker to catch my following weight and keep me on her back. A streak of white as the underbelly of a swallow brushed my hair. Another, a flurry, forcing us back. Millie retreated into the courtyard. The chattering exuberance, the excited joy . . . the summer was approaching, and they had returned. My swallows, swooping, circling in a wide arc and breaking back through the gates into the courtyard.

It was a joy to see them. I would miss them this year on the castle walls, but today I was leaving for Ireland and the horses shied from the gates; they would not let us pass. We sat watching, waiting for this strange display to end.

Fáinleog! My short sword. My hand searched my hip for her scabbard. I jumped from my mare and ran to my chamber, reached under my bed. In the confusion and hurry, I had forgotten her.

When I returned to the courtyard, breathless, the others remained where I had left them, standing and watching the curious behaviour of the swallows, their horses unwilling to chance the gates. I jumped onto Millie's back and, with Fáinleog on my hip, squeezed her gently through to the line of waiting horses, under the towers and out the gates. The swallows did not interfere.

Thank you, my friends. And now to war, to bring Eanna home.

Chapter Fourteen
RETURNING HOME

Wexford
May 1169

The brisk southwesterly wind blew steadily over the port gunnels bellying the sails, pitching the ships slightly. The rolling swell was gentle, not enough to cause the bow to rise a wash of spray over the deck. If it stayed like this, we would soon pass along the south coast of Ireland and make landfall on Bannow Island not long after dawn. We had departed in the early evening on the last day of April.

As it happened, the wind stayed steady as the swell rose slightly in the night, the echo of a storm at sea in some distant southern place. Regardless, there was no mood for sleep in our ships. The men were tense. An army was most vulnerable when landing. If they were not already aware of our plans, our enemies would soon see for themselves, when the dawn would betray our presence.

We had planned to rendezvous with de Prendergast's two ships, sailing from Milford, off the coast of St Davids. With no sighting by late evening, we had no choice but to set the sails and hope they would soon appear in our wake. We needed to land in force if we were to meet any resistance, but equally, we needed the cover of darkness to mask our passage along the southern Irish coastline.

All ship lights were doused, and FitzStephen called for complete quiet as we passed along the dark bulk of the land to our north—the strong wind would easily carry the sounds of heavily manned ships to the land. The only sounds now were the whinnying of the horses, a sound that would quickly betray our presence and purpose to any ears that caught the wind. But there was no avoiding that or the rhythmic scrape of well-sharpened blades on whetstones, more for solace than for any better edge it would give their weapons. Some had no spit to wet their stones, their mouths dry with the apprehension of what the dawn would bring.

When it broke, our three ships sailing in tight formation would arouse immediate suspicion. If our enemies were waiting, they would follow us and be ready to attack. They would plan to let us make shore, then come as we tried to disembark.

In the growing pale light of dawn in the east, we strained for a hint of sail; de Prendergast's ships did not appear.

We had timed our arrival with high tide. With the narrow channel flooded between Bannow Island and the headland where the town of Bannow stood, any attackers would be unable to assault the island until we were fully ashore and arrayed for an assault.

The townsfolk from the small town of Bannow would be alarmed at our approach by now. The wind whisked the smoke from the homes northward, and I could see figures moving along the shore, following our progress. I shuddered at the bitter memory of Eanna kneeling beneath O'Rourke's sword on that very spot almost three years ago. Was it that long? He would have grown so much, changed from a child to a boy. I hoped his joyous, mischievous ways had remained with him. *Not long now,* I sent my promise on the wind; *not long, Eanna, before we come for you.*

As expected, the beach of the island came into view; the narrow channel surged with the flowing tide. Impassable now from the headland, it would remain so until the ebbing tide would, for a brief while, allow a crossing on foot. Now was the time to land; there could be no attack for several hours.

The incessant salty Atlantic wind which scoured the island stunted anything but the coarse grass which offered meagre grazing for the few cattle, which I could see scattered across the exposed shallow rise. The owners of these cattle would doubtless be worried now as they saw us turning our bows for the shore. It was hard to demand payment from an army.

I had pointed FitzStephen to the narrow sandbar that stood westward from the south of the island. There, deep water met the shore, allowing the boats to beach their bows on the sand. We braced against the shudder of the hull scraping over the shingle and crunching to a lurching halt as the loosened sails flapped languidly in the wind.

The men-at-arms, readied for battle, jumped into the shallow wash and surged to the beach to gain sounder ground, the stony surface below the tideline causing many to lose their footing. Although FitzStephen had placed archers on the high decks commanding the strand, I was glad there was no welcoming party—it would not have been an easy landing.

With a clear view across the breadth of the island, and the channel in flood, any threat of an immediate attack was gone. However, ever cautious, the men worked with an urgency to unload the ships. Long wooden gangplanks were placed to guide the horses first from the bellies of the boats and then down from the starboard gunnels and onto the beach. Mounds of provisions steadily appeared: bundles of bowstaves, sheeves of arrows, buckets of arrowheads, kite-shaped shields, lances, swords, breastplates, greaves, maces, flails. Barrels of ale, wine, water, bread, hard cheese, dried meat. Several cages of squawking chickens and alarmed rabbits. The Normans brought them on campaign as a manageable source of fresh meat; they bred quickly and tasted good. We did not have rabbits in Ireland, and I remember seeing a carelessly handled cage falling and breaking on the stones. The rabbits quickly scurried across the sand dunes. *Now* we had rabbits in Ireland.

Our caution proved unnecessary. As the day wore on and no horsemen appeared on the headland, we became more confident. The pace slackened, and several hours later, as the tide receded and the channel became passable, a rider was dispatched to Ferns to alert my father of our arrival. Avoiding the enemy, he would reach Ferns by nightfall. He was to urge my father to hasten to Bannow in force to join with the Norman army.

With the rider on his way and the tide flowing to close the channel, there was little chance we could be assaulted until the light of the following day. A precautionary defensive position was arranged above the channel, but on the whole, the night was passed comfortably in the tents on the shoreline by the ships.

The following morning brought the welcome sight of the full-bellied sails of de Prendergast's two ships from Milford rounding the far head, several miles distant. In the favourable wind, which had held, they made straight for the shore and were soon beached alongside the other three ships. I watched ten knights and over two hundred archers and foot soldiers disembark. They were warmly welcomed by

FitzStephen, whose small army had just doubled in size. He clearly knew many of these men, and he embraced each of the knights and spoke to the men. They were mostly Flemings, as were a sizeable part of his own followers. Gerald de Barry had jokingly referred to us as the Fleet of the Flemings, there were so many of them. But the archers were mostly Welshmen, and there was a scattering of French and a few English too.

As the evening drew in, an alarm was raised when a body of armed horsemen appeared on the headland. The reddening light of dusk reflected from the steel of their weapons. Their numbers swelled as we watched. They remained motionless, watching, not venturing to the channel. The ebbing tide was receding rapidly, and the channel would soon be passable. FitzStephen bawled at the foot soldiers to form even battle lines, two ranks opposite the channel. The archers were arrayed on the higher ground behind the foot soldiers. I could see Rob calmly checking their positions and lines of fire. At almost four hundred, I knew the death they would unleash from the sky; they planted their arrows in reach in the ground around them.

Myler split the knights into two groups of twenty to flank the foot soldiers in the centre. He commanded one flank, and his cousin Miles FitzWilliam the other. Robert FitzStephen sat on his courser behind the foot soldiers, a practiced calm observing a field of battle. I noticed Montmorency yet further back again, surrounded by his own few men. This battle formation was achieved quickly and with minimal fuss. It was one of several I had seen them practice at Chepstow.

The dusk stole the light. A solitary horseman left the headland and approached the channel. I could see Fitz-Stephen, and Myler riding to meet him. They reached the centre of the channel, and through the gathering gloom I was surprised to see Myler reach forward and embrace the rider. They turned, and the three cantered through the ranked army and up the shallow hill to where I stood.

Donal.

❦

As the night closed in and we were alone, Donal told me that upon hearing of our landing, my father had gathered what forces he could overnight, dispatching riders to the kinsmen throughout Leinster. There was understandable reluctance in our allies, as a great many had almost paid with their lives at the debacle at Cill Osnadh. Only the most loyal, or those whom he could coerce, joined him. A meagre force of a few hundred Uí Chennselaig, mostly cavalry, had left Ferns that day at noon to ride to Bannow.

However, as fast as a horse could ride, the word of the arrival of a vast army landing from a fleet of ships had spread quickly, amplified no doubt by the news bearers: *the waters of Bannow Bay barely visible between the crowded ships, vast hordes of steel-clad warriors, belching from the bowels of three masted warships, teeming with men and horses, the shallows churning as they surged ashore*—a messenger's status heightened, at least in their own eyes, by the force of their message.

And so on their journey south they had been joined by the men of two of the smaller dynasties of Leinster, the Uí Lorcáin and the Uí Duibginn, promising loyalty and support to my father. These two families, who had not long before deserted my father, their rightful king, saw no shame in rushing to his side now, for the strongest prevailed; such was the way of Irish affairs. A man knew no greater loyalty above that to his own clan. Beyond that, alliances were decided on the family's best interests; if a side must be chosen, it was the one most likely to win.

And as my father had always acted solely in our family's interest, he expected nothing more from the other dynastic families of Leinster. He had warmly welcomed them. They now stood at over five hundred men, camped on the headland above the channel. They would remain there for the rest of the night as the channel was once again impassable. They would wait until dawn to join their forces.

For my father was also cautious. He had not met any of these Normans for over two years. In addition, apart from the occasional messenger, there had been no contact since Myler, Rob, Conor and I had slipped away from the willow thicket by the monastery more than a year ago. Nevertheless, the arrival of a Norman force on the south coast of his kingdom was welcome if they had indeed come to support his cause. There was nothing to suggest otherwise, but his years as a king had taught him not to trust anyone. Accustomed to the fickle tides of loyalty in Ireland, he needed assurance that his erstwhile allies remained of one mind and true to him. If not, he would be forced to quickly seek the support of O'Connor and O'Rourke to oppose them. He would be loath to do this, but he knew they would agree, it being in their interests to expel these Normans before they gained a foothold. However, O'Connor's burning ambition was to occupy the throne of Ireland as high king by subjugating the other kingdoms to which he had no right, including Leinster. My father would pay a heavy price for his help.

However, Donal was pleased when I reassured him of Strongbow's commitment to us. But he was disappointed with the size of the army we had brought and that Strongbow himself was not present. They had hoped for a much larger force that would weaken the resolve of any opposition we might face; the smaller an army, the more fighting it must do. That said, he understood the prowess in warfare of these Normans. The combined force of over a thousand men would suffice until Strongbow arrived with the rest of his forces..

The following morning, when the channel once again allowed crossing, he rode back to my father with the assurances he required as to the intention of this army. My father was greatly encouraged when he discovered my presence and rode out to meet us as we crossed at the head of the mounted knights, the hooves of the heavy armour-clad animals sucking and popping in the soft sand of the estuary.

As we approached the shoreline, Montmorency splashed forward to greet my father.

'Lord King.' He bowed from the waist. 'You see, as promised.' He turned, gesturing to the army plodding cautiously across the silty causeway. 'I have brought you an army.' My father seemed to acknowledge this.

Surprised at this, but conscious of avoiding ill feeling on campaign, Myler murmured under his breath, 'By Christ, give me patience.' I could see the sentiment was shared by FitzStephen and the other riders around me. He had been a rare sight yesterday when there was the chance of a fight. I heard their grumblings.

The Uí Chennselaig cavalry and their allies waited on the lip of the headland, closely watching the actions of their king. How he behaved would determine if they were to march with or against these Normans today. They would not have relished the prospect of fighting the glittering array of polished steel and well-formed ranks which faced them.

However, having spoken to Donal, my father made a great show of welcoming the Norman leaders. Dismounting, he embraced each in turn, starting with Montmorency, kissing each as an overt show of peace and that no harm should come to these men. Henceforth, they were allies.

I could see the horses of the cavalry on the hill sensing

the release of tension in their riders' bodies. Several dropped their heads and began grazing the sparse salty grass. They ambled down the slope, and two armies mixed along the shore as the remaining Normans struggled through the muddy causeway, cursing in strange tongues, their sentiments clear to the Irish, who helped the heavily laden foot soldiers to the shore.

My father kissed me and held me in a long embrace. Releasing me he said, 'Aoife, *mo chailín. Go raigh maith agat.* Thank you.' His eyes glistened. 'I have missed you. Welcome home,' he said quietly.

'Thank you, father.' I kissed the cheek of the father I knew. Surprised, he looked at me. His fierce dark eyes, sunk in the deep hollows of his furrowed face, hardened by battle and a life under the elements in the saddle. A face I had seen change with life's each trial carving its own mark. But it was not he who had changed now. It was me.

I knew what I would have done and, what's more, what I would do to Montmorency, when the time came—and all for my family. Purity, innocence, virtue—what passes for honourable ways are indulgences when your blood pulls. What other unpalatable choices would I make? Who would judge me? Was failure to secure the interests of our family and our people the ultimate betrayal? Smaller sins, some not so small, were necessities, unavoidable. As said, clean hands or clean sheets seldom grace a throne.

There was a hint of the shape of the man behind the eyes now. A shadowy form I could all but recognise. Vague now . . . translucent, like half-polished steel, but more vivid than before. A reflection perhaps? My destiny?

A barely perceptible nod from him. A recognition. Some things were best left unsaid; private sins should remain so. Putting words on them gives them edges that can hurt. We must each carry our burdens alone.

Still looking at me, he placed his hand on my shoulder and seemed to struggle to find words. 'Tell me of your mother, Aoife? I hope she passed peacefully.' I knew he would have heard of her death these past months now, but I was taken aback at the pain that blazed briefly in his eyes, a momentary glimpse of the grief he held at her loss.

'Did she suffer?' he asked, and I could see the fear in his face at what he might hear.

'I was with her, Father.' I considered my words carefully. Unwilling to speak untruths but seeing his grief, I wanted to spare him. 'In the end, she parted peacefully and contented, holding my hand.' This was true.

I could see the relief releasing him somewhat. 'Thank you, Aoife.' He hesitated as if measuring his words. 'I loved her dearly' was all he said, staring across the sea to her resting place as if reaching out to her. I believed him.

I watched him, lost in his memories of a love of which I knew little but was starting to comprehend.

'Father,' I said, bringing him back. 'She spoke fondly of you.' I paused, unsure if I should speak further of that time long past. Deciding, I continued. 'She told me of Dearbhail, of what happened. That you did not abduct or abuse her.'

He turned to me now, listening intently. 'Why did you not say?' I asked. 'At Cill Osnadh, when O'Rourke humiliated you and the Brehon, Cormac, placed the fine on you? Why did you not say more?'

He sighed and gave a barely noticeable shake of his head.

'Aoife. That day they would have had our blood or our wealth,' he said. 'Cormac knows well what happened, I just had to remind him. I said enough to rile O'Rourke's anger and to let Cormac place a ferocious fine on me to appease O'Rourke. He was insufferable, I know, but we got away with our lives that day.'

I stared at him, dumbfounded. He smiled. 'Aoife, needs

must. Like you now, it's less about what I want or what's good for me than what's right for them.' He swept his arm broadly over the teeming strand. 'They are your people, your family. This is your land,' he said, nodding to the broad green expanse stretching north from where we stood.

'Whatever it takes, no matter how unpleasant or difficult it might be, you must act in their interest. That way you will secure your own.' He held my gaze as if to see my soul to know I understood my responsibility. Eventually, seemingly satisfied, he nodded.

'Good. But now we have matters to attend to,' he finished, and turned back to the beach. I stood there, watching him retreat along the shimmering sand as the tide gurgled rhythmically on the shingle, a man I was gradually coming to know.

Recovering myself, I ran to catch him before we joined the others, who had gathered behind a bramble thicket for some shelter from the persistent wind.

'Father, now that they are here, we must march straight to Osraige, to free Eanna. Mac Giolla Patrick will not harm him now. He will negotiate his release if we are quick, before he can be joined by O'Connor and O'Rourke.'

He stopped and looked at me. 'Aoife, I suspect you are right in that. But these men'—he gestured to FitzStephen, Montmorency and the other Normans waiting for us to join them—'these men have more to concern them than Eanna. I must give them the taste of the spoils of war quickly to whet their appetites.'

I knew he was right. FitzStephen and Myler's other uncle, Maurice FitzGerald, had been promised the lordship of Wexford, a lucrative prize; the taxes and customs levies from such a prosperous trading town would make them wealthy. Even though Eanna was now in more danger than at any moment, there needs had to be satisfied first.

'So we must move quickly, take Wexford and move immediately on Osraige to free Eanna. It's the only way, Aoife.' He walked on.

We joined the others. It was quickly decided that we would march to Wexford, twenty miles to the northeast. Although Waterford was an equal distance, it had better defences and a larger garrison. It would best be tackled with a larger force than we had gathered around us today. Besides, FitzStephen rightly pointed out that leaving such an important post as Wexford in hostile hands in our rear was not prudent. It was also agreed, at my father's insistence, that we would not dally in Wexford but would assault Mac Giolla Patrick in Osraige without delay. He too wanted his son back in the safety of Ferns.

Early success would also hasten others to join us and discourage our enemies, so orders were given that camp would be broken immediately after the men had eaten. FitzStephen insisted on this delay, knowing a hard day's marching and fighting lay ahead; there was nothing like an empty belly to dampen a man's enthusiasm for battle. We would reach Wexford by noon.

※

As our army marched slowly towards the town, we were, as expected, approached by several bodies of men from some of the lower families of South Leinster wishing to join our ranks. Known to my father, they had been, in better times, his vassals, who had then abandoned him to his fate after our defeat at Ferns and our hurried flight to Wales. However, seeing my father's return at the head of a strong army, they judged that his fortunes had turned and unashamedly offered their support and expected to be welcomed into his army. And they were.

Chapter Fifteen
A RACE AGAINST TIME

Wexford
May 1169

The Norsemen of Wexford had long resented the oversight of my father as king of Leinster. There was only ever a begrudging recognition of his authority—or any authority, for that matter—on the island. Their origins, although long past, were Scandinavian, and while their ways intertwined ever more with ours as the years passed, they retained a fiercely independent spirit that was first to abandon any subordination to the Leinster kings when the opportunity arose. Not seven years past, Donal had led a force to their strong stone walls to call to order some overly assertive Norse Tangs, forcing them by negotiation to temper their ambitions and to continue their recognition of my father as their overlord.

My father's current difficulties were their opportunity, and they had, as expected, taken the opportunity to forsake his authority once again. Being fully aware of our landing and the approach of our army and ever confident in their superior numbers, they had decided to meet us to settle the matter in an open field approximately a mile southwest of the town.

As we approached we could see their force, a darker mass gathered on the rising land of the low hill that lay between us and the town itself. They had chosen the ground well, with the slope below them and a small stream to their left flank that gave out to open marshy ground, which would impede any cavalry from that approach. The dense woodlands on their right flank served the same purpose, which would ultimately force our attack into a frontal assault into their well-arranged shield wall. Several ranks deep, the Norsemen knew they could withstand any assault from an Irish cavalry. They would wait behind the impenetrable layer of overlapping shields, gradually exhausting our horsemen on their bristling spears, glinting ominously in the midday sun. Then, advancing slowly down the hill, they could realistically anticipate victory.

But that was not what confronted them today. Without fuss, FitzStephen calmly proceeded at the head of the column to within five hundred paces and surveyed their ranks. He then ordered the army to assume the same formation as the previous evening, except the archers were to form up in front of the foot soldiers at two hundred paces from the Norse shield wall. The twin ranks of the soldiers were placed twenty paces to their rear, with the Norman knights flanking them, ready to assail any horsemen who might ride from the Norsemen to interfere with the work of the archers. FitzStephen asked my father and Donal to form up behind them and to act as reserves when he requested their intervention, should it be necessary.

FitzStephen and the Normans were not impressed with what they saw.

'I see no cavalry?' he asked Donal as they watched the silent Norse ranks on the slope.

'No,' he replied. 'They fight on foot. They are townsmen. Traders and craftsmen for the most part. They don't willingly venture too far from behind their walls, and they can disappear behind them just as quick. I'm surprised they've ventured out to meet us today.'

The early afternoon sun had dulled behind a thin cloud bank. It would take some heat from the sweating men-at-arms and knights taking their positions in the battlelines. The layers of padded jerkins, heavy chain mail and body armour took its toll on strength in the midday sun. Worse still, the knights sat encased in their helmeted cauldron of the woollen arming cap covered with the chainmail aventail, topped with the weight of the heavy helmets. They spared themselves until the last, with their visors raised to release what heat they could from their reddened faces.

However, in a fight it was always better to have the sun on your back, in your enemies' eyes. But today, hidden behind clouds, it would offer no help to the Normans or hindrance to the Norsemen who faced into it.

I watched as our battle formation quickly fell into place. It must have been chilling for the Norsemen to watch the minimalist efficiency of it all. What moments before had been an open grazed meadow, harmlessly sloping down a kindly hill, was now filled with an ominously silent, disciplined force of warriors who were wholly unfamiliar to the Norsemen. This was not what they had been expecting.

The soldiers drawn up in even ranks, covered in chain mail and helmeted to the last, their kite-shaped, brightly painted shields at the ready, were entirely new to them. The horsemen, their glistening armour draped with the coloured surcoats of their lords, held their lances skyward, their long swords, maces and flails at their sides. Such a body of archers, many hundreds, with the longbows of which they had heard so much, raining death from the sky. An ominous silence hung over the meadow.

'No archers to speak of,' FitzStephen observed. FitzGodebert's reports had been correct. This army was simply a mass of men gathered in one spot. From what FitzStephen could see, their tactic would be to use their superiority in numbers and the slope to bludgeon a defeat on us. There was no order to their ranks, no archers or cavalry for combined arms use with their foot soldiers. They fought today as the Anglo-Saxons had fought at Hastings over a hundred years ago. The battle that had decided the fate of England in one single afternoon, when six thousand Normans, led by William the Conqueror, had defeated and killed their king, Harold Godwinson, despite facing an army of over forty thousand men. Likewise, these Norsemen today expected their enemies to fight as they had always done.

'Well.' He seemed to shrug his shoulders. 'We will not oblige them. And the odds are far better today.' Turning to the man on his right, he ordered him to tell Rob Smith to have the archers ready. He was to have each archer loose twenty arrows in a continuous volley into the Norsemen on his command.

'Tell him to spare his bodkin arrowheads. They are unarmoured, from what I can see. So broadheads will serve adequately. He can recover the arrows from the bodies later.'

I shuddered at hearing this. The bodkin heads were narrow and heavy, designed for piercing armour. The broadheads, flat with swallow-tail shapes, were intended for tearing the flesh of men and animals. Once stuck, they were impossible to remove, ripping flesh and arteries if the victim survived and fled.

From watching them practice in the dell at Chepstow, I knew each archer could, at this distance, accurately unleash twenty arrows in the time it took to draw twenty breaths. So at twenty arrows a man, it would take these five hundred archers no time to rain ten thousand arrows into the two thousand Norsemen.

While they could scrape some protection from the round shields that many of them carried, particularly those in the front rank, FitzStephen told Donal he could confidently expect at least half the Norsemen to fall in the first volley.

Depending on the level of disarray in their ranks, he would order the mounted knights or the foot soldiers forward, but possibly another volley from the archers first. FitzStephen was chillingly casual in his manner.

While Rob prepared his archers, there was a shuffling in the ranks of the Norsemen. A rider passed repeatedly behind the ranks, bellowing orders we could not catch, the southerly breeze whisking his words to the north. A trickle of men in the rear ranks turned up the slope and began making their way over the low crest of the hill. Although it was not visible from this lower slope, I knew the town sat a short distance over the rise, stretching over the steeper slope that reached down to the shore of the estuary of the Slaney River.

Then their forward ranks began retreating quickly up the slope, keeping a watchful eye on us. They were soon out of bowshot; that advantage was lost to us. FitzStephen would not commit the cavalry, fearing the ruse of a feigned retreat, commonly used by the Normans to lure their opponents into an ambush. He flattered the Norsemen; they had no such plan.

Not liking what they saw arrayed before them, wiser heads had prevailed. They had decided to withdraw behind the proven barrier of their tall stone walls. They were quickly over the crest, and as we advanced slowly in formation up the slope, we could see plumes of smoke rising over the hill. When we reached the flat summit, the Norsemen were setting fire to the thatched roofs of the remaining timber buildings not yet ablaze in the suburb outside the town walls. They would destroy any cover the buildings might afford to us in an attack. With the fire raging, they withdrew over the wooden bridges that spanned the deep ditch beneath the high castellated stone walls. The bridges were destroyed; the heavy gates closed and barred.

'I don't know why they came out in the first place,' Donal said, a while later as we rode along the walls out of bowshot. FitzStephen nodded his head in agreement. This was a formidable fortress. The walls were teeming with warriors, confident now in their security behind them. Long built, of cut stone at the height of three or four men in places, with turrets interspaced and well-protected gates, it would not be easily taken if they defended well.

The shock force of mounted knights was of no use against stone walls; chain mail, armour and heavy weapons were a lot heavier when a man is struggling out of a muddy ditch to a sheer wall under a hail of fire from above. In addition, the men on the walls could easily shelter from archers when not under attack from an infantry. Our task had just become a whole lot harder.

The army FitzStephen had brought to Ireland was best suited to the open field, where they could use their heavy cavalry, their archers and the well-honed tactics I had seen them rehearse exhaustively at Chepstow. They had brought none of their siege weapons: the catapult, the trebuchet or the ballista, the bolt thrower. Regardless, we did not have time for a siege. We needed the momentum of victory. More importantly, I thought, each moment we were delayed in Wexford would further endanger Eanna. Hours mattered.

Knowing Donal had not long previously contested the town with the Norsemen, FitzStephen asked him to tell him what he knew of its layout and defences. He could tell from what he could see that as long as the town retained access to the sea with their fleet of boats, we could not starve them into submission. We must find a way to defeat them in an assault or to force their surrender.

Donal told FitzStephen the town had never been taken by force. The Norsemen had chosen the site well. Completely enclosed by the high walls, it was narrow and long. He had walked it at five hundred paces along the shore and the opposite wall, which faced us now. It was approximately two hundred paces deep, stretching down a steep slope from this wall to the quays. A small stream ran into the town, and it had ample freshwater wells to sustain the inhabitants in a siege. The ground on which we now stood was on a level with the south-westerly wall and offered no advantage in overlooking the town.

A larger stream ran to the southeast of the walls into a marshy basin beside the shoreline. Any approach from that side of the town was impossible in the soft ground. Likewise, the ground to the northwest was not favourable; the shorter stretch of wall there would be more easily defended by concentrating their fire from the walls on the narrow approach. He had been of the view that if an attack was necessary, it would be costly in the lives of his men, but it would best be made from where we now stood, from the southwest. FitzStephen nodded. He favoured an assault as opposed to putting the town to fire. He would do so if necessary, but he would be destroying the town and people who were to be the source of his wealth, as promised to him by my father. A successful assault would encourage the surrender of the town with minimal damage to property and his army.

Listening to Donal, FitzStephen rode with the rest of the Norman leaders around the walls. The defenders watched, throwing nothing more than the occasional insult. They were ignored by the Normans. They concentrated on the defences, maintaining a constant stream of questions at Donal and my father. I helped when I could, knowing the layout of the town well enough.

'You are a wise general, Donal. I see no better way,' Fitz-Stephen said finally.

While it would be difficult, I was pleased to see them agree that an immediate assault was preferable. It would not only demonstrate our intent to the Norsemen, but it would also test their resolve.

The entire army was put to work gathering stone and soil, which was to be used to form two causeways four-men wide that would span the ditch beneath the walls. The material was placed just out of bowshot from the walls and carried forward and dumped into the ditch by the foot soldiers, who had some protection from their chain mail and helmets. Some carried shields to protect the others, and the task was completed remarkably quickly. The defenders held their fire for the most part, doubtless aware of the attack that was coming. To quell their enthusiasm, Rob positioned a few archers to ensure that the men on the walls would be reluctant to show their heads for fear of their accurate fire.

'Rob, I need you to keep a lot of arrows pouring onto the wall above us when we get across,' Myler said, as I helped him strap the shoulder buckles on his breast plate.

'When!' Rob looked sceptical. '*If* you get across!' He said before continuing, 'And if you do, what then? You've no cover, and they'll have bowmen in those turrets on either side shooting at you.' Rob was not convinced at all by this plan.

'That's why I need you to keep their heads down until we get up the ladders.' Myler had volunteered to lead the attack over the causeway directly to the bottom of the wall. They had assembled a few ladders and would use them to surge across in an attempt to overwhelm the Norsemen. The second causeway led directly to a gate, where his cousin, Miles FitzDavid, would lead a group of knights and foot soldiers to try to force the gates. Rob's archers were to concentrate their fire to pin the defenders back from the walls and prevent them, as much as was possible, from interfering with the attackers. Rob shook his head on hearing what they were to attempt.

'Hold still,' I told Myler as I attached the moulded epaulettes which would protect his shoulders. He was wearing his upper body armour, as the greatest threat would come from above their heads today. Needing to be nimble scrambling over the causeway and up the ladder, he dispensed with the greaves, which normally protected his lower legs. The chainmail chausses that covered them would suffice. He detached the visor from his helmet, saying he'd need to see the bastards coming, and left his scabbard behind. He would have no need for it for the rest of the day. He laughed, kissed me, and, after embracing Rob, picked up his large kite-shaped shield and strode to take his position in the front rank of attack.

Myler seemed invigorated by the prospect of battle. His eyes took on an intensity, matching the vivid alertness which overtook him. I was to learn in time that he was probably the bravest man I had ever known, bordering on reckless. It was not that he felt no fear; he did. Any man who claims otherwise is lying or drunk—most probably the latter, as it was how most men summoned the courage to face the horror of close combat. For a man whom I knew and loved as a caring, gentle man, he was transformed into an unfamiliar, fierce, efficient killer in battle, as I was to witness many times.

He had told me his fear was heightened in the moments before the fight started. You could not but think they could be your last, he said, as we lay in my bed early one morning in Chepstow. Sweating in his battledress, his mouth dry as sand, he admitted he would sometimes piss himself, as would most others around him, and worse. The smell of men waiting to fight was not pleasant. Many would vomit; that's why it was best to leave your visor open till the last second. It was hard enough to breathe in them without a sea of your own sick splashing around.

'There is not a lot to like before a battle starts, Aoife. It's the worst time, the waiting,' he told me. 'But everything changes for me once it starts. I don't understand it.' He described how there was a flow, almost a rhythm, in combat. He moved without thinking, probably from the constant drilling. He could see what an opponent was thinking before he knew himself. Head up; watch the eyes, not the weapon. Hesitation was death; move forward with controlled aggression. Preserve your energy, use your enemies' weight to unbalance and strike, move forward again. Gradually there came a joy in it, a battle joy. Some called it bloodlust; perhaps that's all it was.

'It's the second most exhilarating feeling I have ever had, Aoife,' he said with a smile. 'Shall I show you the first?' He laughed and rolled me on top of him.

I was learning much about men these days. In this they struck me as remarkably like horses, which I knew far better at that age, having ridden and handled them all my life. There was not one in ten horses who was truly brave. A horse who could not stay in the pack but would barge its way to the front, accepting no horse to be ahead. It would head into any jump or the widest ditch without hesitation once put to it. All other animals, more timid by nature, would follow this horse. Yet that horse could be the most docile lamb of an animal to handle in the stable or meadow.

So it was that I watched Myler jostle his way through the

assembled men to the front rank, ready to lead the attack. They stood aside, willing to let him pass.

Rob stood beside me watching him go. 'What a lad, Aoife,' he said, shaking his head, and then he was gone too.

On a signal from FitzStephen, the two attacking groups surged forward. Myler was several paces in front of his men, leaping across the freshly placed loose soil. Some of the following men fell and brought down several others. By now the defenders were gathered densely on the walls above them. They were well prepared; they produced large wooden platforms, which several men held above the heads of those waiting to attack Myler as he reached the wall. I could see Rob's archers pouring arrows onto the walls; they were useless. They thumped harmlessly into the platforms protecting the Norsemen. Myler was quickly joined at the base of the wall, the men pressing themselves against the stone for what little protection it gave. This also proved pointless. The defenders hoisted enormous oak timbers onto the wall and tipped them over, each large beam felling several men sheltering against the wall. It was hard to watch; armour was no protection against such weight.

I watched as Myler and Robert de Barry, hoisted a ladder against the wall. It was quickly thrown aside, and I was sickened to see an enormous Norseman hurl a heavy cut stone down on them. It caught de Barry square on the helmet; he tumbled back into the trench, motionless. I did not know if he could survive such a crushing blow. Dropping his sword, Myler jumped into the trench and, covering de Barry from the bowshots from the turrets with his shield, he and two other men dragged him from the trench and out of harm's way.

By now, under the continuous rain of stone, timber and arrows, several Norman knights and foot soldiers lay strewn at the foot of the walls and in the bottom of the ditch. The group who had assaulted the gate was struggling to inflict any damage on the strong oak timbers.

With de Barry in safe hands, Myler rushed back across the causeway. They huddled under the meagre protection of their shields while others tried to hoist the ladders. Not one got a foot to a rung before it was quickly thrown back. I saw one ladder being pulled up onto the wall by the defenders. It was hopeless.

Realising that continuing the attack was pointless, Fitz-Stephen called on them to withdraw. The Norsemen jeered as they retreated over the causeways, taking their dead and wounded with them.

It had not only been pointless; it had also been costly. As the evening closed in, we gathered around a campfire near my tent; we needed to eat. We had lost eighteen men, with many more wounded. This was a lot for a force our size; they were the irreplaceable knights and foot soldiers. Myler's uncle had regained consciousness and would survive, although his helmet would not. Worse still, Rob reckoned he had hardly put a scratch on a man on the walls. The Norsemen would take heart at today's fighting, as we could hear from the laughter drifting over the walls of the town in the still evening.

'We'll be attacking again at first light,' Myler said gloomily. 'Ladders and timber platforms to give us some cover are being built.' We all turned to the sound of the hammering coming from where Rob's archers were camped. They were woodsmen and farmers for the most part and would make easy work of it.

However, none of us were encouraged by the sound. We sat in silence.

'Myler. We're not going to take this place by force,' Donal said eventually. 'Well, not quickly anyway. It's never been done. I told you that.' He shook his head. 'They can stay in there forever, resupplying themselves from the sea as they want.'

Rob nodded his head in agreement. 'He's right, Myler. These Norsemen know what they are doing. We need another plan.'

Myler knew they were right. He looked at each of them in turn. 'OK, but what? What do you suggest?' A long silence. Nothing. The baleful hammering droned on, ominous, like the sound of a scaffold being built for the condemned. What could be done? Another day lost; another defeat would be ruinous for our campaign. More so for Eanna, I thought.

'The boats,' I said. Their faces, sculpted by the glowing flame of the fire against the dark night, turned to me.

'What?' Rob asked.

It was clear to me now, suddenly clear.

'The boats.' I jumped up. 'We destroy the boats on the quays.'

Shaking heads. Dismissive sighs. Donal threw the remnants of a rabbit leg he was eating into the fire. The long scrape of the whetstone on steel resumed as Myler honed his well-sharpened blade.

'No, listen,' I insisted. Pausing, Myler looked at me, more out of loyalty than any real sense of hope in my plan.

'They are fighting because they think they can hold out until help arrives. If they doubt that, they will talk,' I said. Donal nodded but shrugged at the obvious.

I continued. 'Right now, they think time is on their side. Without the boats to resupply, time is with us. They don't particularly care who claims to be their overlords, as long as they are left to their trade.' Myler looked to Donal, who nodded his agreement. He said nothing, expecting me to continue.

I went on to explain to him that the Norsemen do not seek enemies. They would ally with any force that best suits their interests, and equally fight ferociously against any that endangered them. Their desire was to be left unmolested in their towns and hinterlands, allowing them to continue their seagoing trade in all manner of goods with places far and near. They would quickly come to terms and offer support to any lord who would guarantee these freedoms. They had, until recently, been subjects of my father and many kings of Leinster before him. It was understandable that they were weary of the unknown, particularly if that *unknown* presents itself as a formidable armed force beneath your walls.

'Well, why not just send messengers to them now,' Rob asked, 'telling them they can keep their town if they support us.'

'They won't. Why would they? They can sit behind their walls until an army arrives at our rear. They'd be a lot more certain in their future then,' I said. I had their attention now. 'We don't have time. We need to tip the balance in our favour a bit. Make them think again. Burn their boats and then offer to talk.' They were all silent now. They knew it made sense.

'They'll be well guarded. Under the walls. Risky,' Donal said. 'Anyway, not all the boats are on the quays. There's a good few anchored in the bay.'

Rob said that they were close enough to set alight with fire arrows. After a bit of talk, Myler eventually agreed that it was worth a try, and if it didn't work, they'd be attacking the walls in the morning regardless. It would need to be done by stealth in the dark with a small group, creeping silently around the town through the marshland to the east, up the shoreline to the quays. It would have to be quick, and hopefully the guards had brazier fires and torches on the quays for the flame they'd need to fire the boats.

Knowing they might have to swim and needing surprise, there would be no armour or heavy chain mail; reflected light and clinking metal would quickly betray them—if it didn't drown them first. Rob said that wouldn't work for him, as the pitch on his arrows could not get wet. So it was agreed that he would take his men to the northwest side of the town and create a diversion for the men on the walls by lighting some fires. He would be ready to fire into the anchored boats when he saw those on the quay ablaze, all going to plan.

With that agreed, Donal and Myler went to get the agreement of my father and FitzStephen. Rob and I sat silently listening to the crackling fire, our appetites gone in anticipation of what was to come. Returning quickly, they both simply nodded their heads. They could try it, but they had to be quick.

'Ten men,' Myler said. 'Five of mine and five of yours, Donal. Bring quiet ones that can swim.'

As they were leaving to their tasks, they stopped when I suddenly said, 'I'm coming,' to the surprise of everyone.

'No, you're not,' Donal said.

'Yes, I am. It's my plan.'

'No, you're not!' he said, raising his voice.

'Stop me so!' I shouted back at him. Donal looked to Myler, certain sense would prevail.

Myler looked at me. Then he simply shrugged his shoulders and opened his hands, powerless.

'Gods!' Donal cursed and stomped off to gather his men.

THE MEN CARRIED short swords and daggers. Fáinleog was tucked into a thick leather belt I wore over a tanned leather tunic and rugged breeches.

'Grow a beard quickly, Aoife, or blacken your skin with this mud.' Myler handed me a bowl of a foul-smelling substance with the consistency of thick gruel. It reminded me of the monks' food we had survived on during that long winter at the monastery in Ferns.

'And you too, Padraig,' Donal said, pointing to the young lad he had brought as one of his five men. He was one of the young buachaills Rob had trained with the longbow in Ferns, one of the boys who had fired him into the mill pond that day. I smiled at the memory. Padraig was turning out to be a valued warrior in all manner of ways. He was probably a couple of years younger than me. I knew his sisters and mother well.

'There's barely a shade of a hair on your chin,' Donal teased him. 'Have your balls dropped at all yet?'

Even then, Padraig managed to look a bit embarrassed. We all smiled and laughed as best we could. We needed the diversion of humour now to lessen the tension gripping our stomachs.

The clouds covered any moonlight, and the weak light from the lanterns swaying in the wind on the walls would not betray us. Our night eyes gradually opened to the darkness; Myler whispered to me to stop looking at the lanterns after I had stumbled as we moved through the marshy ground. The squelching of our footfalls boomed like thunder to me when I saw the guards on the walls peering our way, but the gusting wind was kind, breaking and disguising any sound we made. The flurry of the occasional nesting bird we disturbed was lost in the wind.

The water deepened, and we were soon wading waist deep in high rushes. Three hundred paces away over the water, we could see the boats tied to the heavy timber quays that stretched along the sea wall of the town. As expected, there were several guards gathered around one of the flaming braziers arranged along the dock; the nights still held their spring chill in early May. The braziers added to the light thrown from the flaming torches leaning from the walls.

The reeds would cover our approach for half the distance. Beyond that, we would be in open water, well-lit from the quays. Out of our depth, we would be swimming, visible and vulnerable. We needed Rob to distract the men on the walls and the quays with his fires before we struck out.

The cold of the water sucked the warmth from my body as we waited. The wind stripped what little heat remained. I shivered, a slight tremor at first, then quickly it turned into a shuddering racking of my body.

The wind was rising, choppy waves splashing around us. We couldn't wait much longer. If we didn't go soon, we would not have the strength to swim to the quays in this sea, never mind the fight that would follow.

'We either go now or we go back,' Donal whispered to Myler. 'Where the hell is Rob?'

'Wait. Look,' Myler said, gesturing towards the dim shore of the estuary beyond the town where Rob should be by now. First one, then several fires flickered into the night. In the blackness on the land beyond the light thrown from the walls, they burst into being. We could hear the men on the walls calling to the guards on the quay, who took up their arms and drifted towards the other end, closer to Rob's fires.

This was it.

We pushed through the reeds, the movement giving some life to my numb limbs. Toe tipping, then nothing. The others swam hard at the quay, covering the distance quickly. I could see Myler climbing a ladder and waiting for the others before he jumped onto the dock. I was not halfway across, and the waves were biting. Eventually, under the dock, I grasped the ladder, exhausted. I could hear shouting and men grappling on the boards above me. As I hauled myself up, a man fell past me into the water. He surfaced, gasping, gulping for air, aimlessly, his throat open, the sea filling his lungs.

Onto the quay on all fours, I panted, shattered. All was quiet. I looked up. The guards lay strewn in expanding pools of blood. Myler and the others were firing the torches and dumping the contents of the braziers into the boats, some of which, laden with dry goods, burst into flames.

But standing with his back to me at this end of the dock, not ten paces away, was a helmeted Norseman. He held Padraig by the hair, kneeling with a blade to his throat. One move from Donal, who stood facing him, sword by his side, would leave another mother in Ferns grieving for her youngest son.

Time slowed. Donal did not look at me, but held the Norseman's gaze. I rose slowly. Slipping Fáinleog from my belt, no shadows to betray me, I moved quickly, silently, toward his back. I gripped the hilt in two hands and threw my weight forward, driving her blade through his tunic into his heart. He did not see her tip burst through his chest, for by then Donal had his sword in his throat. The Norseman slumped lifeless onto the dock.

By now the boats were all ablaze. Volleys of fire arrows streaked from the shore, finding the dark ships anchored on the bay. Once an arrow stuck, it betrayed the boat's presence, and it was easy work to rain fire down to set it alight.

We could hear the Norsemen working to open the heavy gates that led to the docks. It was too late to save their boats, but they would want to make us pay for this. Cutting loose all the smaller skiffs on the dock, we jumped into the last and pushed out into the darkness of the bay, away from the quay. Soon out of bowshot, we made for the firmer ground beyond the marsh we had crossed. Exhausted, we had not lost a man.

Padraig, sitting in the bottom of the boat, lifted my hand and kissed it silently.

THE WEAK YELLOW light of the dawn rose quickly. Unobstructed by the sea, it cast a pale blue light over our army, standing in orderly battle formation beneath the walls. It would not have been a welcome sight for the Norsemen on the walls.

Sleep would not have come easy to the inhabitants of the town that night. The lingering stench of smouldering, damp timbers from the smoking ships and quays hung in the air, adding to their gloom. The constant hammering through the night, foreboding in the dark, heightened their dread of what the dawn would bring. The hammering stopped abruptly before the dawn. The silence, louder still, amplified the tension.

FitzStephen had wanted the dawn to present the defenders with the enormity of the assault they faced that day and inevitability of our victory. With their fleet destroyed and any hopes of resupply in the event of a siege gone, they could not hold out for long in the hope that a relieving army would arrive. That possibility was, in any case, by no means a certainty for the defenders. They prided themselves on their independence from the Irish lords and stood separate from the other Norse towns of Dublin and Waterford. None had any obligation to come to their aid, and regardless, if they did choose to do so, it would take time for any alliance to form and muster the required forces to march to the rear of the army standing under their walls. They also knew they would pay a high price if the town was taken by force. Any of the surviving defenders could be expected to be summarily executed; their women and children would suffer abuses from soldiers not to be contemplated and then sold into slavery.

FitzStephen arranged his army that morning so that as the cloak of the restless night lifted for the traumatised people of Wexford, the sight that would greet them would make sure they turned their thoughts to that price should they continue to defy us.

The ditch had been filled in two more places during the night. There would now be four points of attack. In four parts, the army stood in full battle dress, ranked and silent. Protective wooden hoarding had been brought forward and erected at the crossing points of each causeway. Stacks of sturdy wooden ladders lay close at hand, ready to be carried across. Each column of the mail-clad men preparing to attack was to be protected by large timber trellises carried by other men and joined in an apex over their heads. They would deflect the barrage of missiles and absorb arrows.

We had learned from the men who joined us on our march that there were two visiting bishops in the town. These were influential men and well disposed towards my father. For all his sins, he was clever enough to have been generous to the church, exceedingly generous. Leinster was awash with the abbeys, nunneries and churches he had endowed, and the treasuries of the bishops brimmed with his gold. Bishops could be surprisingly forgiving of a king's transgressions, contorting themselves with remarkable dexterity with their scriptures in the absolution of a benevolent king's sins.

My father suggested we find a priest, and as the sun rose the men on the walls saw our army kneel and receive mass in a great show of piety. The bishops would be relieved to know that at least it was a Christian army at their gates. It would do no harm in the talks that were to be offered.

To avoid unsettling the defenders, it was decided it was best to present them with the familiar. Rather than the threatening presence of an armoured Norman delegation, Donal and I, who were well known and respected by them, would approach the gates. Montmorency had insisted that one Norman accompany us. I think FitzStephen misunderstood that he was volunteering for this task, and he agreed he should go with us. Unhappy but unable to withdraw, Montmorency agreed. I too would have preferred that he did not accompany us, for of all the Normans, he was the most unsympathetic to the urgency with which we needed to march on Mac Giolla Patrick in Osraige to secure Eanna's release. We had to take Wexford now.

Before we had left, I rode over to Rob on the pretence of getting a better view of the walls from the slightly higher ground on which the Welsh archers were massed. I told him that on my signal from the gates, he was to have the bowmen light fire arrows from the braziers and hoist them in their bows, ready to shoot, in a display fully obvious to the men on the walls. I might have unwittingly left him with the impression that this order came directly from FitzStephen.

As we approached the ditch carrying willow branches as a sign for parley, the gates opened slightly. It was the two bishops who squeezed through and stepped cautiously forward as the gates were closed and barred behind them. I knew one as Joseph Ua hAedha, the bishop of Ferns. He glanced uneasily over his shoulder at the closed gates. He was the bishop whose robe Rob had relieved of its intricately embroidered hem for the silk it provided for attaching the fletching to his arrows. I could not easily unsee his pale, spindly legs—the vision did not add to the high dignity of his office.

His eyes darted nervously over the army arrayed behind us. 'Donal, Aoife, my children,' he gushed, all smiles. 'Such a joy to see men kneeling in God's praise. An army, a Christian army. God be praised!' He gestured, open armed, to the heavens.

'I see you have a new robe, Bishop,' I said. I could feel Donal's disapproval, but it was hard to miss the opportunity. I'd apologise later.

Ignoring my comment, the bishop looked to Montmorency. Taking the prompt, Donal introduced him and took the opportunity to describe the nature of the army and our purpose here today—our father, the rightful king of Leinster, was the legitimate overlord of this town in his kingdom. The men opposing him were rebels defying his authority. He demanded their submission, the surrender of the town.

'I see, Donal, yes, I see . . . but I think things may have changed somewhat,' he said. 'I'm not sure the men of Wexford would fully agree with that right now . . .'

Donal interrupted, 'Let me be clear, Bishop: we will attack if you do not agree. You will give us hostages and agree to fight with our army when we call. In return, we will spare the town.'

'Hmm.' He rubbed his stubbled chin in his hand. 'Well, I'm sure they are willing to be reasonable, but your terms will have to be discussed. I will deliver your offer to the Tengs, and I am sure we can resume our parley at first light tomorrow.' He smiled, exuding an air of calm reasonableness.

They were playing for time. If they could hold out, there was a chance an army would presently appear at our rear. Donal hesitated.

'Bishop,' I said, squeezing my mare forward. 'You will accept our terms immediately and in full or we will attack the city now.' Donal and Montmorency looked at me, as surprised as the look on the bishop's face.

'Excuse me?'

'You heard me. If we do not return to our lines with your full acceptance of our terms, we will attack. They are my father's words.'

He looked to Donal, who remained stony-faced.

'You would not attack a town and put the lives of two defenceless men of the cloth at risk, bishops no less?' He gestured to his colleague, who shivered slightly.

'You are free to leave,' I said. 'But you must do so immediately.'

At this, Montmorency intervened. He spoke loudly, for he knew that the town elders would be listening behind the gates.

'Be also aware that the accepted conventions of the siege will apply, should you continue with your insolence. If you are unfamiliar with these, let me remind you: all men will be put to the sword, and our soldiers will be given the customary three days of their pleasure with the women, girls and boys of the town.' His voice boomed. I shuddered at what he had said, for I knew it was true—and that this cruel man would satisfy his appetites on many a poor soul.

But the bishops hesitated. We could hear murmuring voices behind the gates. So I turned and waved my signal to Rob. Men with torches passed along the ranks of archers, lighting the pitched tips of the fire arrows. In moments, five hundred bowmen stood with strained bows, arrows pointed skywards, ready to unleash the inferno on the thatch-roofed buildings within the walls.

'You have as long as it takes for the flames to singe the fingers of the bowmen to agree, Bishop,' I said.

He stood transfixed, staring at the archers. I could see the shock on his face. I leant forward on my horse. 'Bishop! I suggest you talk to the Norsemen. Quickly!'

He scrambled to the gate. The Norsemen had heard the exchange. They knew their town would be quickly ablaze and they would be hard pressed to withstand a determined attack. There was a quick mumbled conversation before the bishop scurried back. They accepted our terms.

'Open the gates!' I shouted, relieved. Wexford was ours.

THE VIEW from the walls over our camp was impressive. Behind us, over the town, the estuary of the Slaney River opened out into the shallow bay. With the tide out, the maze of sandbars was just visible as the evening light fled west. Myler was very glad we had not had to storm these walls. They were well built, with a wide walkway that served as a more than adequate fighting platform. There were piles of heavy stones and timbers placed at regular intervals, prepared by the Norsemen to crash onto the heads of any who attempted to scale the ladders. Bundles of spears and sheeves of arrows were strewn around. The Norsemen were big men by nature, well skilled in the use of their double-headed war axes. It would not have been easy.

The chaotic normality that was a town like Wexford quickly reasserted itself after the initial caution of the Norse. Their weariness faded as they realised my father was true to his word and no harm would come to the inhabitants if they accepted his authority. In return for generous provisions for our camp, no injury would befall any man, and no woman or child would be molested.

FitzStephen removed any doubts in this regard by placing several of his own men in stocks by the gates for their unwelcome pursuit of a young woman; there they would spend the night cooling their loins with their breeches around their ankles.

The women of the town were thus assured their virtue would not be abused. The whores, as common as beggars in every town and port, were equally happy their virtue was being thoroughly abused. They charged well for their services.

The common people of our races held no particular animosity towards one another. They fought at the behest of their lords, as they must, but once declared as allies, they moved freely amongst each other: Flemings, French, Irish, Welsh, Normans, Norse and English.

The raucous singing, drunkenness and brawling that follow a battle is only surpassed by that when the battle has been avoided. They would do as men always did then, deep into the night, knowing full well they would be marching at first light.

It had been agreed that we would not delay and would march for Osraige at dawn. There was no time to lose as a party of Mac Giolla Patrick's men had been seen in the camp. In the confusion after the surrender of the town, they had initially gone unnoticed, their purpose unclear, Myler told us. My father paled on hearing this, like me he knew these hours were perilous for Eanna. Mac Giolla Patrick and his masters, O'Connor and O'Rourke, would be quick to murder or mutilate Eanna now. Our hope lay in getting to Mac Giolla Patrick first, to persuade him otherwise by whatever means. But my father knew he could not march a drunken army through the night to fight at dawn.

The Normans readily agreed to march on Osraige as my father had also proven true to his word to them. Myler's uncles, FitzStephen and Maurice FitzGerald, who would follow with Strongbow, were given the lucrative lordship of Wexford as he had promised. However, there was considerable surprise and disquiet amongst the Norman leaders when he also announced that Montmorency was to be given two cantreds of land stretching along the coast from Wexford to the other Norse town of Waterford. No one understood why he had favoured him in this way; he certainly had not earned it through valour. De Prendergast was particularly unhappy at this, as he had brought a considerable part of the Norman force in the two ships from Milford.

However, there would be ample spoils to distribute to the Normans as we regained our kingdom. De Prendergast was somewhat placated when I told Myler to inform him that the lands my father had given to Montmorency were sparsely populated with no towns. There was little wealth there and no people to work the land. My father had not been as generous to Montmorency as it might seem.

Thinking of Eanna as I stood with Myler on the turret overlooking the chaos in the camp, I could take no joy in our success. In the fading light, drunken men, brawled or embraced, I couldn't tell. Barrels of ale rolled through whores serving their clients in the half-light. Taking their coin and, when they could, not fulfilling their side of the bargain; most of the men were none the wiser. Beggars and thieves skulking in the dark, watched the drunks rummage in their purses, stealthily removing them when the men slumped on a bench or stumbled to the ground, senseless.

A small, drunken man emerged from the half-light and stumbled towards the causeway, arms outstretched. He walked slowly, arms grasping at nothing, until he lost his footing and fell to the ground. Rising, he continued for a moment before falling again. He began to crawl through the semidarkness. His face was soiled and bloody. The shifting light from the torches caught the face, then snatched it away . . . His lips were moving, mouthing unheard words, as he crawled slowly, tortuously, to stop just beneath me. The wind stilled, the light full, the head bowed. Lifting, the blood mixed with dirt and the puss seeping from what had been the eyes. The light hard and clear now on the face . That face, forever seared into my mind's eye. Not a man, a drunken man, but a boy... Eanna.

'Aoife,' he cried. I heard him now. 'Aoife,' again and again. Myler ran from the turret, but I stood watching, weeping. I would weep for him now, for he would never hear me weep for him again. I would spare him that. I ran to him.

MY FATHER HOWLED when I brought Eanna to him, a guttural primeval howl from the depths of his soul. I grasped Eanna to my chest to cover his ears from the frightening sound and the unceasing profanities he spat venomously as he smashed everything within his grasp. He drew his sword and slashed wildly at the furniture and tableware. Those in the room fled to the walls, and several servants ran from the room. Amidst his madness, he swore to find the men who did this. He would castrate them, feed them their balls, pierce their eyeballs with hot irons before ripping the flesh from their faces with his own teeth.

'On this, I swear. On everything sacred and true, on this I swear,' He screamed.

No, you won't, Father, I thought. *Not if I get to them first.*

THE END

Author's Note

I have always been captivated by the immersive experience of historical fiction and its ability to transport me to times and places long past. As photographs of family holidays are better with someone in them, history is best taught and understood with the people of the times firmly in the frame. Dry historical records quickly slip the mind, but tell the human stories behind the events and our own emotions help burn them into our memories.

As a fan of the genre, I have always been surprised that vast swaths of Irish history have been neglected by the writing fraternity, particularly for a country that cherishes the writer and is well represented in the ranks of the literary greats.

Allied with our obsessive interest in our history, you would think the field would be well exhausted by now. Yet this is not so, quite the opposite in fact. A precursory glance at our neighbours will reveal the veritable libraries of novels piled high, exhaustively exploring every conceivable nuance of English history.

AUTHOR'S NOTE

We, on the other hand, have been delinquent. Why, I ask myself?

Well, there might be aspects of Irish history into which *we* would not welcome prying eyes dragging up long-forgotten and embarrassing family secrets. We are happy to bang our drums and wave our flags at the great injustices visited upon us in our history. Ireland, a nation of innocent types, disenfranchised and abused by an invader who despoiled a happy land and people, corrupted a unique culture and set the country on a spiral of conflict lasting over eight hundred years.

Well, at least one clause of the last sentence holds true—Ireland may have had a somewhat unique culture at the time in European terms. The island had avoided, for the most part, the waves of conquerors which continually swept across the continent of Europe and Britain. While avoiding the inevitable conflict and destruction which accompanied these events, the island also never benefitted from the administrative, judicial and technical innovations that usually came, part and parcel, with the victors. The surviving political entities of these upheavals gradually rose in power and stability as a creeping unity spread across the land.

There was good and bad in this for Ireland. From a military perspective, the Irish kings were many and disunited, and for that reason they could be overcome, one by one, by an invader. However, for the same reason it was difficult to conquer the island in its entirety; the lack of a dominant power meant there was no single king whose head and capital, once taken, would bring the island to heel.

In addition, there were some surprisingly enlightened aspects to the ancient Brehon law that was in use in Ireland at the time. This body of law was fundamentally different in origin to Justinian law, which formed the basis of the dominant judicial systems in Europe at the end of the twelfth century. (Justinian law had its origins in Rome, and its adoption followed the Roman legions as that empire expanded.) Contemporary readers will find many Brehon laws remarkably apt for the modern zeitgeist in terms of the care of animals, the environment and women's rights. By way of example, Brehon law allowed a woman to easily divorce her husband for a multitude of reasons and take her share of the wealth—reasons that included obesity and impotence. However, there were unsavoury aspects to the law, such as the acceptance of slavery, which was legal and widespread—a practice which had long been outlawed as barbaric by the Normans.

Any assertion that life in Ireland at the time approached any kind of an ideal is questionable. In truth, it was harsh and uncertain. Indeed, the only certainty was the incessant seasonal warring, with all the unpleasantness it brought for both men and women. And if they were lucky enough to avoid the spear, slavery or famine would await.

Furthermore, any attempt by the Irish—or Celts, as they were known—to tarnish the Norman arrival with illegitimacy would be to condemn themselves. Their own ancestors had arrived centuries beforehand from the continent to take the island from the first tribes, the Tuatha Dé Danann. The Normans arrived and did much the same, but at least the Normans who stayed could claim lineage from the high kings of Ireland, stretching back to the most revered high king of all, Brian Boru, Ard Rí. If that wasn't enough, they could solemnly claim lineage to a man created from some clay by God on the sixth day of the universe, Adam. That's hard to best.

This novel is my attempt to weave these nuances into an account of the whirlwind events of late twelfth-century

AUTHOR'S NOTE

Ireland that I would have enjoyed reading. It is the first in a series, to be collectively known as The Hiberno-Norman Chronicles.

I have taken some liberties with the characters and their relationships, motivations, passions and flaws. However, I have remained closely loyal to the historical facts as recorded in the primary records. The most attentive enthusiasts will spot one or two mild transgressions on my part to aid the narrative flow. For these, and any errors or omissions, which are entirely mine, I ask your forgiveness. However, the book is a work of historical fiction; please view it as such and refer to the appropriate records and academic works as required.

In my defence, I wanted to keep up the pace and maintain the interest of the reader. I think any story is enhanced with a little of the shocking unpredictability of *A Game of Thrones* and unnerving tension of *Peaky Blinders*. I doubt I've reached those heights yet, but I hope I'm at least heading in that direction and you'll stick with me.

To further help the interested reader, I've produced some detailed maps which place events in their geographical context and trace the movements of the characters as the story unfolds. These maps can be viewed in Google Earth and can be accessed from my website seanjfitzgerald.com on the Places & History page. You'll also find some photos and videos in which I touch upon some of the history and important events which take place in the book.

My motives in seeking the attention of readers are not purely selfish, as I do believe that the history of these times is compelling. These stories are as riveting as anything George R. R. Martin could write but have the added advantage of being factual. However, we have not exploited this history to the same extent as our neighbours and other countries have done to entice tourists. As a country, we have a fabulous but neglected asset in this history, which I'm sure we could better use to tell our story and attract visitors to the country and places where these momentous events unfolded.

SF

December 2023

Acknowledgments

I'd like to thank my son Derry and my friends Keelan O'Donnell and Kevin Jennings for suffering the experience of reviewing early drafts of the novel. They will recognise their invaluable course corrections and ideas in the work.

My nephew, Luke Fitzgerald went beyond the requirements of familial relations in his excellent detailed critique; many thanks.

Niall, my youngest son travelled the southeast of Ireland with me putting his drone flying skills to good use in producing the drone footage of the places where the events of the novel occurred. This footage will be available on my website on the Places&History page.

Of the many research materials I used, the following three are the most reader-friendly; Strongbow by Conor Kostick, Brehon Laws by Jo Kerrigan and Fin Dwyer's irish-historypodcast.com.

And to my wife, Deirdre, who has endured the creative process more than anyone and now knows far more about the Norman invasion of Ireland than she thought possible or ever truly wanted.

About the Author

Sean J. Fitzgerald is a Dubliner. He started work at the age of thirteen on a milk float delivering door to door in the suburbs of north Dublin; he can remember the horse rearing and the crates of pint glass bottles shattering the quiet silence before dawn. He spent years travelling and working as an engineer, salesman and ultimately as an entrepreneur in places as diverse as Moscow, through Edinburgh to Boston and onward to California.

Today he lives in Kildare in Ireland with his wife, children, dogs and horses having returned home to do what he always wanted…to write.

Aoife of Leinster is the first book in The Hiberno-Norman Chronicles by Sean J. Fitzgerald. It combines detailed historical research with an infusion of the humanity of the men and women who shaped these events, bringing the dry historical record to life. While remaining true to the historical record of events, this novel explores the motivations, passions and flaws that drove these people while offering keen insights into the political, social and cultural backdrop that informed them.

The novel is brought to life with the media material produced by the author of the landscape in which the events described took place. Enthusiasts can follow the course of the novel with videos, photographs, additional historical information and detailed Google Earth maps. This material is available on the author's website www.seanjfitzgerald.com

Printed in Great Britain
by Amazon